W9-CPQ-577

THE MACHINERIES OF JOY

RAY BRADBURY

SHORT STORIES

BANTAM BOOKS · TORONTO · NEW YORK · LONDON

A NATIONAL GENERAL COMPANY

THE MACHINERIES OF JOY

*A Bantam Book / published by arrangement with
Simon and Schuster, Inc.*

PRINTING HISTORY
Simon and Schuster edition published February 1964
Bantam edition published July 1965

2nd printing ..... January 1966	5th printing .... July 1968
3rd printing ..... October 1966	6th printing .... July 1969
4th printing .... July 1967	7th printing ..... October 1969
	8th printing .... July 1970	

Bantam Books are published by Bantam Books, Inc., a National
General company. Its trade-mark, consisting of the words "Bantam
Books" and the portrayal of a bantam, is registered in the United
States Patent Office and in other countries. Marca Registrada.
Bantam Books, Inc., 666 Fifth Avenue, New York, N.Y. 10019.

For *Ramona*,
who cried when she heard
that the Hound of the
Baskervilles was dead . . .

For *Susan*,
who snorted at the same news . . .

For *Bettina*,
who laughed . . .

And for *Alexandra*,
who told everyone to
just get out of the way . . .

This book, dear daughters,
with four different kinds
of love, for you.

CONTENTS

the machineries of joy   / 1

the one who waits   / 14

tyrannosaurus rex   / 21

the vacation   / 34

the drummer boy of shiloh   / 41

boys! raise giant mushrooms in <u>your</u> cellar!   / 47

almost the end of the world   / 63

perhaps we are going away   / 71

and the sailor, home from the sea   / 75

el día de muerte   / 83

the illustrated woman   / 93

some live like lazarus   / 104

a miracle of rare device   / 115

and so died riabouchinska   / 129

the beggar on o'connell bridge   / 142

death and the maiden   / 157

a flight of ravens   / 165

the best of all possible worlds   / 176

the lifework of juan díaz   / 183

to the chicago abyss   / 193

the anthem sprinters   / 203

"Somewhere," said Father Vittorini, "did Blake not speak of the Machineries of Joy? That is, did not God promote environments, then intimidate these Natures by provoking the existence of flesh, toy men and women, such as are we all? And thus happily sent forth, at our best, with good grace and fine wit, on calm noons, in fair climes, are we not God's Machineries of Joy?"

"If Blake said that," said Father Brian, "he never lived in Dublin."

THE MACHINERIES OF JOY

Father Brian delayed going below to breakfast because he thought he heard Father Vittorini down there, laughing. Vittorini, as usual, was dining alone. So who was there to laugh with, or at?

Us, thought Father Brian, *that's who*.

He listened again.

Across the hall Father Kelly too was hiding, or meditating, rather, in his room.

They never let Vittorini finish breakfast, no, they always managed to join him as he chewed his last bit of toast. Otherwise they could not have borne their guilt through the day.

Still, that was laughter, was it not, belowstairs? Father Vittorini had ferreted out something in the morning *Times*. Or, worse, had he stayed up half the night with the unholy ghost, that television set which stood in the entry like an unwelcome guest, one foot in whimsy, the other in the doldrums? And, his mind bleached by the electronic beast, was Vittorini now planning some bright fine new devilment, the cogs wheeling in his soundless mind, seated and deliberately fasting, hoping to lure them down curious at the sound of his Italian humors?

"Ah, God." Father Brian sighed and fingered the envelope he had prepared the previous night. He had tucked it in his coat as a protective measure should he decide to hand it to Pastor Sheldon. Would Father Vittorini detect it through the cloth with his quick dark X-ray vision?

Father Brian pressed his hand firmly along his lapel to squash any merest outline of his request for transferral to another parish.

"Here goes."

And, breathing a prayer, Father Brian went downstairs.

1

"Ah, Father Brian!"

Vittorini looked up from his still full cereal bowl. The brute had not even so much as sugared his corn flakes yet.

Father Brian felt as if he had stepped into an empty elevator shaft.

Impulsively he put out a hand to save himself. It touched the top of the television set. The set was warm. He could not help saying, "Did you have a seance here last night?"

"I sat up with the set, yes."

"Sat up is right!" snorted Father Brian. "One does sit up, doesn't one, with the sick, or the dead? I used to be handy with the ouija board myself. There was more brains in that." He turned from the electrical moron to survey Vittorini. "And did you hear far cries and banshee wails from, what is it? Canaveral?"

"They called off the shot at three A.M."

"And you here now, looking daisy-fresh." Father Brian advanced, shaking his head. "What's true is not always what's fair."

Vittorini now vigorously doused his flakes with milk. "But you, Father Brian, you look as if you made the grand tour of Hell during the night."

Fortunately, at this point Father Kelly entered. He froze when he too saw how little along Vittorini was with his fortifiers. He muttered to both priests, seated himself, and glanced over at the perturbed Father Brian.

"True, William, you look half gone. Insomnia?"

"A touch."

Father Kelly eyed both men, his head to one side. "What goes on here? Did something happen while I was out last night?"

"We had a small discussion," said Father Brian, toying with the dread flakes of corn.

"Small discussion!" said Father Vittorini. He might have laughed, but caught himself and said simply, "The Irish priest is worried by the Italian Pope."

"Now, Father Vittorini," said Kelly.

"Let him run on," said Father Brian.

"Thank you for your permission," said Vittorini, very politely and with a friendly nod. "Il Papa is a constant source of reverent irritation to at least some if not all of the Irish clergy. Why not a pope named Nolan? Why not a green instead of a red hat? Why not, for that matter, move Saint

Peter's Cathedral to Cork or Dublin, come the twenty-fifth century?"

"I hope nobody said *that*," said Father Kelly.

"I am an angry man," said Father Brian. "In my anger I might have *inferred* it."

"Angry, why? And inferred for what reason?"

"Did you hear what he just said about the twenty-fifth century?" asked Father Brian. "Well, it's when Flash Gordon and Buck Rogers fly in through the baptistry transom that yours truly hunts for the exits."

Father Kelly sighed. "Ah, God, is it *that* joke again?"

Father Brian felt the blood burn his cheeks, but fought to send it back to cooler regions of his body.

"Joke? It's off and beyond that. For a month now it's Canaveral this and trajectories and astronauts that. You'd think it was Fourth of July, he's up half each night with the rockets. I mean, now, what kind of life is it, from midnight on, carousing about the entryway with that Medusa machine which freezes your intellect if ever you stare at it? I cannot sleep for feeling the whole rectory will blast off any minute."

"Yes, yes," said Father Kelly. "But what's all this about the Pope?"

"Not the new one, the one before the last," said Brian wearily. "Show him the clipping, Father Vittorini."

Vittorini hesitated.

"Show it," insisted Brian, firmly.

Father Vittorini brought forth a small press clipping and put it on the table.

Upside down, even, Father Brian could read the bad news: "POPE BLESSES ASSAULT ON SPACE."

Father Kelly reached one finger out to touch the cutting gingerly. He intoned the news story half aloud, underlining each word with his fingernail:

CASTEL GANDOLFO, ITALY, SEPT. 20.—Pope Pius XII gave his blessing today to mankind's efforts to conquer space.

The Pontiff told delegates to the International Astronautical Congress, "God has no intention of setting a limit to the efforts of man to conquer space."

The 400 delegates to the 22-nation congress were received by the Pope at his summer residence here.

"This Astronautic Congress has become one of great importance at this time of man's exploration of outer space," the Pope said. "It should concern all humanity. . . . Man has to make the effort to put himself in new orientation with God and his universe."

Father Kelly's voice trailed off.

"When did this story appear?"

"In 1956."

"*That* long back?" Father Kelly laid the thing down. "*I* didn't read it."

"It seems," said Father Brian, "you and I, Father, don't read much of anything."

"Anyone could overlook it," said Kelly. "It's a teeny-weeny article."

"With a very large idea in it," added Father Vittorini, his good humor prevailing.

"The point is—"

"The point is," said Vittorini, "when first I spoke of this piece, grave doubts were cast on my veracity. Now we see I have cleaved close by the truth."

"Sure," said Father Brian quickly, "but as our poet William Blake put it, 'A truth that's told with bad intent beats all the lies you can invent.' "

"Yes." Vittorini relaxed further into his amiability. "And didn't Blake also write

He who doubts from what he sees,
Will ne'er believe, do what you please.
If the Sun and Moon should doubt
They'd immediately go out.

Most appropriate," added the Italian priest, "for the Space Age."

Father Brian stared at the outrageous man.

"I'll thank you not to quote our Blake at us."

"*Your* Blake?" said the slender pale man with the softly glowing dark hair. "Strange, I'd always thought him English."

"The poetry of Blake," said Father Brian, "was always a great comfort to my mother. It was she told me there was Irish blood on his maternal side."

"I will graciously accept that," said Father Vittorini. "But back to the newspaper story. Now that we've found it, it seems a good time to do some research on Pius the Twelfth's encyclical."

Father Brian's wariness, which was a second set of nerves under his skin, prickled alert.

"What encyclical is that?"

"Why, the one on space travel."

"He *didn't* do that?"

"He did."

"On space travel, a special encyclical?"

"A special one."

Both Irish priests were near onto being flung back in their chairs by the blast.

Father Vittorini made the picky motions of a man cleaning up after a detonation, finding lint on his coat sleeve, a crumb or two of toast on the tablecloth.

"Wasn't it enough," said Brian, in a dying voice, "he shook hands with the astronaut bunch and told them well done and all that, but he had to go on and write at length about it?"

"It was not enough," said Father Vittorini. "He wished, I hear, to comment further on the problems of life on other worlds, and its effect on Christian thinking."

Each of these words, precisely spoken, drove the two other men farther back in their chairs.

"You *hear?*" said Father Brian. "You haven't read yourself yet?"

"No, but I intend—"

"You intend everything and mean worse. Sometimes, Father Vittorini, you do not talk, and I hate to say this, like a priest of the Mother Church at all."

"I talk," replied Vittorini, "like an Italian priest somehow caught and trying to preserve surface tension treading an ecclesiastical bog where I am outnumbered by a great herd of clerics named Shaughnessy and Nulty and Flannery that mill and stampede like caribou or bison every time I so much as whisper 'papal bull.' "

"There is no doubt in my mind"—and here Father Brian squinted off in the general direction of the Vatican, itself— "that it was you, if you could've been there, might've put the Holy Father up to this whole space-travel monkeyshines."

"I?"

"You! It's you, it is not, certainly not us, that lugs in the magazines by the carload with the rocket ships on the shiny covers and the filthy green monsters with six eyes and seventeen gadgets chasing after half-draped females on some moon or other? You I hear late nights doing the countdowns from ten, nine, eight on down to one, in tandem with the beast TV, so we lie aching for the dread concussions to knock the fillings from our teeth. Between one Italian here and another at Castel Gondolfo, may God forgive me, you've managed to depress the entire Irish clergy!"

"Peace," said Father Kelly at last, "both of you."

"And peace it is, one way or another I'll have it," said Father Brian, taking the envelope from his pocket.

"Put that away," said Father Kelly, sensing what must be in the envelope.

"Please give this to Pastor Sheldon for me."

Father Brian rose heavily and peered about to find the door and some way out of the room. He was suddenly gone.

"Now see what you've done!" said Father Kelly.

Father Vittorini, truly shocked, had stopped eating. "But, Father, all along I thought it was an amiable squabble, with him putting on and me putting on, him playing it loud and me soft."

"Well, you've played it too long, and the blasted fun turned serious!" said Kelly. "Ah, you don't know William like I do. You've really torn him."

"I'll do my best to mend—"

"You'll mend the seat of your pants! Get out of the way, this is my job now." Father Kelly grabbed the envelope off the table and held it up to the light, "The X ray of a poor man's soul. Ah, God."

He hurried upstairs. "Father Brian?" he called. He slowed. "Father?" He tapped at the door. "William?"

In the breakfast room, alone once more, Father Vittorini remembered the last few flakes in his mouth. They now had no taste. It took him a long slow while to get them down.

It was only after lunch that Father Kelly cornered Father Brian in the dreary little garden behind the rectory and handed back the envelope.

"Willy, I want you to tear this up. I won't have you quitting in the middle of the game. How long has all this gone on between you two?"

Father Brian sighed and held but did not rip the envelope. "It sort of crept upon us. It was me at first spelling the Irish writers and him pronouncing the Italian operas. Then me describing the Book of Kells in Dublin and him touring me through the Renaissance. Thank God for small favors, he didn't discover the papal encyclical on the blasted space traveling sooner, or I'd have transferred myself to a monkery where the fathers keep silence as a vow. But even there, I fear, he'd follow and count down the Canaveral blastoffs in sign language. What a Devil's advocate that man would make!"

"Father!"

"I'll do penance for that later. It's just this dark otter, this seal, he frolics with Church dogma as if it was a candy-striped bouncy ball. It's all very well to have seals cavorting, but I say don't mix them with the true fanatics, such as you and me! Excuse the pride, Father, but there does seem to be a variation on the true theme every time you get them piccolo players in amongst us harpers, and don't you agree?"

"What an enigma, Will. We of the Church should be examples for others on how to get along."

"Has anyone told Father Vittorini that? Let's face it, the Italians are the Rotary of the Church. You couldn't have trusted one of them to stay sober during the Last Supper."

"I wonder if we Irish could?" mused Father Kelly.

"We'd wait until it was over, at least!"

"Well, now, are we priests or barbers? Do we stand here splitting hairs, or do we shave Vittorini close with his own razor? William, have you no plan?"

"Perhaps to call in a Baptist to mediate."

"Be off with your Baptist! Have you researched the encyclical?"

"The encyclical?"

"Have you let grass grow since breakfast between your toes? You have! Let's read that space-travel edict! Memorize it, get it pat, then counterattack the rocket man in his own territory! This way, to the library. What is it the youngsters cry these days? Five, four, three, two, one, blast off?"

"Or the rough equivalent."

"Well, say the rough equivalent, then, man. And follow me!"

They met Pastor Sheldon, going into the library as he was coming out.

"It's no use," said the pastor, smiling, as he examined the fever in their faces. "You won't find it in there."

"Won't find what in there?" Father Brian saw the pastor looking at the letter which was still glued to his fingers, and hid it away, fast. "Won't find what, sir?"

"A rocket ship is a trifle too large for our small quarters," said the pastor in a poor try at the enigmatic.

"Has the Italian bent your ear, then?" cried Father Kelly in dismay.

"No, but echoes have a way of ricocheting about the place. I came to do some checking myself."

"Then," gasped Brian with relief, "you're on *our* side?"

Pastor Sheldon's eyes became somewhat sad. "Is there a side to this, Fathers?"

They all moved into the little library room, where Father Brian and Father Kelly sat uncomfortably on the edges of the hard chairs. Pastor Sheldon remained standing, watchful of their discomfort.

"Now. Why are you afraid of Father Vittorini?"

"Afraid?" Father Brian seemed surprised at the word and cried softly, "It's more like angry."

"One leads to the other," admitted Kelly. He continued, "You see, Pastor, it's mostly a small town in Tuscany shunting stones at Meynooth, which is, as you know, a few miles out from Dublin."

"I'm Irish," said the pastor, patiently.

"So you are, Pastor, and all the more reason we can't figure your great calm in this disaster," said Father Brian.

"I'm California Irish," said the pastor.

He let this sink in. When it had gone to the bottom, Father Brian groaned miserably. "Ah. We *forgot.*"

And he looked at the pastor and saw there the recent dark, the tan complexion of one who walked with his face like a sunflower to the sky, even here in Chicago, taking what little light and heat he could to sustain his color and being. Here stood a man with the figure, still, of a badminton and tennis player under his tunic, and with the firm lean hands of the handball expert. In the pulpit, by the look of his arms moving in the air, you could see him swimming under warm California skies.

Father Kelly let forth one sound of laughter.

"Oh, the gentle ironies, the simple fates. Father Brian, here is our Baptist!"

"Baptist?" asked Pastor Sheldon.

"No offense, Pastor, but we were off to find a mediator, and here you are, an Irishman from California, who has known the wintry blows of Illinois so short a time, you've still the look of rolled lawns and January sunburn. We, we were born and raised on lumps in Cork and Kilcock, Pastor. Twenty years in Hollywood would not thaw us out. And now, well, they do say, don't they, that California is much . . ." here he paused, "like Italy?"

"I see where you're driving," mumbled Father Brian.

Pastor Sheldon nodded, his face both warm and gently sad. "My blood is like your own. But the climate I was shaped in is like Rome's. So you see, Father Brian, when I asked *are* there any sides, I spoke from my heart."

"Irish yet not Irish," mourned Father Brian. "Almost but not quite Italian. Oh, the world's played tricks with our flesh."

"Only if we let it, William, Patrick."

Both men started a bit at the sound of their Christian names.

"You still haven't answered: Why are you afraid?"

Father Brian watched his hands fumble like two bewildered wrestlers for a moment. "Why, it's because just when we get things settled on Earth, just when it looks like victory's in sight, the Church on a good footing, along comes Father Vittorini—"

"Forgive me, Father," said the pastor. "Along comes reality. Along comes space, time, entropy, progress, along come a million things, always. Father Vittorini didn't invent space travel."

"No, but he makes a good thing of it. With him 'everything begins in mysticism and ends in politics.' Well, no matter. I'll stash my shillelagh if he'll put away his rockets."

"No, let's leave them out in the open," replied the pastor. "Best not to hide violence or special forms of travel. Best to work with them. Why don't we climb in that rocket, Father, and learn from it?"

"Learn what? That most of the things we've taught in the past on Earth don't fit out there on Mars or Venus or wherever in hell Vittorini would push us? Drive Adam and Eve out of some new Garden, on Jupiter, with our very own rocket fires? Or worse, find there's no Eden, no Adam, no Eve, no damned Apple nor Serpent, no Fall, no Original Sin, no Annunciation, no Birth, no Son, you go on with the list, no nothing at all! on one blasted world tailing another? Is *that* what we must learn, Pastor?"

"If need be, yes," said Pastor Sheldon. "It's the Lord's space and the Lord's worlds *in* space, Father. We must not try to take our cathedrals with us, when all we need is an overnight case. The Church can be packed in a box no larger than is needed for the articles of the Mass, as much as these hands can carry. Allow Father Vittorini this, the people of the southern climes learned long ago to build in wax which melts and takes its shape in harmony with the motion and need of man. William, William, if you insist on building in hard ice, it will shatter when we break the sound barrier or melt and leave you nothing in the fire of the rocket blast."

"That," said Father Brian, "is a hard thing to learn at fifty years, Pastor."

"But learn, I know you will," said the pastor, touching his shoulder. "I set you a task: to make peace with the Italian priest. Find some way tonight for a meeting of minds. Sweat at it, Father. And, first off, since our library is meager, hunt for and find the space encyclical, so we'll know what we're yelling about."

A moment later the pastor was gone.

Father Brian listened to the dying sound of those swift feet—as if a white ball were flying high in the sweet blue air and the pastor were hurrying in for a fine volley.

"Irish but not Irish," he said. "Almost but not quite Italian. And now what are we, Patrick?"

"I begin to wonder," was the reply.

And they went away to a larger library wherein might be hid the grander thoughts of a Pope on a bigger space.

A long while after supper that night, in fact almost at bedtime, Father Kelly, sent on his mission, moved about the rectory tapping on doors and whispering.

Shortly before ten o'clock, Father Vittorini came down the stairs and gasped with surprise.

Father Brian, at the unused fireplace, warming himself at the small gas heater which stood on the hearth, did not turn for a moment.

A space had been cleared and the brute television set moved forward into a circle of four chairs, amongst which stood two small taborettes on which stood two bottles and four glasses. Father Brian had done it all, allowing Kelly to do nothing. Now he turned, for Kelly and Pastor Sheldon were arriving.

The pastor stood in the entryway and surveyed the room. "Splendid." He paused and added, "I think. Let me see now . . ." He read the label on one bottle. "Father Vittorini is to sit here."

"By the Irish Moss?" asked Vittorini.

"The same," said Father Brian.

Vittorini, much pleased, sat.

"And the rest of us will sit by the Lachryma Christi, I take it?" said the pastor.

"An *Italian* drink, Pastor."

"I think I've heard of it," said the pastor, and sat.

"Here." Father Brian hurried over and, without looking at Vittorini, poured his glass a good way up with the Moss. "An Irish transfusion."

"Allow me." Vittorini nodded his thanks and arose, in turn, to pour the others' drinks. "The tears of Christ and the sunlight of Italy," he said. "And now, before we drink, I have something to say."

The others waited, looking at him.

"The papal encyclical on space travel," he said at last, "does not exist."

"We discovered that," said Kelly, "a few hours ago."

"Forgive me, Fathers," said Vittorini. "I am like the fisherman on the bank who, seeing fish, throws out more bait. I suspected, all along, there was no encyclical. But every time it was brought up, about town, I heard so many priests from Dublin deny it existed, I came to think it *must!* They would not go check the item, for they feared it existed. I would not, in my pride, do research, for I feared it *did not* exist. So Roman pride or Cork pride, it's all the same. I shall go on retreat soon and be silent for a week, Pastor, and do penance."

"Good, Father, good." Pastor Sheldon rose. "Now I've a small announcement. A new priest arrives here next month. I've thought long on it. The man is Italian, born and raised in Montreal."

Vittorini closed one eye and tried to picture this man to himself.

"If the Church must be all things to all people," said the pastor, "I am intrigued with the thought of hot blood raised in a cold climate, as this new Italian was, even as I find it fascinating to consider myself, cold blood raised in California. We've needed another Italian here to shake things up, and this Latin looks to be the sort will shake even Father Vittorini. Now will someone offer a toast?"

"May I, Pastor?" Father Vittorini rose again, smiling gently, his eyes darkly aglow, looking at this one and now that of the three. He raised his glass. "Somewhere did Blake not speak of the Machineries of Joy? That is, did not God promote environments, then intimidate those Natures by provoking the existence of flesh, toy men and women, such as are we all? And thus happily sent forth, at our best, with good grace and fine wit, on calm noons, in fair climes, are we not God's Machineries of Joy?"

"If Blake said that," said Father Brian, "I take it all back. He never lived in Dublin!"

All laughed together.

Vittorini drank the Irish Moss and was duly speechless.

The others drank the Italian wine and grew mellow, and in his mellowness Father Brian cried softly, "Vittorini, now, will you, unholy as it is, tune on the ghost?"

"Channel Nine?"

"Nine it is!"

And while Vittorini dialed the knobs Father Brian mused over his drink, "Did Blake *really* say that?"

"The fact is, Father," said Vittorini, bent to the phantoms coming and going on the screen, "he might have, if he'd lived today. I wrote it down myself tonight."

All watched the Italian with some awe. Then the TV gave a hum and came clear, showing a rocket, a long way off, getting ready.

"The machineries of joy," said Father Brian. "Is that one of them you're tuning in? And is that another sitting there, the rocket on its stand?"

"It could be, tonight," murmured Vittorini. "If the thing goes up, and a man in it, all around the world, and him still alive, and us with him, though we just sit here. That would be joyful indeed."

The rocket was getting ready, and Father Brian shut his eyes for a moment. Forgive me, Jesus, he thought, forgive an old man his prides, and forgive Vittorini his spites, and help me to understand what I see here tonight, and let me stay awake if need be, in good humor, until dawn, and let the thing go well, going up and coming down, and think of the man in that contraption, Jesus, *think* of and be with him. And help me, God, when the summer is young, for, sure as fate on Fourth of July evening there will be Vittorini and the kids from around the block, on the rectory lawn, lighting skyrockets. All of them there watching the sky, like the morn of the Redemption, and help me, O Lord, to be as those children before the great night of time and void where you abide. And help me to walk forward, Lord, to light the next rocket Independence Night, and stand with the Latin father, my face suffused with that same look of the delighted child in the face of the burning glories you put near our hand and bid us savor.

He opened his eyes.

Voices from far Canaveral were crying in a wind of time. Strange phantom powers loomed upon the screen. He was drinking the last of the wine when someone touched his elbow gently.

"Father," said Vittorini, near. "Fasten your seat belt."

"I will," said Father Brian. "I will. And many thanks."

He sat back in his chair. He closed his eyes. He waited for the thunder. He waited for the fire. He waited for the concussion and the voice that would teach a silly, a strange, a wild and miraculous thing:

How to count back, ever backward . . . to zero.

THE ONE WHO WAITS

I live in a well. I live like smoke in the well. Like vapor in a stone throat. I don't move. I don't do anything but wait. Overhead I see the cold stars of night and morning, and I see the sun. And sometimes I sing old songs of this world when it was young. How can I tell you what I am when I don't know? I cannot. I am simply waiting. I am mist and moonlight and memory. I am sad and I am old. Sometimes I fall like rain into the well. Spider webs are startled into forming where my rain falls fast, on the water surface. I wait in cool silence and there will be a day when I no longer wait.

Now it is morning. I hear a great thunder. I smell fire from a distance. I hear a metal crashing. I wait. I listen.

Voices. Far away.

"All right!"

One voice. An alien voice. An alien tongue I cannot know. No word is familiar. I listen.

"Send the men out!"

A crunching in crystal sands.

"Mars! So this is it!"

"Where's the flag?"

"Here, sir."

"Good, good."

The sun is high in the blue sky and its golden rays fill the well and I hang like a flower pollen, invisible and misting in the warm light.

Voices.

"In the name of the Government of Earth, I proclaim this to be the Martian Territory, to be equally divided among the member nations."

What are they saying? I turn in the sun, like a wheel, invisible and lazy, golden and tireless.

"What's over here?"

14

"A well!"

"No!"

"Come on. Yes!"

The approach of warmth. Three objects bend over the well mouth, and my coolness rises to the objects.

"Great!"

"Think it's good water?"

"We'll see."

"Someone get a lab test bottle and a dropline."

"I will!"

A sound of running. The return.

"Here we are."

I wait.

"Let it down. Easy."

Glass shines, above, coming down on a slow line.

The water ripples softly as the glass touches and fills. I rise in the warm air toward the well mouth.

"Here we are. You want to test this water, Regent?"

"Let's have it."

"What a beautiful well. Look at that construction. How old you think it is?"

"God knows. When we landed in that other town yesterday Smith said there hasn't been life on Mars in ten thousand years."

"Imagine."

"How is it, Regent? The water."

"Pure as silver. Have a glass."

The sound of water in the hot sunlight. Now I hover like a dust, a cinnamon, upon the soft wind.

"What's the matter, Jones?"

"I don't know. Got a terrible headache. All of a sudden."

"Did you drink the water yet?"

"No, I haven't. It's not that. I was just bending over the well and all of a sudden my head split. I feel better now."

Now I know who I am.

My name is Stephen Leonard Jones and I am twenty-five years old and I have just come in a rocket from a planet called Earth and I am standing with my good friends Regent and Shaw by an old well on the planet Mars.

I look down at my golden fingers, tan and strong. I look at my long legs and at my silver uniform and at my friends.

"What's wrong, Jones?" they say.

"Nothing," I say, looking at them. "Nothing at all."

The food is good. It has been ten thousand years since food. It touches the tongue in a fine way and the wine with the food is warming. I listen to the sound of voices. I make words that I do not understand but somehow understand. I test the air.

"What's the matter, Jones?"

I tilt this head of mine and rest my hands holding the silver utensils of eating. I feel everything.

"What do you mean?" this voice, this new thing of mine, says.

"You keep breathing funny. Coughing," says the other man.

I pronounce exactly. "Maybe a little cold coming on."

"Check with the doc later."

I nod my head and it is good to nod. It is good to do several things after ten thousand years. It is good to breathe the air and it is good to feel the sun in the flesh deep and going deeper and it is good to feel the structure of ivory, the fine skeleton hidden in the warming flesh, and it is good to hear sounds much clearer and more immediate than they were in the stone deepness of a well. I sit enchanted.

"Come out of it, Jones. Snap to it. We got to move!"

"Yes," I say, hypnotized with the way the word forms like water on the tongue and falls with slow beauty out into the air.

I walk and it is good walking. I stand high and it is a long way to the ground when I look down from my eyes and my head. It is like living on a fine cliff and being happy there.

Regent stands by the stone well, looking down. The others have gone murmuring to the silver ship from which they came.

I feel the fingers of my hand and the smile of my mouth.

"It is deep," I say.

"Yes."

"It is called a Soul Well."

Regent raises his head and looks at me. "How do you know that?"

"Doesn't it look like one?"

"I never heard of a Soul Well."

"A place where waiting things, things that once had flesh, wait and wait," I say, touching his arm.

The sand is fire and the ship is silver fire in the hotness

of the day and the heat is good to feel. The sound of my feet in the hard sand. I listen. The sound of the wind and the sun burning the valleys. I smell the smell of the rocket boiling in the noon. I stand below the port.

"Where's Regent?" someone says.

"I saw him by the well," I reply.

One of them runs toward the well. I am beginning to tremble. A fine shivering tremble, hidden deep, but becoming very strong. And for the first time I hear it, as if it too were hidden in a well. A voice calling deep within me, tiny and afraid. And the voice cries, *Let me go, let me go,* and there is a feeling as if something is trying to get free, a pounding of labyrinthine doors, a rushing down dark corridors and up passages, echoing and screaming.

"Regent's in the well!"

The men are running, all five of them. I run with them but now I am sick and the trembling is violent.

"He must have fallen. Jones, you were here with him. Did you see? Jones? Well, speak up, man."

"What's wrong, Jones?"

I fall to my knees, the trembling is so bad.

"He's sick. Here, help me with him."

"The sun."

"No, not the sun," I murmur.

They stretch me out and the seizures come and go like earthquakes and the deep hidden voice in me cries, *This is Jones, this is me, that's not him, that's not him, don't believe him, let me out, let me out!* And I look up at the bent figures and my eyelids flicker. They touch my wrists.

"His heart is acting up."

I close my eyes. The screaming stops. The shivering ceases. I rise, as in a cool well, released.

"He's dead," says someone.

"Jones is dead."

"From what?"

"Shock, it looks like."

"What kind of shock?" I say, and my name is Sessions and my lips move crisply, and I am the captain of these men. I stand among them and I am looking down at a body which lies cooling on the sands. I clap both hands to my head.

"Captain!"

"It's nothing," I say, crying out. "Just a headache. I'll be all right. There. There," I whisper. "It's all right now."

"We'd better get out of the sun, sir."

"Yes," I say, looking down at Jones. "We should never have come. Mars doesn't want us."

We carry the body back to the rocket with us, and a new voice is calling deep in me to be let out.

Help, help. Far down in the moist earthen-works of the body. *Help, help!* in red fathoms, echoing and pleading.

The trembling starts much sooner this time. The control is less steady.

"Captain, you'd better get in out of the sun, you don't look too well, sir."

"Yes," I say. "Help," I say.

"What, sir?"

"I didn't say anything."

"You said 'Help,' sir."

"Did I, Matthews, did I?"

The body is laid out in the shadow of the rocket and the voice screams in the deep underwater catacombs of bone and crimson tide. My hands jerk. My mouth splits and is parched. My nostrils fasten wide. My eyes roll. *Help, help, oh help, don't, don't, let me out, don't, don't.*

"Don't," I say.

"What, sir?"

"Never mind," I say. "I've got to get free," I say. I clap my hand to my mouth.

"How's that, sir?" cries Matthews.

"Get inside, all of you, go back to Earth!" I shout.

A gun is in my hand. I lift it.

"Don't, sir!"

An explosion. Shadows run. The screaming is cut off. There is a whistling sound of falling through space.

After ten thousand years, how good to die. How good to feel the sudden coolness, the relaxation. How good to be like a hand within a glove that stretches out and grows wonderfully cold in the hot sand. Oh, the quiet and the loveliness of gathering, darkening death. But one cannot linger on.

A crack, a snap.

"Good God, he's killed himself!" I cry, and open my eyes and there is the captain lying against the rocket, his skull split by a bullet, his eyes wide, his tongue protruding between his white teeth. Blood runs from his head. I bend to him and touch him. "The fool," I say. "Why did he do that?"

The men are horrified. They stand over the two dead men and turn their heads to see the Martian sands and the distant well where Regent lies lolling in deep waters. A croaking comes out of their dry lips, a whimpering, a childish protest against this awful dream.

The men turn to me.

After a long while, one of them says, "That makes you captain, Matthews."

"I know," I say slowly.

"Only six of us left."

"Good God, it happened so quick!"

"I don't want to stay here, let's get out!"

The men clamor. I go to them and touch them now, with a confidence which almost sings in me. "Listen," I say, and touch their elbows or their arms or their hands.

We all fall silent.

We are one.

No, no, no, no, no, no! Inner voices crying, deep down and gone into prisons beneath exteriors.

We are looking at each other. We are Samuel Matthews and Raymond Moses and William Spaulding and Charles Evans and Forrest Cole and John Summers, and we say nothing but look upon each other and our white faces and shaking hands.

We turn, as one, and look at the well.

"Now," we say.

No, no, six voices scream, hidden and layered down and stored forever.

Our feet walk in the sand and it is as if a great hand with twelve fingers were moving across the hot sea bottom.

We bend to the well, looking down. From the cool depths six faces peer back up at us.

One by one we bend until our balance is gone, and one by one drop into the mouth and down through cool darkness into the cold waters.

The sun sets. The stars wheel upon the night sky. Far out, there is a wink of light. Another rocket coming, leaving red marks on space.

I live in a well. I live like smoke in a well. Like vapor in a stone throat. Overhead I see the cold stars of night and morning, and I see the sun. And sometimes I sing old songs of this world when it was young. How can I tell you what I am when even I don't know? I cannot.

I am simply waiting.

TYRANNOSAURUS REX

He opened a door on darkness. A voice cried, "Shut it!" It was like a blow in the face. He jumped through. The door banged. He cursed himself quietly. The voice, with dreadful patience, intoned, "Jesus. You Terwilliger?"

"Yes," said Terwilliger. A faint ghost of screen haunted the dark theater wall to his right. To his left, a cigarette wove fiery arcs in the air as someone's lips talked swiftly around it.

"You're five minutes late!"

Don't make it sound like five years, thought Terwilliger.

"Shove your film in the projection room door. Let's *move*." Terwilliger squinted.

He made out five vast loge seats that exhaled, breathed heavily as amplitudes of executive life shifted, leaning toward the middle loge where, almost in darkness, a little boy sat smoking.

No, thought Terwilliger, not a boy. That's him, Joe Clarence. Clarence the Great.

For now the tiny mouth snapped like a puppet's, blowing smoke. "Well?"

Terwilliger stumbled back to hand the film to the projectionist, who made a lewd gesture toward the loges, winked at Terwilliger and slammed the booth door.

"Jesus," sighed the tiny voice. A buzzer buzzed. "Roll it, projection!"

Terwilliger probed the nearest loge, struck flesh, pulled back and stood biting his lips.

Music leaped from the screen. His film appeared in a storm of drums:

TYRANNOSAURUS REX: The Thunder Lizard.

Photographed in stop-motion animation with miniatures created by John Terwilliger. A study in life-forms on Earth one billion years before Christ.

21

Faint ironic applause came softly patting from the baby hands in the middle loge.

Terwilliger shut his eyes. New music jerked him alert. The last titles faded into a world of primeval sun, mist, poisonous rain and lush wilderness. Morning fogs were strewn along eternal seacoasts where immense flying dreams and dreams of nightmare scythed the wind. Huge triangles of bone and rancid skin, of diamond eye and crusted tooth, pterodactyls, the kites of destruction, plunges, struck prey, and skimmed away, meat and screams in their scissor mouths.

Terwilliger gazed, fascinated.

In the jungle foliage now, shiverings, creepings, insect jitterings, antennae twitchings, slime locked in oily fatted slime, armor skinned to armor, in sun glade and shadow moved the reptilian inhabitors of Terwilliger's mad remembrance of vengeance given flesh and panic taking wing.

Brontosaur, stegosaur, triceratops. How easily the clumsy tonnages of name fell from one's lips.

The great brutes swung like ugly machineries of war and dissolution through moss ravines, crushing a thousand flowers at one footfall, snouting the mist, ripping the sky in half with one shriek.

My beauties, thought Terwilliger, my little lovelies. All liquid latex, rubber sponge, ball-socketed steel articulature; all nightdreamed, clay-molded, warped and welded, riveted and slapped to life by hand. No bigger than my fist, half of them; the rest no larger than this head they sprang from.

"Good Lord," said a soft admiring voice in the dark.

Step by step, frame by frame of film, stop motion by stop motion, he, Terwilliger, had run his beasts through their postures, moved each a fraction of an inch, photographed them, moved them another hair, photographed them, for hours and days and months. Now these rare images, this eight hundred scant feet of film, rushed through the projector.

And lo! he thought. I'll never get used to it. Look! They come *alive!*

Rubber, steel, clay, reptilian latex sheath, glass eye, porcelain fang, all ambles, trundles, strides in terrible prides through continents as yet unmanned, by seas as yet unsalted, a billion years lost away. They *do* breathe. They *do* smite air with thunders. Oh, uncanny!

I feel, thought Terwilliger, quite simply, that there stands *my* Garden, and these my animal creations which I love on this Sixth Day, and tomorrow, the Seventh, I must rest.

"Lord," said the soft voice again.

Terwilliger almost answered, "Yes?"

"This is beautiful footage, Mr. Clarence," the voice went on.

"Maybe," said the man with a boy's voice.

"Incredible animation."

"I've seen better," said Clarence the Great.

Terwilliger stiffened. He turned from the screen where his friends lumbered into oblivion, from butcheries wrought on architectural scales. For the first time he examined his possible employers.

"Beautiful stuff."

This praise came from an old man who sat to himself far across the theater, his head lifted forward in amazement toward that ancient life.

"It's jerky. Look there!" The strange boy in the middle loge half rose, pointing with the cigarette in his mouth. "Hey, was *that* a bad shot. You *see?*"

"Yes," said the old man, tired suddenly, fading back in his chair. "I see."

Terwilliger crammed his hotness down upon a suffocation of swiftly moving blood.

"Jerky," said Joe Clarence.

White light, quick numerals, darkness; the music cut, the monsters vanished.

"Glad that's over." Joe Clarence exhaled. "Almost lunchtime. Throw on the next reel, Walter! That's all, Terwilliger." Silence. "Terwilliger?" Silence. "Is that dumb bunny still here?"

"Here." Terwilliger ground his fists on his hips.

"Oh," said Joe Clarence. "It's not bad. But don't get ideas about money. A dozen guys came here yesterday to show stuff as good or better than yours, tests for our new film, *Prehistoric Monster*. Leave your bid in an envelope with my secretary. Same door out as you came in. Walter, what the hell are you waiting for? Roll the next one!"

In darkness, Terwilliger barked his shins on a chair, groped for and found the door handle, gripped it tight, tight.

Behind him the screen exploded: an avalanche fell in great flourings of stone, whole cities of granite, immense edifices of marble piled, broke and flooded down. In this thunder, he heard voices from the week ahead:

"We'll pay you one thousand dollars, Terwilliger."

"But I need a thousand for my equipment alone!"

"Look, we're giving you a break. Take it or leave it!"

With the thunder dying, he knew he would take, and he knew he would hate it.

Only when the avalanche had drained off to silence behind him and his own blood had raced to the inevitable decision and stalled in his heart, did Terwilliger pull the immensely weighted door wide to step forth into the terrible raw light of day.

Fuse flexible spine to sinuous neck, pivot neck to death's-head skull, hinge jaw from hollow cheek, glue plastic sponge over lubricated skeleton, slip snake-pebbled skin over sponge, meld seams with fire, then rear upright triumphant in a world where insanity wakes but to look on madness—Tyrannosaurus Rex!

The Creator's hands glided down out of arc-light sun. They placed the granuled monster in false green summer wilds, they waded it in broths of teeming bacterial life. Planted in serene terror, the lizard machine basked. From the blind heavens the Creator's voice hummed, vibrating the Garden with the old and monotonous tune about the foot-bone connected to the . . . anklebone, anklebone connected to the . . . legbone, legbone connected to the . . . kneebone, kneebone connected to the . . .

A door burst wide.

Joe Clarence ran in very much like an entire Cub Scout pack. He looked wildly around as if no one were there.

"My God!" he cried. "Aren't you set up yet? This costs me money!"

"No," said Terwilliger dryly. "No matter how much time I take, I get paid the same."

Joe Clarence approached in a series of quick starts and stops. "Well, shake a leg. And make it real horrible."

Terwilliger was on his knees beside the miniature jungle set. His eyes were on a straight level with his producer's as he said, "How many feet of blood and gore would you like?"

"Two thousand feet of each!" Clarence laughed in a kind of gasping stutter. "Let's look." He grabbed the lizard.

"Careful!"

"Careful?" Clarence turned the ugly beast in careless and nonloving hands. "It's my monster, ain't it? The contract—"

"The contract says you use this model for exploitation advertising, but the animal reverts to me after the film's in release."

"Holy cow." Clarence waved the monster. "That's wrong. We just signed the contracts four days ago—"

"It feels like four years." Terwilliger rubbed his eyes. "I've been up two nights without sleep finishing this beast so we can start shooting."

Clarence brushed this aside. "To hell with the contract. What a slimy trick. It's my monster. You and your agent give me heart attacks. Heart attacks about money, heart attacks about equipment, heart attacks about—"

"This camera you gave me is ancient."

"So if it breaks, fix it; you got hands? The challenge of the shoestring operation is using the old brain instead of cash. Getting back to the point, this monster, it should've been specified in the deal, is my baby."

"I never let anyone own the things I make," said Terwilliger honestly. "I put too much time and affection in them."

"Hell, okay, so we give you fifty bucks extra for the beast, and throw in all this camera equipment free when the film's done, right? Then you start your own company. Compete with me, get even with me, right, using my own machines!" Clarence laughed.

"If they don't fall apart first," observed Terwilliger.

"Another thing." Clarence put the creature on the floor and walked around it. "I don't like the way this monster shapes up."

"You don't like *what?*" Terwilliger almost yelled.

"His expression. Needs more fire, more . . . goombah. More mazash!"

"Mazash?"

"The old bimbo! Bug the eyes more. Flex the nostrils. Shine the teeth. Fork the tongue sharper. You can *do* it! Uh, the monster ain't mine, huh?"

"Mine." Terwilliger arose.

His belt buckle was now on a line with Joe Clarence's eyes. The producer stared at the bright buckle almost hypnotically for a moment.

"God damn the goddam lawyers!"

He broke for the door.

"Work!"

The monster hit the door a split second after it slammed shut.

Terwilliger kept his hand poised in the air from his overhand throw. Then his shoulders sagged. He went to pick up his beauty. He twisted off its head, skinned the latex flesh off the skull, placed the skull on a pedestal and, painstakingly, with clay, began to reshape the prehistoric face.

"A little goombah," he muttered. "A touch of mazash."

. . .

They ran the first film test on the animated monster a week later.

When it was over, Clarence sat in darkness and nodded imperceptibly.

"Better. But . . . more horrorific, bloodcurdling. Let's scare the hell out of Aunt Jane. Back to the drawing board!"

"I'm a week behind schedule now," Terwilliger protested. "You keep coming in, change this, change that, you say, so I change it, one day the tail's all wrong, next day it's the claws—"

"You'll find a way to make me happy," said Clarence. "Get in there and fight the old aesthetic fight!"

At the end of the month they ran the second test.

"A near miss! Close!" said Clarence. "The face is just almost right. Try again, Terwilliger!"

Terwilliger went back. He animated the dinosaur's mouth so that it said obscene things which only a lip reader might catch, while the rest of the audience thought the beast was only shrieking. Then he got the clay and worked until 3 A.M. on the awful face.

"That's it!" cried Clarence in the projection room the next week. "Perfect! Now *that's* what I call a monster!"

He leaned toward the old man, his lawyer, Mr. Glass, and Maury Poole, his production assistant.

"You *like* my creature?" He beamed.

Terwilliger, slumped in the back row, his skeleton as long as the monsters he built, could feel the old lawyer shrug.

"You seen one monster, you seen 'em all."

"Sure, sure, but this one's special!" shouted Clarence happily. "Even *I* got to admit Terwilliger's a genius!"

They all turned back to watch the beast on the screen, in

a titanic waltz, throw its razor tail wide in a vicious harvesting that cut grass and clipped flowers. The beast paused now to gaze pensively off into mists, gnawing a red bone.

"That monster," said Mr. Glass at last, squinting. "He sure looks familiar."

"Familiar?" Terwilliger stirred, alert.

"It's got such a look," drawled Mr. Glass in the dark, "I couldn't forget, from someplace."

"Natural Museum exhibits?"

"No, no."

"Maybe," laughed Clarence, "you read a book once, Glass?"

"Funny . . ." Glass, unperturbed, cocked his head, closed one eye. "Like detectives, I don't forget a face. But, that Tyrannosaurus Rex—where before did I meet *him?*"

"Who cares?" Clarence sprinted. "He's great. And all because I booted Terwilliger's behind to make him do it right. Come on, Maury!"

When the door shut, Mr. Glass turned to gaze steadily at Terwilliger. Not taking his eyes away, he called softly to the projectionist. "Walt? Walter? Could you favor us with that beast again?"

"Sure thing."

Terwilliger shifted uncomfortably, aware of some bleak force gathering in blackness, in the sharp light that shot forth once more to ricochet terror off the screen.

"Yeah. Sure," mused Mr. Glass. "I almost remember. I almost know him. But . . . *who?*"

The brute, as if answering, turned and for a disdainful moment stared across one hundred thousand million years at two small men hidden in a small dark room. The tyrant machine named itself in thunder.

Mr. Glass quickened forward, as if to cup his ear.

Darkness swallowed all.

With the film half finished, in the tenth week, Clarence summoned thirty of the office staff, technicians and a few friends to see a rough cut of the picture.

The film had been running fifteen minutes when a gasp ran through the small audience.

Clarence glanced swiftly about.

Mr. Glass, next to him, stiffened.

Terwilliger, scenting danger, lingered near the exit, not

knowing why; his nervousness was compulsive and intuitive. Hand on the door, he watched.

Another gasp ran through the crowd.

Someone laughed quietly. A woman secretary giggled. Then there was instantaneous silence.

For Joe Clarence had jumped to his feet.

His tiny figure sliced across the light on the screen. For a moment, two images gesticulated in the dark: Tyrannosaurus, ripping the leg from a Pteranodon, and Clarence, yelling, jumping forward as if to grapple with these fantastic wrestlers.

"Stop! Freeze it right there!"

The film stopped. The image held.

"What's wrong?" asked Mr. Glass.

"Wrong?" Clarence crept up on the image. He thrust his baby hand to the screen, stabbed the tyrant jaw, the lizard eye, the fangs, the brow, then turned blindly to the projector light so that reptilian flesh was printed on his furious cheeks. "What goes? What *is* this?"

"Only a monster, Chief."

"Monster, hell!" Clarence pounded the screen with his tiny fist. "That's *me!*"

Half the people leaned forward, half the people fell back, two people jumped up, one of them Mr. Glass, who fumbled for his other spectacles, flexed his eyes and moaned, "So *that's* where I saw him before!"

"That's where you what?"

Mr. Glass shook his head, eyes shut. "That face, I *knew* it was familiar."

A wind blew in the room.

Everyone turned. The door stood open.

Terwilliger was gone.

They found Terwilliger in his animation studio cleaning out his desk, dumping everything into a large cardboard box, the Tyrannosaurus machine-toy model under his arm. He looked up as the mob swirled in, Clarence at the head.

"What did I do to deserve this!" he cried.

"I'm sorry, Mr. Clarence."

"You're sorry?! Didn't I pay you well?"

"No, as a matter of fact."

"I took you to lunches—"

"Once. I picked up the tab."

"I gave you dinner at home, you swam in my pool, and now *this!* You're fired!"

"You can't fire me, Mr. Clarence. I've worked the last week free and overtime, you forgot my check—"

"You're fired anyway, oh, you're *really* fired! You're black-balled in Hollywood. Mr. Glass!" He whirled to find the old man. "Sue him!"

"There is nothing," said Terwilliger, not looking up any more, just looking down, packing, keeping in motion, "nothing you can sue me for. Money? You never paid enough to save on. A house? Could never afford that. A wife? I've worked for people like you all my life. So wives are out. I'm an unencumbered man. There's nothing you can do to me. If you attach my dinosaurs, I'll just go hole up in a small town somewhere, get me a can of latex rubber, some clay from the river, some old steel pipe, and make new monsters. I'll buy stock film raw and cheap. I've got an old beat-up stop-motion camera. Take that away, and I'll build one with my own hands. I can do anything. And that's why you'll never hurt me again."

"You're fired!" cried Clarence. "Look at me. Don't look away. You're fired! You're fired!"

"Mr. Clarence," said Mr. Glass, quietly, edging forward. "Let me talk to him just a moment."

"So talk to him!" said Clarence. "What's the use? He just stands there with that monster under his arm and the god-dam thing looks like me, so get out of the way!"

Clarence stormed out the door. The others followed.

Mr. Glass shut the door, walked over to the window and looked out at the absolutely clear twilight sky.

"I wish it would rain," he said. "That's one thing about California I can't forgive. It never really lets go and cries. Right now, what wouldn't I give for a little something from that sky? A bolt of lightning, even."

He stood silent, and Terwilliger slowed in his packing. Mr. Glass sagged down into a chair and doodled on a pad with a pencil, talking sadly, half aloud, to himself.

"Six reels of film shot, pretty good reels, half the film done, three hundred thousand dollars down the drain, hail and farewell. Out the window all the jobs. Who feeds the starving mouths of boys and girls? Who will face the stock-holders? Who chucks the Bank of America under the chin? Anyone for Russian roulette?"

He turned to watch Terwilliger snap the locks on a brief-case.

"What hath God wrought?"

Terwilliger, looking down at his hands, turning them over to examine their texture, said, "I didn't know I was doing it, I swear. It came out in my fingers. It was all subconscious. My fingers do everything for me. They did *this.*"

"Better the fingers had come in my office and taken me direct by the throat," said Glass. "I was never one for slow motion. The Keystone Kops, at triple speed, was my idea of living, or dying. To think a rubber monster has stepped on us all. We are now so much tomato mush, ripe for canning!"

"Don't make me feel any guiltier than I feel," said Terwilliger.

"What do you want, I should take you dancing?"

"It's just," cried Terwilliger. "He kept at me. Do this. Do that. Do it the other way. Turn it inside out, upside down, he said. I swallowed my bile. I was angry all the time. Without knowing, I must've changed the face. But right up till five minutes ago, when Mr. Clarence yelled, I didn't see it. I'll take all the blame."

"No," sighed Mr. Glass, "we should *all* have seen. Maybe we did and couldn't admit. Maybe we did and laughed all night in our sleep, when we couldn't hear. So where are we now? Mr. Clarence, he's got investments he can't throw out. You got your career from this day forward, for better or worse, you can't throw out. Mr. Clarence right now is aching to be convinced it was all some horrible dream. Part of his ache, ninety-nine per cent, is in his wallet. If you could put one per cent of your time in the next hour convincing him of what I'm going to tell you next, tomorrow morning there will be no orphan children staring out of the want ads in *Variety* and the *Hollywood Reporter*. If you would go tell him—"

"Tell me *what?*"

Joe Clarence, returned, stood in the door, his cheeks still inflamed.

"What he just told me." Mr. Glass turned calmly. "A touching story."

"I'm listening!" said Clarence.

"Mr. Clarence." The old lawyer weighed his words carefully. "This film you just saw is Mr. Terwilliger's solemn and silent tribute to you."

"It's *what?*" shouted Clarence.

Both men, Clarence and Terwilliger, dropped their jaws. The old lawyer gazed only at the wall and in a shy voice said, "Shall I go on?"

The animator closed his jaw. "If you want to."

"This film—" the lawyer arose and pointed in a single motion toward the projection room— "was done from a feeling of honor and friendship for you, Joe Clarence. Behind your desk, an unsung hero of the motion picture industry, unknown, unseen, you sweat out your lonely little life while who gets the glory? The stars. How often does a man in Atawanda Springs, Idaho, tell his wife, 'Say, I was thinking the other night about Joe Clarence—a great producer, that man'? How often? Should I tell? Never! So Terwilliger brooded. How could he present the real Clarence to the world? The dinosaur is there; boom! it hits him! This is it! he thought, the very thing to strike terror to the world, here's a lonely, proud, wonderful, awful symbol of independence, power, strength, shrewd animal cunning, the true democrat, the individual brought to its peak, all thunder and big lightning. Dinosaur: Joe Clarence. Joe Clarence: Dinosaur. Man embodied in Tyrant Lizard!"

Mr. Glass sat down, panting quietly.

Terwilliger said nothing.

Clarence moved at last, walked across the room, circled Glass slowly, then came to stand in front of Terwilliger, his face pale. His eyes were uneasy, shifting up along Terwilliger's tall skeleton frame.

"You said *that?*" he asked faintly.

Terwilliger swallowed.

"To me he said it. He's shy," said Mr. Glass. "You ever hear him say much, ever talk back, swear? anything? He likes people, he can't say. But, immortalize them? That he can do!"

"Immortalize?" said Clarence.

"What else?" said the old man. "Like a statue, only moving. Years from now people will say, 'Remember that film, *The Monster from the Pleistocene?*' And people will say, 'Sure! why?' 'Because,' the others say, 'it was the one monster, the one brute, in all Hollywood history had real guts, real personality. And why is this? Because one genius had enough imagination to base the creature on a real-life, hard-hitting, fast-thinking businessman of A-one caliber.' You're one with history, Mr. Clarence. Film libraries will carry you in good supply. Cinema societies will ask for you. How lucky can you get? Nothing like this will ever happen to Immanuel Glass, a lawyer. Every day for the next two hundred, five hundred years, you'll be starring somewhere in the world!"

"*Every* day?" asked Clarence softly. "For the next—"

"Eight hundred, even; why not?"

"I never thought of that."

"Think of it!"

Clarence walked over to the window and looked out at the Hollywood Hills, and nodded at last.

"My God, Terwilliger," he said. "You really like me *that* much?"

"It's hard to put in words," said Terwilliger, with difficulty.

"So do we finish the mighty spectacle?" asked Glass. "Starring the tyrant terror striding the earth and making all quake before him, none other than Mr. Joseph J. Clarence?"

"Yeah. Sure." Clarence wandered off, stunned, to the door, where he said, "You know? I always *wanted* to be an actor!"

Then he went quietly out into the hall and shut the door.

Terwilliger and Glass collided at the desk, both clawing at a drawer.

"Age before beauty," said the lawyer, and quickly pulled forth a bottle of whisky.

At midnight on the night of the first preview of *Monster from the Stone Age*, Mr. Glass came back to the studio, where everyone was gathering for a celebration, and found Terwilliger seated alone in his office, his dinosaur on his lap.

"You weren't *there?*" asked Mr. Glass.

"I couldn't face it. Was there a riot?"

"A riot? The preview cards are all superdandy extra plus! A lovelier monster nobody saw before! So now we're talking sequels! Joe Clarence as the Tyrant Lizard in *Return of the Stone Age Monster*, Joe Clarence and/or Tyrannosaurus Rex in, maybe, *Beast from the Old Country*—"

The phone rang. Terwilliger got it.

"Terwilliger, this is Clarence! Be there in five minutes! We've done it! Your animal! Great! Is he mine now? I mean, to hell with the contract, as a favor, can I have him for the mantel?"

"Mr. Clarence, the monster's yours."

"Better than an Oscar! So long!"

Terwilliger stared at the dead phone.

"God bless us all, said Tiny Tim. He's laughing, almost hysterical with relief."

"So maybe I know why," said Mr. Glass. "A little girl, after the preview, asked him for an autograph."

"An *autograph?*"

"Right there in the street. Made him sign. First autograph he ever gave in his life. He laughed all the while he wrote his name. Somebody knew him. There he was, in front of the theater, big as life, Rex Himself, so sign the name. So he did."

"Wait a minute," said Terwilliger slowly, pouring drinks. "That little girl . . . ?"

"My youngest daughter," said Glass. "So who knows? And who will tell?"

They drank.

"Not me," said Terwilliger.

Then, carrying the rubber dinosaur between them, and bringing the whisky, they went to stand by the studio gate, waiting for the limousines to arrive all lights, horns and annunciations.

THE VACATION

It was a day as fresh as grass growing up and clouds going over and butterflies coming down can make it. It was a day compounded from silences of bee and flower and ocean and land, which were not silences at all, but motions, stirs, flutters, risings, fallings, each in its own time and matchless rhythm. The land did not move, but moved. The sea was not still, yet was still. Paradox flowed into paradox, stillness mixed with stillness, sound with sound. The flowers vibrated and the bees fell in separate and small showers of golden rain on the clover. The seas of hill and the seas of ocean were divided, each from the other's motion, by a railroad track, empty, compounded of rust and iron marrow, a track on which, quite obviously, no train had run in many years. Thirty miles north it swirled on away to further mists of distance, thirty miles south it tunneled islands of cloud-shadow that changed their continental positions on the sides of far mountains as you watched.

Now, suddenly, the railroad track began to tremble.

A blackbird, standing on the rail, felt a rhythm grow faintly, miles away, like a heart beginning to beat.

The blackbird leaped up over the sea.

The rail continued to vibrate softly until, at long last, around a curve and along the shore came a small workman's handcar, its two-cylinder engine popping and spluttering in the great silence.

On top of this small four-wheeled car, on a double-sided bench facing in two directions and with a little surrey roof above for shade, sat a man, his wife and their small seven-year-old son. As the handcar traveled through lonely stretch after lonely stretch, the wind whipped their eyes and blew their hair, but they did not look back but only ahead. Sometimes they looked eagerly as a curve unwound itself, some-

34

times with great sadness, but always watchful, ready for the next scene.

As they hit a level straightaway, the machine engine gasped and stopped abruptly. In the now crushing silence, it seemed that the quiet of earth, sky and sea itself, by its friction, brought the car to a wheeling halt.

"Out of gas."

The man, sighing, reached for the extra can in the small storage bin and began to pour it into the tank.

His wife and son sat quietly looking at the sea, listening to the muted thunder, the whisper, the drawing back of huge tapestries of sand, gravel, green weed, and foam.

"Isn't the sea nice?" said the woman.

"I like it," said the boy.

"Shall we picnic here, while we're at it?"

The man focused some binoculars on the green peninsula ahead.

"Might as well. The rails have rusted badly. There's a break ahead. We may have to wait while I set a few back in place."

"As many as there are," said the boy, "we'll have picnics!"

The woman tried to smile at this, then turned her grave attention to the man. "How far have we come today?"

"Not ninety miles." The man still peered through the glasses, squinting. "I don't like to go farther than that any one day, anyway. If you rush, there's no time to see. We'll reach Monterey day after tomorrow, Palo Alto the next day, if you want."

The woman removed her great shadowing straw hat, which had been tied over her golden hair with a bright yellow ribbon, and stood perspiring faintly, away from the machine. They had ridden so steadily on the shuddering rail car that the motion was sewn into their bodies. Now, with the stopping, they felt odd, on the verge of unraveling.

"Let's eat!"

The boy ran the wicker lunch basket down to the shore.

The boy and the woman were already seated by a spread tablecloth when the man came down to them, dressed in his business suit and vest and tie and hat as if he expected to meet someone along the way. As he dealt out the sandwiches and exhumed the pickles from their cool green Mason jars, he began to loosen his tie and unbutton his vest, always looking around as if he should be careful and ready to button up again.

"Are we all alone, Papa?" said the boy, eating.

"Yes."

"No one else, anywhere?"

"No one else."

"Were there people before?"

"Why do you keep asking that? It wasn't that long ago. Just a few months. You remember."

"Almost. If I try hard, then I don't remember at all." The boy let a handful of sand fall through his fingers. "Were there as many people as there is sand here on the beach? What *happened* to them?"

"I don't know," the man said, and it was true.

They had wakened one morning and the world was empty. The neighbors' clothesline was still strung with blowing white wash, cars gleamed in front of other 7-A.M. cottages, but there were no farewells, the city did not hum with its mighty arterial traffics, phones did not alarm themselves, children did not wail in sunflower wildernesses.

Only the night before, he and his wife had been sitting on the front porch when the evening paper was delivered, and, not even daring to open the headlines out, he had said, "I wonder when He will get tired of us and just rub us all out?"

"It has gone pretty far," she said. "On and on. We're such fools, aren't we?"

"Wouldn't it be nice—" he lit his pipe and puffed it— "if we woke tomorrow and everyone in the world was gone and everything was starting over?" He sat smoking, the paper folded in his hand, his head resting back on the chair.

"If you could press a button right now and make it happen, would you?"

"I think I would," he said. "Nothing violent. Just have everyone vanish off the face of the earth. Just leave the land and the sea and the growing things, like flowers and grass and fruit trees. And the animals, of course, let them stay. Everything except man, who hunts when he isn't hungry, eats when full, and is mean when no one's bothered him."

"Naturally, we would be left." She smiled quietly.

"I'd like that," he mused. "All of time ahead. The longest summer vacation in history. And us out for the longest picnic-basket lunch in memory. Just you, me and Jim. No commuting. No keeping up with the Joneses. Not even a car.

I'd like to find another way of traveling, an older way. Then, a hamper full of sandwiches, three bottles of pop, pick up supplies where you need them from empty grocery stores in empty towns, and summertime forever up ahead . . ."

They sat a long while on the porch in silence, the newspaper folded between them.

At last she opened her mouth.

"Wouldn't we be *lonely?*" she said.

So that's how it was the morning of the new world. They had awakened to the soft sounds of an earth that was now no more than a meadow, and the cities of the earth sinking back into seas of saber-grass, marigold, marguerite and morning-glory. They had taken it with remarkable calm at first, perhaps because they had not liked the city for so many years, and had had so many friends who were not truly friends, and had lived a boxed and separate life of their own within a mechanical hive.

The husband arose and looked out the window and observed very calmly, as if it were a weather condition, "Everyone's gone," knowing this just by the sounds the city had ceased to make.

They took their time over breakfast, for the boy was still asleep, and then the husband sat back and said, "Now I must plan what to do."

"Do? Why . . . why, you'll go to work, of course."

"You still don't believe it, do you?" He laughed. "That I won't be rushing off each day at eight-ten, that Jim won't go to school again ever. School's out for all of us! No more pencils, no more books, no more boss's sassy looks! We're let out, darling, and we'll never come back to the silly damn dull routines. Come on!"

And he had walked her through the still and empty city streets.

"They didn't die," he said. "They just . . . went away."

"What about the other cities?"

He went to an outdoor phone booth and dialed Chicago, then New York, then San Francisco.

Silence. Silence. Silence.

"That's it," he said, replacing the receiver.

"I feel guilty," she said. "Them gone and us here. And . . . I feel happy. Why? I *should* be unhappy."

"Should you? It's no tragedy. They weren't tortured or

blasted or burned. They went easily and they didn't know. And now we owe nothing to no one. Our only responsibility is being happy. Thirty more years of happiness, wouldn't that be good?"

"But . . . then we must have more children!"

"To repopulate the world?" He shook his head slowly, calmly. "No. Let Jim be the last. After he's grown and gone let the horses and cows and ground squirrels and garden spiders have the world. They'll get on. And someday some other species that can combine a natural happiness with a natural curiosity will build cities that won't even look like cities to us, and survive. Right now, let's go pack a basket, wake Jim, and get going on that long thirty-year summer vacation. I'll beat you to the house!"

He took a sledge hammer from the small rail car, and while he worked alone for half an hour fixing the rusted rails into place the woman and the boy ran along the shore. They came back with dripping shells, a dozen or more, and some beautiful pink pebbles, and sat and the boy took school from the mother, doing homework on a pad with a pencil for a time, and then at high noon the man came down, his coat off, his tie thrown aside, and they drank orange pop, watching the bubbles surge up, glutting, inside the bottles. It was quiet. They listened to the sun tune the old iron rails. The smell of hot tar on the ties moved about them in the salt wind, as the husband tapped his atlas map lightly and gently.

"We'll go to Sacramento next month, May, then work up toward Seattle. Should make that by July first, July's a good month in Washington, then back down as the weather cools, to Yellowstone, a few miles a day, hunt here, fish there . . ."

The boy, bored, moved away to throw sticks into the sea and wade out like a dog to retrieve them.

The man went on: "Winter in Tucson, then, part of the winter, moving toward Florida, up the coast in the spring, and maybe New York by June. Two years from now, Chicago in the summer. Winter, three years from now, what about Mexico City? Anywhere the rails lead us, anywhere at all, and if we come to an old offshoot rail line we don't know anything about, what the hell, we'll just take it, go down it, to see where it goes. And some year, by God, we'll boat down the Mississippi, always wanted to do that. Enough to last us a lifetime. And that's just how long I want to take to do it all . . ."

His voice faded. He started to fumble the map shut, but, before he could move, a bright thing fell through the air and hit the paper. It rolled off into the sand and made a wet lump.

His wife glanced at the wet place in the sand and then swiftly searched his face. His solemn eyes were too bright. And down one cheek was a track of wetness.

She gasped. She took his hand and held it, tight.

He clenched her hand very hard, his eyes shut now, and slowly he said, with difficulty, "Wouldn't it be nice if we went to sleep tonight and in the night, somehow, it all came back. All the foolishness, all the noise, all the hate, all the terrible things, all the nightmares, all the wicked people and stupid children, all the mess, all the smallness, all the confusion, all the hope, all the need, all the love. Wouldn't it be nice."

She waited and nodded her head once.

Then both of them started.

For standing between them, they knew not for how long, was their son, an empty pop bottle in one hand.

The boy's face was pale. With his free hand he reached out to touch his father's cheek, where the single tear had made its track.

"You," he said. "Oh, Dad, you. You haven't anyone to play with, *either*."

The wife started to speak.

The husband moved to take the boy's hand.

The boy jerked back. "Silly! Oh, silly! Silly fools! Oh, you dumb, dumb!" And, whirling, he rushed down to the ocean and stood there crying loudly.

The wife rose to follow, but the husband stopped her.

"No. Let him."

And then they both grew cold and quiet. For the boy, below on the shore, crying steadily, now was writing on a piece of paper and stuffing it in the pop bottle and ramming the tin cap back on and taking the bottle and giving it a great glittering heave up in the air and out into the tidal sea.

What, thought the wife, what did he write on the note? What's in the bottle?

The bottle moved out in the waves.

The boy stopped crying.

After a long while he walked up the shore, to stand looking at his parents. His face was neither bright nor dark, alive nor dead, ready nor resigned; it seemed a curious mixture that simply made do with time, weather and these people. They looked at him and beyond to the bay, where the bottle containing the scribbled note was almost out of sight now, shining in the waves.

Did he write what *we* wanted? thought the woman, did he write what he heard us just wish, just say?

Or did he write something for only himself, she wondered, that tomorrow he might wake and find himself alone in an empty world, no one around, no man, no woman, no father, no mother, no fool grownups with fool wishes, so he could trudge up to the railroad tracks and take the handcar motoring, a solitary boy, across the continental wilderness, on eternal voyages and picnics?

Is that what he wrote in the note?

Which?

She searched his colorless eyes, could not read the answer; dared not ask.

Gull shadows sailed over and kited their faces with sudden passing coolness.

"Time to go," someone said.

They loaded the wicker basket onto the rail car. The woman tied her large bonnet securely in place with its yellow ribbon, they set the boy's pail of shells on the floorboards, then the husband put on his tie, his vest, his coat, his hat, and they all sat on the benches of the car looking out at the sea where the bottled note was far out, blinking, on the horizon.

"Is asking enough?" said the boy. "Does wishing work?"

"Sometimes . . . *too* well."

"It depends on what you ask for."

The boy nodded, his eyes far away.

They looked back at where they had come from, and then ahead to where they were going.

"Goodbye, place," said the boy, and waved.

The car rolled down the rusty rails. The sound of it dwindled, faded. The man, the woman, the boy dwindled with it in distance, among the hills.

After they were gone, the rail trembled faintly for two minutes, and ceased. A flake of rust fell. A flower nodded.

The sea was very loud.

THE DRUMMER BOY OF SHILOH

In the April night, more than once, blossoms fell from the orchard trees and lit with rustling taps on the drumskin. At midnight a peach stone left miraculously on a branch through winter, flicked by a bird, fell swift and unseen, struck once, like panic, which jerked the boy upright. In silence he listened to his own heart ruffle away, away, at last gone from his ears and back in his chest again.

After that, he turned the drum on its side, where its great lunar face peered at him whenever he opened his eyes.

His face, alert or at rest, was solemn. It was indeed a solemn time and a solemn night for a boy just turned fourteen in the peach field near the Owl Creek not far from the church at Shiloh.

". . . thirty-one, thirty-two, thirty-three . . ."

Unable to see, he stopped counting.

Beyond the thirty-three familiar shadows, forty thousand men, exhausted by nervous expectation, unable to sleep for romantic dreams of battles yet unfought, lay crazily askew in their uniforms. A mile yet farther on, another army was strewn helter-skelter, turning slow, basting themselves with the thought of what they would do when the time came: a leap, a yell, a blind plunge their strategy, raw youth their protection and benediction.

Now and again the boy heard a vast wind come up, that gently stirred the air. But he knew what it was, the army here, the army there, whispering to itself in the dark. Some men talking to others, others murmuring to themselves, and all so quiet it was like a natural element arisen from south or north with the motion of the earth toward dawn.

What the men whispered the boy could only guess, and he guessed that it was: Me, I'm the one, I'm the one of all the rest won't die. I'll live through it. I'll go home. The band will play. And I'll be there to hear it.

Yes, thought the boy, that's all very well for them, they can give as good as they get!

For with the careless bones of the young men harvested by night and bindled around campfires were the similarly strewn steel bones of their rifles, with bayonets fixed like eternal lightning lost in the orchard grass.

Me, thought the boy, I got only a drum, two sticks to beat it, and no shield.

There wasn't a man-boy on this ground tonight did not have a shield he cast, riveted or carved himself on his way to his first attack, compounded of remote but nonetheless firm and fiery family devotion, flag-blown patriotism and cocksure immortality strengthened by the touchstone of very real gunpowder, ramrod, minnieball and flint. But without these last the boy felt his family move yet farther off away in the dark, as if one of those great prairie-burning trains had chanted them away never to return, leaving him with this drum which was worse than a toy in the game to be played tomorrow or some day much too soon.

The boy turned on his side. A moth brushed his face, but it was peach blossom. A peach blossom flicked him, but it was a moth. Nothing stayed put. Nothing had a name. Nothing was as it once was.

If he lay very still, when the dawn came up and the soldiers put on their bravery with their caps, perhaps they might go away, the war with them, and not notice him lying small here, no more than a toy himself.

"Well, by God, now," said a voice.

The boy shut up his eyes, to hide inside himself, but it was too late. Someone, walking by in the night, stood over him.

"Well," said the voice quietly, "here's a soldier crying *before* the fight. Good. Get it over. Won't be time once it all starts."

And the voice was about to move on when the boy, startled, touched the drum at his elbow. The man above, hearing this, stopped. The boy could feel his eyes, sense him slowly bending near. A hand must have come down out of the night, for there was a little rat-tat as the fingernails brushed and the man's breath fanned his face.

"Why, it's the drummer boy, isn't it?"

The boy nodded, not knowing if his nod was seen. "Sir, is that *you?*" he said.

"I assume it is." The man's knees cracked as he bent still closer.

He smelled as all fathers should smell, of salt sweat, ginger tobacco, horse and boot leather, and the earth he walked upon. He had many eyes. No, not eyes, brass buttons that watched the boy.

He could only be, and was, the General.

"What's your name, boy?" he asked.

"Joby," whispered the boy, starting to sit up.

"All right, Joby, don't stir." A hand pressed his chest gently, and the boy relaxed. "How long you been with us, Joby?"

"Three weeks, sir."

"Run off from home or joined legitimately, boy?"

Silence.

"Damn-fool question," said the General. "Do you shave yet, boy? Even more of a damn-fool. There's your cheek, fell right off the tree overhead. And the others here not much older. Raw, raw, damn raw, the lot of you. You ready for tomorrow or the next day, Joby?"

"I think so, sir."

"You want to cry some more, go on ahead. I did the same last night."

"*You,* sir?"

"God's truth. Thinking of everything ahead. Both sides figuring the other side will just give up, and soon, and the war done in weeks, and us all home. Well, that's not how it's going to be. And maybe that's why I cried."

"Yes, sir," said Joby.

The General must have taken out a cigar now, for the dark was suddenly filled with the Indian smell of tobacco unlit as yet, but chewed as the man thought what next to say.

"It's going to be a crazy time," said the General. "Counting both sides, there's a hundred thousand men, give or take a few thousand out there tonight, not one as can spit a sparrow off a tree, or knows a horse clod from a minnieball. Stand up, bare the breast, ask to be a target, thank them and sit down, that's us, that's them. We should turn tail and train four months, they should do the same. But here we are, taken with spring fever and thinking it blood lust, taking our sulphur with cannons instead of with molasses as it should be, going to be a hero, going to live forever. And I can see all of them over there nodding agreement, save the other way around. It's wrong, boy, it's wrong as a head put on hind side front and a man marching backward through life. It will be a double massacre if one of their itchy generals decides to picnic his lads on our grass. More innocents will get shot out of pure Cherokee enthusiasm than ever got shot before. Owl Creek was full of boys splashing around in the noonday sun just a few hours ago. I fear it will be full of boys again, just floating, at sundown tomorrow, not caring where the tide takes them."

The General stopped and made a little pile of winter leaves and twigs in the darkness, as if he might at any moment strike fire to them to see his way through the coming days when the sun might not show its face because of what was happening here and just beyond.

The boy watched the hand stirring the leaves and opened his lips to say something, but did not say it. The General heard the boy's breath and spoke himself.

"Why am I telling you this? That's what you wanted to ask, eh? Well, when you got a bunch of wild horses on a loose rein somewhere, somehow you got to bring order, rein them in. These lads, fresh out of the milkshed, don't know what I know, and I can't tell them: men actually die, in war. So each is his own army. I got to make *one* army of them. And for that, boy, I need you."

"Me!" The boy's lips barely twitched.

"Now, boy," said the General quietly, "you are the heart of the army. Think of that. You're the heart of the army. Listen, now."

And, lying there, Joby listened.

And the General spoke on.

If he, Joby, beat slow tomorrow, the heart would beat slow in the men. They would lag by the wayside. They would drowse in the fields on their muskets. They would sleep forever, after that, in those same fields, their hearts slowed by a drummer boy and stopped by enemy lead.

But if he beat a sure, steady, ever faster rhythm, then, then their knees would come up in a long line down over that hill, one knee after the other, like a wave on the ocean shore! Had he seen the ocean ever? Seen the waves rolling in like a well-ordered cavalry charge to the sand? Well, that was it, that's what he wanted, that's what was needed! Joby was his right hand and his left. He gave the orders, but Joby set the pace!

So bring the right knee up and the right foot out and the left knee up and the left foot out. One following the other in good time, in brisk time. Move the blood up the body and make the head proud and the spine stiff and the jaw resolute. Focus the eye and set the teeth, flare the nostrils and tighten the hands, put steel armor all over the men, for blood moving fast in them does indeed make men feel as they'd put on steel. He must keep at it, at it! Long and steady, steady and long! Then, even though shot or torn, those wounds got in hot blood—in blood he'd helped stir—would feel less pain. If their blood was cold, it would be more than slaughter, it would be murderous nightmare and pain best not told and no one to guess.

The General spoke and stopped, letting his breath slack off. Then, after a moment, he said, "So there you are, that's it. Will you do that, boy? Do you know now you're general of the army when the General's left behind?"

The boy nodded mutely.

"You'll run them through for me then, boy?"

"Yes, sir."

"Good. And, God willing, many nights from tonight, many years from now, when you're as old or far much older than me, when they ask you what you did in this awful time, you will tell them—one part humble and one part proud—'I was the drummer boy at the battle of Owl Creek,' or the Tennessee River, or maybe they'll just name it after the church there. 'I was the drummer boy at Shiloh.' Good grief, that has a beat and sound to it fitting for Mr. Longfellow. 'I was the drummer boy at Shiloh.' Who will ever hear those words and not know you, boy, or what you thought this night, or what you'll think tomorrow or the next day when we must get up on our legs and *move!*"

The general stood up. "Well, then. God bless you, boy. Good night."

"Good night, sir."

And, tobacco, brass, boot polish, salt sweat and leather, the man moved away through the grass.

Joby lay for a moment, staring but unable to see where the man had gone.

He swallowed. He wiped his eyes. He cleared his throat.

He settled himself. Then, at last, very slowly and firmly, he turned the drum so that it faced up toward the sky.

He lay next to it, his arm around it, feeling the tremor, the touch, the muted thunder as, all the rest of the April night in the year 1862, near the Tennessee River, not far from the Owl Creek, very close to the church named Shiloh, the peach blossoms fell on the drum.

BOYS! RAISE GIANT MUSHROOMS IN YOUR CELLAR!

Hugh Fortnum woke to Saturday's commotions and lay, eyes shut, savoring each in its turn.

Below, bacon in a skillet; Cynthia waking him with fine cookings instead of cries.

Across the hall, Tom *actually* taking a shower.

Far off in the bumblebee dragonfly light, whose voice was already damning the weather, the time, and the tides? Mrs. Goodbody? Yes. That Christian giantess, six foot tall with her shoes off, the gardener extraordinary, the octogenarian dietitian and town philosopher.

He rose, unhooked the screen and leaned out to hear her cry, "There! Take *that! This'll* fix you! Hah!"

"Happy Saturday, Mrs. Goodbody!"

The old woman froze in clouds of bug spray pumped from an immense gun.

"Nonsense!" she shouted. "With these fiends and pests to watch for?"

"What kind *this* time?" called Fortnum.

"I don't want to shout it to the jaybirds, but"—she glanced suspiciously around—"what would you say if I told you I was the first line of defense concerning flying saucers?"

"Fine," replied Fortnum. "There'll be rockets between the worlds any year now."

"There already *are!*" She pumped, aiming the spray under the hedge. "There! Take that!"

He pulled his head back in from the fresh day, somehow not as high-spirited as his first response had indicated. Poor soul, Mrs. Goodbody. Always the essence of reason. And now what? Old age?

The doorbell rang.

He grabbed his robe and was half down the stairs when he heard a voice say, "Special delivery. Fortnum?" and saw

47

Cynthia turn from the front door, a small packet in her hand.

"Special-delivery airmail for your son."

Tom was downstairs like a centipede.

"Wow! That must be from the Great Bayou Novelty Greenhouse!"

"I wish I were as excited about ordinary mail," observed Fortnum.

"Ordinary!" Tom ripped the cord and paper wildly. "Don't you read the back pages of *Popular Mechanics?* Well, here *they* are!"

Everyone peered into the small open box.

"Here," said Fortnum, "*what* are?"

"The Sylvan Glade Jumbo-Giant Guaranteed Growth Raise-Them-in-Your-Cellar-for-Big-Profit Mushrooms!"

"Oh, of course," said Fortnum. "How silly of me."

Cynthia squinted. "Those little teeny bits?"

" 'Fabulous growth in twenty-four hours,' " Tom quoted from memory. " 'Plant them in your cellar . . .' "

Fortnum and wife exchanged glances.

"Well," she admitted, "It's better than frogs and green snakes."

"Sure is!" Tom ran.

"Oh, Tom," said Fortnum lightly.

Tom paused at the cellar door.

"Tom," said his father. "Next time, fourth-class mail would do fine."

"Heck," said Tom. "They must've made a mistake, thought I was some rich company. Airmail special, who can afford that?"

The cellar door slammed.

Fortnum, bemused, scanned the wrapper a moment then dropped it into the wastebasket. On his way to the kitchen, he opened the cellar door.

Tom was already on his knees, digging with a hand rake in the dirt.

He felt his wife beside him, breathing softly, looking down into the cool dimness.

"Those *are* mushrooms, I hope. Not . . . toadstools?"

Fortnum laughed. "Happy harvest, farmer!"

Tom glanced up and waved.

Fortnum shut the door, took his wife's arm and walked her out to the kitchen, feeling fine.

Toward noon, Fortnum was driving toward the nearest market when he saw Roger Willis, a fellow Rotarian and a teacher of biology at the town high school, waving urgently from the sidewalk.

Fortnum pulled his car up and opened the door.

"Hi, Roger, give you a lift?"

Willis responded all too eagerly, jumping in and slamming the door.

"Just the man I want to see. I've put off calling for days. Could you play psychiatrist for five minutes, God help you?"

Fortnum examined his friend for a moment as he drove quietly on.

"God help you, yes. Shoot."

Willis sat back and studied his fingernails. "Let's just drive a moment. There. Okay. Here's what I want to say: Something's wrong with the world."

Fortnum laughed easily. 'Hasn't there always been?"

"No, no, I mean . . . something strange—something unseen —is happening."

"Mrs. Goodbody," said Fortnum, half to himself, and stopped.

"Mrs. Goodbody?"

"This morning, gave me a talk on flying saucers."

"No." Willis bit the knuckle of his forefinger nervously. "Nothing like saucers. At least, I don't think. Tell me, what exactly is intuition?"

"The conscious recognition of something that's been subconscious for a long time. But don't quote this amateur psychologist!" He laughed again.

"Good, good!" Willis turned, his face lighting. He readjusted himself in the seat. "That's it! Over a long period, things gather, right? All of a sudden, you have to spit, but you don't remember saliva collecting. Your hands are dirty, but you don't know how they got that way. Dust falls on you everyday and you don't feel it. But when you get enough dust collected up, there it is, you see and name it. That's intuition, as far as I'm concerned. Well, what kind of dust has been falling on *me?* A few meteors in the sky at night? funny weather just before dawn? I don't know. Certain colors, smells, the way the house creaks at three in the morning? Hair prickling on my arms? All I know is, the damn dust has collected. Quite suddenly I know."

"Yes," said Fortnum, disquieted. "But what *is* it you know?"

Willis looked at his hands in his lap. "I'm afraid. I'm not afraid. Then I'm afraid again, in the middle of the day. Doctor's checked me. I'm A-one. No family problems. Joe's a fine boy, a good son. Dorothy? She's remarkable. With her I'm not afraid of growing old or dying."

"Lucky man."

"But beyond my luck now. Scared stiff, really, for myself, my family; even right now, for you."

"Me?" said Fortnum.

They had stopped now by an empty lot near the market. There was a moment of great stillness, in which Fortnum turned to survey his friend. Willis' voice had suddenly made him cold.

"I'm afraid for everybody," said Willis. "Your friends, mine, and their friends, on out of sight. Pretty silly, eh?"

Willis opened the door, got out and peered in at Fortnum.

Fortnum felt he had to speak. "Well, what do we do about it?"

Willis looked up at the sun burning blind in the sky. "Be aware," he said slowly. "Watch everything for a few days."

"Everything?"

"We don't use half what God gave us, ten per cent of the time. We ought to hear more, feel more, smell more, taste more. Maybe there's something wrong with the way the wind blows these weeds there in the lot. Maybe it's the sun up on those telephone wires or the cicadas singing in the elm trees. If only we could stop, look, listen, a few days, a few nights, and compare notes. Tell me to shut up then, and I will."

"Good enough," said Fortnum, playing it lighter than he felt. "I'll look around. But how do I know the thing I'm looking for when I see it?"

Willis peered in at him, sincerely. "You'll know. You've got to know. Or we're done for, all of us," he said quietly.

Fortnum shut the door and didn't know what to say. He felt a flush of embarrassment creeping up his face. Willis sensed this.

"Hugh, do you think I'm . . . off my rocker?"

"Nonsense!" said Fortnum, too quickly. "You're just nervous, is all. You should take a week off."

Willis nodded. "See you Monday night?"

"Any time. Drop around."

"I hope I will, Hugh. I really hope I will."

Then Willis was gone, hurrying across the dry weed-grown lot toward the side entrance of the market.

Watching him go, Fortnum suddenly did not want to move. He discovered that very slowly he was taking deep breaths, weighing the silence. He licked his lips tasting the salt. He looked at his arm on the doorsill, the sunlight burning the golden hairs. In the empty lot the wind moved all alone to itself. He leaned out to look at the sun, which stared back with one massive stunning blow of intense power that made him jerk his head in. He exhaled. Then he laughed out loud. Then he drove away.

• • •

The lemonade glass was cool and deliciously sweaty. The ice made music inside the glass, and the lemonade was just sour enough, just sweet enough on his tongue. He sipped, he savored, he tilted back in the wicker rocking chair on the twilight front porch, his eyes closed. The crickets were chirping out on the lawn. Cynthia, knitting across from him on the porch, eyed him curiously; he could feel her attention.

"What are you up to?" she said at last.

"Cynthia," he said, "is your intuition in running order? Is this earthquake weather? Is the land going to sink? Will war be declared? Or is it only that our delphinium will die of the blight?"

"Hold on. Let me feel my bones."

He opened his eyes and watched Cynthia in turn closing hers and sitting absolutely statue-still, her hands on her knees. Finally she shook her head and smiled.

"No. No war declared. No land sinking. Not even a blight. Why?"

"I've met a lot of doom talkers today. Well, two anyway, and—"

The screen door burst wide. Fortnum's body jerked as if he had been struck. "What—!"

Tom, a gardener's wooden flat in his arms, stepped out on the porch.

"Sorry," he said. "What's wrong, Dad?"

"Nothing." Fortnum stood up, glad to be moving. "Is that the crop?"

Tom moved forward eagerly. "Part of it. Boy, they're

doing great. In just seven hours, with lots of water, look how big the darn things are!" He set the flat on the table between his parents.

The crop was indeed plentiful. Hundreds of small grayish-brown mushrooms were sprouting up in the damp soil.

"I'll be damned," said Fortnum, impressed.

Cynthia put out her hand to touch the flat, then took it away uneasily.

"I hate to be a spoilsport, but . . . there's no way for these to be anything else but mushrooms, is there?"

Tom looked as if he had been insulted. "What do you think I'm going to feed you? Poisoned fungoids?"

"That's just it," said Cynthia quickly. "How do you tell them apart?"

"Eat 'em," said Tom. "If you live, they're mushrooms. If you drop dead—*well!*"

He gave a great guffaw, which amused Fortnum but only made his mother wince. She sat back in her chair.

"I—I don't like them," she said.

"Boy, oh, boy." Tom seized the flat angrily. "When are we going to have the next wet-blanket sale in *this* house?"

He shuffled morosely away.

"Tom—" said Fortnum.

"Never mind," said Tom. "Everyone figures they'll be ruined by the boy entrepreneur. To heck with it!"

Fortnum got inside just as Tom heaved the mushrooms, flat and all, down the cellar stairs. He slammed the cellar door and ran out the back door.

Fortnum turned back to his wife, who, stricken, glanced away.

"I'm sorry," she said. "I don't know why, I just *had* to say that to Tom. I—"

The phone rang. Fortnum brought the phone outside on its extension cord.

"Hugh?" It was Dorothy Willis' voice. She sounded suddenly very old and very frightened. "Hugh, Roger isn't there, is he?"

"Dorothy? No."

"He's gone!" said Dorothy. "All his clothes were taken from the closet." She began to cry.

"Dorothy, hold on, I'll be there in a minute."

"You must help, oh, you must. Something's happened to

him, I know it," she wailed. "Unless you do something, we'll never see him alive again."

Very slowly he put the receiver back on its hook, her voice weeping inside it. The night crickets quite suddenly were very loud. He felt the hairs, one by one, go up on the back of his neck.

Hair can't do that, he thought. Silly, silly. It can't do that, not in *real* life, it can't!

But, one by slow prickling one, his hair did.

•   •   •

The wire hangers were indeed empty. With a clatter, Fortnum shoved them aside and down along the rod, then turned and looked out of the closet at Dorothy Willis and her son Joe.

"I was just walking by," said Joe, "and saw the closet empty, all Dad's clothes gone!"

"Everything was fine," said Dorothy. "We've had a wonderful life. I don't understand, I don't, I don't!" She began to cry again, putting her hands to her face.

Fortnum stepped out of the closet.

"You didn't hear him leave the house?"

"We were playing catch out front," said Joe. "Dad said he had to go in for a minute. I went around back. Then he was gone!"

"He must have packed quickly and walked wherever he was going, so we wouldn't hear a cab pull up in front of the house."

They were moving out through the hall now.

"I'll check the train depot and the airport." Fortnum hesitated. "Dorothy, is there anything in Roger's background—"

"It wasn't insanity took him." She hesitated. "I feel, somehow, he was kidnapped."

Fortnum shook his head. "It doesn't seem reasonable he would arrange to pack, walk out of the house and go meet his abductors."

Dorothy opened the door as if to let the night or the night wind move down the hall as she turned to stare back through the rooms, her voice wandering.

"No. Somehow they came into the house. Right in front of us, they stole him away."

And then: "A terrible thing has happened."

Fortnum stepped out into the night of crickets and rustling trees. The doom talkers, he thought, talking their dooms. Mrs. Goodbody, Roger, and now Roger's wife. Something terrible *has* happened. But what, in God's name? And how?

He looked from Dorothy to her son. Joe, blinking the wetness from his eyes, took a long time to turn, walk along the hall and stop, fingering the knob of the cellar door.

Fortnum felt his eyelids twitch, his iris flex, as if he were snapping a picture of something he wanted to remember.

Joe pulled the cellar door wide, stepped down out of sight, gone. The door tapped shut.

Fortnum opened his mouth to speak, but Dorothy's hand was taking his now, he had to look at her.

"Please," she said. "Find him for me."

He kissed her cheek. "If it's humanly possible."

If it's humanly possible. Good Lord, why had he picked *those* words?

He walked off into the summer night.

A gasp, an exhalation, a gasp, an exhalation, an asthmatic insuck, a vaporing sneeze. Somebody dying in the dark? No.

Just Mrs. Goodbody, unseen beyond the hedge, working late, her hand pump aimed, her bony elbow thrusting. The sick-sweet smell of bug spray enveloped Fortnum as he reached his house.

"Mrs. Goodbody? Still at it?"

From the black hedge her voice leaped. "Damn it, yes! Aphids, water bugs, woodworms, and now the *Marasmius oreades*. Lord, it grows fast!"

"What does?"

"The *Marasmius oreades*, of course! It's me against them, and I intend to win! There! There! There!"

He left the hedge, the gasping pump, the wheezing voice, and found his wife waiting for him on the porch almost as if she were going to take up where Dorothy had left off at her door a few minutes ago.

Fortnum was about to speak when a shadow moved inside. There was a creaking noise. A knob rattled.

Tom vanished into the basement.

Fortnum felt as if someone had set off an explosion in

his face. He reeled. Everything had the numbed familiarity of those waking dreams where all motions are remembered before they occur, all dialogue known before it falls from the lips.

He found himself staring at the shut basement door. Cynthia took him inside, amused.

"What? Tom? Oh, I relented. The darn mushrooms meant so much to him. Besides, when he threw them into the cellar they did nicely, just lying in the dirt—"

"Did they?" Fortnum heard himself say.

Cynthia took his arm. "What about Roger?"

"He's gone, yes."

"Men, men, men," she said.

"No, you're wrong," he said. "I saw Roger every day the last ten years. When you know a man that well, you can tell how things are at home, whether things are in the oven or the Mixmaster. Death hadn't breathed down his neck yet; he wasn't running scared after his immortal youth, picking peaches in someone else's orchards. No, no, I swear, I'd bet my last dollar on it, Roger—"

The doorbell rang behind him. The delivery boy had come up quietly onto the porch and was standing there with a telegram in his hand.

"Fortnum?"

Cynthia snapped on the hall light as he ripped the envelope open and smoothed it out for reading.

TRAVELING NEW ORLEANS. THIS TELEGRAM POSSIBLE OFF-GUARD MOMENT. YOU MUST REFUSE, REPEAT REFUSE, ALL SPECIAL-DELIVERY PACKAGES. ROGER

Cynthia glanced up from the paper.

"I don't understand. What does he mean?"

But Fortnum was already at the telephone, dialing swiftly, once. "Operator? The police, and hurry!"

At ten-fifteen that night the phone rang for the sixth time during the evening. Fortnum got it and immediately gasped. "Roger! Where are you?"

"Where am I, hell," said Roger lightly, almost amused. "You know very well where I am, you're responsible for this. I should be angry!"

Cynthia, at his nod, had hurried to take the extension phone in the kitchen. When he heard the soft click, he went on.

"Roger, I swear I don't know. I got that telegram from you—"

"What telegram?" said Roger jovially. "I sent no telegram. Now, of a sudden, the police come pouring onto the south-bound train, pull me off in some jerk-water, and I'm calling you to get them off my neck. Hugh, if this is some joke—"

"But, Roger, you just vanished!"

"On a business trip, if you can call that vanishing. I told Dorothy about this, and Joe."

"This is all very confusing, Roger. You're in no danger? Nobody's blackmailing you, forcing you into this speech?"

"I'm fine, healthy, free and unafraid."

"But, Roger, your premonitions?"

"Poppycock! Now, look, I'm being very good about this, aren't I?"

"Sure, Roger—"

"Then play the good father and give me permission to go. Call Dorothy and tell her I'll be back in five days. How *could* she have forgotten?"

"She did, Roger. See you in five days, then?"

"Five days, I swear."

The voice was indeed winning and warm, the old Roger again. Fortnum shook his head.

"Roger," he said, "this is the craziest day I've ever spent. You're not running off from Dorothy? Good Lord, you can tell *me*."

"I love her with all my heart. Now here's Lieutenant Parker of the Ridgetown police. Goodbye, Hugh."

"Good—"

But the lieutenant was on the line, talking, talking angrily. What had Fortnum meant putting them to this trouble? What was going on? Who did he think he was? Did or didn't he want this so-called friend held or released?

"Released," Fortnum managed to say somewhere along the way, and hung up the phone and imagined he heard a voice call all aboard and the massive thunder of the train leaving the station two hundred miles south in the somehow increasingly dark night.

Cynthia walked very slowly into the parlor.

"I feel so foolish," she said.

"How do you think I feel?"

"Who could have sent that telegram, and why?"

He poured himself some Scotch and stood in the middle of the room looking at it.

"I'm glad Roger is all right," his wife said at last.

"He isn't," said Fortnum.

"But you just said—"

"I said nothing. After all, we couldn't very well drag him off that train and truss him up and send him home, could we, if he insisted he was okay? No. He sent that telegram, but changed his mind after sending it. Why, why, why?" Fortnum paced the room, sipping the drink. "Why warn us against special-delivery packages? The only package we've got this *year* which fits that description is the one Tom got this morning. . . ." His voice trailed off.

Before he could move, Cynthia was at the wastepaper basket taking out the crumpled wrapping paper with the special-delivery stamps on it.

The postmark read: NEW ORLEANS, LA.

Cynthia looked up from it. "New Orleans. Isn't that where Roger is heading right now?"

A doorknob rattled, a door opened and closed in Fortnum's mind. Another doorknob rattled, another door swung wide and then shut. There was a smell of damp earth.

He found his hand dialing the phone. After a long while Dorothy Willis answered at the other end. He could imagine her sitting alone in a house with too many lights on. He talked quietly with her a while, then cleared his throat and said, "Dorothy, look. I know it sounds silly. Did any special-delivery packages arrive at your house the last few days?"

Her voice was faint. "No." Then: "No, wait. Three days ago. But I thought you *knew!* All the boys on the block are going in for it."

Fortnum measured his words carefully.

"Going in for what?"

"But why ask?" she said. "There's nothing wrong with raising mushrooms, is there?"

Fortnum closed his eyes.

"Hugh? Are you still there?" asked Dorothy. "I said there's nothing wrong with—"

"Raising mushrooms?" said Fortnum at last. "No. Nothing wrong. Nothing wrong."

And slowly he put down the phone.

The curtains blew like veils of moonlight. The clock ticked. The after-midnight world flowed into and filled the bedroom. He heard Mrs. Goodbody's clear voice on this morning's air, a million years gone now. He heard Roger putting a cloud over the sun at noon. He heard the police damning him by phone from down state. Then Roger's voice again, with the locomotive thunder hurrying him away and away, fading. And, finally, Mrs. Goodbody's voice behind the hedge:

"Lord, it grows fast!"

"What does?"

"The *Marasmius oreades!*"

He snapped his eyes open. He sat up.

Downstairs, a moment later, he flicked through the unabridged dictionary.

His forefinger underlined the words:

"Marasmius oreades; a mushroom commonly found on lawns in summer and early autumn . . ."

He let the book fall shut.

Outside, in the deep summer night, he lit a cigarette and smoked quietly.

A meteor fell across space, burning itself out quickly. The trees rustled softly.

The front door tapped shut.

Cynthia moved toward him in her robe.

"Can't sleep?"

"Too warm, I guess."

"It's not warm."

"No," he said, feeling his arms. "In fact, it's cold." He sucked on the cigarette twice, then, not looking at her, said, "Cynthia, what if . . ." He snorted and had to stop. "Well, what if Roger was right this morning. Mrs. Goodbody, what if she's right, too? Something terrible *is* happening. Like, well," —he nodded at the sky and the million stars— "Earth being invaded by things from other worlds, maybe."

"Hugh—"

"No, let me run wild."

"It's quite obvious we're not being invaded, or we'd notice."

"Let's say we've only half noticed, become uneasy about something. What? How could we be invaded? By what means would creatures invade?"

Cynthia looked at the sky and was about to try something when he interrupted.

"No, not meteors or flying saucers, things we can see. What about bacteria? That comes from outer space, too, doesn't it?"

"I read once, yes."

"Spores, seeds, pollens, viruses probably bombard our atmosphere by the billions every second and have done so for millions of years. Right now we're sitting out under an invisible rain. It falls all over the country, the cities, the towns, and right now, our lawn."

"*Our* lawn?"

"*And* Mrs. Goodbody's. But people like her are always pulling weeds, spraying poison, kicking toadstools off their grass. It would be hard for any strange life form to survive in cities. Weather's a problem, too. Best climate might be South: Alabama, Georgia, Louisiana. Back in the damp bayous they could grow to a fine size."

But Cynthia was beginning to laugh now.

"Oh, really, you don't believe, do you, that this Great Bayou or Whatever Greenhouse Novelty Company that sent Tom his package is owned and operated by six-foot-tall mushrooms from another planet?"

"If you put it that way, it sounds funny."

"Funny! It's hilarious!" She threw her head back, deliciously.

"Good grief!" he cried, suddenly irritated. "*Something's* going on! Mrs. Goodbody is rooting out and killing *Marasmius oreades*. What *is Marasmius oreades*? A certain kind of mushroom. Simultaneously, and I suppose *you'll* call it coincidence, by special delivery, what arrives the same day? Mushrooms for Tom! What *else* happens? Roger fears he may soon cease to be! Within hours, he vanishes, then telegraphs us, warning us not to accept what? The special-delivery mushrooms for Tom! Has Roger's son got a similar package in the last few days? He has! Where do the packages come from? New Orleans! And where is Roger going when he vanishes? New Orleans! Do you see, Cynthia, do you see? I wouldn't be upset if all these separate things didn't lock together! Roger, Tom, Joe, mushrooms, Mrs. Goodbody, packages, destinations, everything in one pattern!"

She was watching his face now, quieter, but still amused. "Don't get angry."

"I'm not!" Fortnum almost shouted. And then he simply could not go on. He was afraid that if he did he would find himself shouting with laughter too, and somehow he did not want that. He stared at the surrounding houses up and down the block and thought of the dark cellars and the neighbor boys who read *Popular Mechanics* and sent their money in by the millions to raise the mushrooms hidden away. Just as he, when a boy, had mailed off for chemicals, seeds, turtles, numberless salves and sickish ointments. In how many million American homes tonight were billions of mushrooms rousing up under the ministrations of the innocent?

"Hugh?" His wife was touching his arm now. "Mushrooms, even big ones, can't think, can't move, don't have arms and legs. How could they run a mail-order service and 'take over' the world? Come on, now, let's look at your terrible fiends and monsters!"

She pulled him toward the door. Inside, she headed for the cellar, but he stopped, shaking his head, a foolish smile shaping itself somehow to his mouth. "No, no, I know what we'll find. You win. The whole thing's silly. Roger will be back next week and we'll all get drunk together. Go on up to bed now and I'll drink a glass of warm milk and be with you in a minute."

"That's better!" She kissed him on both cheeks, squeezed him and went away up the stairs.

In the kitchen, he took out a glass, opened the refrigerator, and was pouring the milk when he stopped suddenly.

Near the front of the top shelf was a small yellow dish. It was not the dish that held his attention, however. It was what lay in the dish.

The fresh-cut mushrooms.

He must have stood there for half a minute, his breath frosting the air, before he reached out, took hold of the dish, sniffed it, felt the mushrooms, then at last, carrying the dish, went out into the hall. He looked up the stairs, hearing Cynthia moving about in the bedroom, and was about to call up to her, "Cynthia, did you put *these* in the refrigerator?" Then he stopped. He knew her answer. She had not.

He put the dish of mushrooms on the newel-upright at the bottom of the stairs and stood looking at them. He imagined himself in bed later, looking at the walls, the open windows, watching the moonlight sift patterns on the ceiling. He heard himself saying, Cynthia? And her answering, Yes? And him saying, There *is* a way for mushrooms to grow arms and legs. What? she would say, silly, silly man, what? And he would gather courage against her hilarious reaction and go on, What if a man wandered through the swamp, picked the mushrooms and *ate* them. . . ?

No response from Cynthia.

Once inside the man, would the mushrooms spread through his blood, take over every cell and change the man from a man to a—Martian? Given this theory, would the mushroom *need* its own arms and legs? No, not when it could borrow people, live inside and become them. Roger ate mushrooms given him by his son. Roger became 'something else.' He kidnapped himself. And in one last flash of sanity, of being himself, he telegraphed us, warning us not to accept the special-delivery mushrooms. The 'Roger' that telephoned later was no longer Roger but a captive of what he had eaten! Doesn't that figure, Cynthia, doesn't it, doesn't it?

No, said the imagined Cynthia, no, it doesn't figure, no, no, no. . . .

There was the faintest whisper, rustle, stir from the cellar. Taking his eyes from the bowl, Fortnum walked to the cellar door and put his ear to it.

"Tom?"

No answer.

"Tom, are you down there?"

No answer.

"Tom?"

After a long while, Tom's voice came up from below.

"Yes, Dad?"

"It's after midnight," said Fortnum, fighting to keep his voice from going high. "What are you doing down there?"

No answer.

"I said—"

"Tending to my crop," said the boy at last, his voice cold and faint.

"Well, get the hell *out* of there! You hear me?"

Silence.

"Tom? Listen! Did you put some mushrooms in the refrigerator tonight? If so, why?"

Ten seconds must have ticked by before the boy replied from below, "For you and Mom to eat, of course."

Fortnum heard his heart moving swiftly and had to take three deep breaths before he could go on.

"Tom? You didn't . . . that is, you haven't by any chance *eaten* some of the mushrooms yourself, *have* you?"

"Funny you ask that," said Tom. "Yes. Tonight. On a sandwich. After supper. Why?"

Fortnum held to the doorknob. Now it was his turn not to answer. He felt his knees beginning to melt and he fought the whole silly senseless fool thing. No reason, he tried to say, but his lips wouldn't move.

"Dad?" called Tom, softly from the cellar. "Come on down." Another pause. "I want you to see the harvest."

Fortnum felt the knob slip in his sweaty hand. The knob rattled. He gasped.

"Dad?" called Tom softly.

Fortnum opened the door.

The cellar was completely black below.

He stretched his hand in toward the light switch.

As if sensing this from somewhere, Tom said, "Don't. Light's bad for the mushrooms."

He took his hand off the switch.

He swallowed. He looked back at the stair leading up to his wife. I suppose, he thought, I should go say goodbye to Cynthia. But why should I think that! Why, in God's name, should I think that at all? No reason, *is* there?

None.

"Tom?" he said, affecting a jaunty air. "Ready or not, here I come!"

And stepping down in darkness, he shut the door.

ALMOST THE END OF THE WORLD

Sighting Rock Junction, Arizona, at noon on August 22, 1967, Willy Bersinger let his miner's boot rest easy on the jalopy's accelerator and talked quietly to his partner, Samuel Fitts.

"Yes, sir, Samuel, it's great hitting town. After a couple of months out at the Penny Dreadful Mine, a jukebox looks like a stained-glass window to me. We need the town; without it, we might wake some morning and find ourselves all jerked beef and petrified rock. And then, of course, the town needs us, too."

"How's that?" asked Samuel Fitts.

"Well, we bring things into town that it hasn't got—mountains, creeks, desert night, stars, things like that . . ."

And it was true, thought Willy, driving along. Set a man 'way out in the strange lands and he fills with wellsprings of silence. Silence of sagebrush, or a mountain lion purring like a warm beehive at noon. Silence of the river shallows deep in the canyons. All this a man takes in. Opening his mouth, in town, he breathes it out.

"Oh, how I love to climb into that old barbershop chair," Willy admitted, "and see all those city men lined up under the naked-lady calendars, staring back at me, waiting while I chew over my philosophy of rocks and mirages and the kind of Time that just sits out there in the hills waiting for man to go away. I exhale—and that wilderness settles in a fine dust on the customers. Oh, it's nice, me talking, soft and easy, up and down, on and on . . ."

In his mind he saw the customers' eyes strike fire. Someday they would yell and rabbit for the hills, leaving families and time-clock civilization behind.

"It's good to feel wanted," said Willy. "You and me, Samuel, are basic necessities for those city-dwelling folks. Gangway, Rock Junction!"

And with a tremulous tin whistling they steamed across city limits into awe and wonder.

They had driven perhaps a hundred feet through town when Willy kicked the brakes. A great shower of rust flakes sifted from the jalopy fenders. The car stood cowering in the road.

"Something's wrong," said Willy. He squinted his lynx eyes this way and that. He snuffed his huge nose. "You feel it? You smell it?"

"Sure," said Samuel, uneasily, "but what?"

Willy scowled. "You ever see a sky-blue cigar-store Indian?"

"Never did."

"There's one over there. Ever see a pink dog kennel, an orange outhouse, a lilac-colored birdbath? There, there, and over there!"

Both men had risen slowly now to stand on the creaking floorboards.

"Samuel," whispered Willy, "the whole damn shooting match, every kindling pile, porch rail, gewgaw gingerbread, fence, fireplug, garbage truck, the *whole blasted town,* look at it! It was painted just an hour ago!"

"No!" said Samuel Fitts.

But there stood the band pavilion, the Baptist church, the firehouse, the Oddfellows' orphanage, the railroad depot, the county jail, the cat hospital and all the bungalows, cottages, greenhouses, gazebos, shop signs, mailboxes, telephone poles and trashbins, around and in between, and they all blazed with corn yellow, crab-apple greens, circus reds. From water tank to tabernacle, each building looked as if God had jig-sawed it, colored it and set it out to dry a moment ago.

Not only that, but where weeds had always been, now cabbages, green onions, and lettuce crammed every yard, crowds of curious sunflowers clocked the noon sky, and pansies lay under unnumbered trees cool as summer puppies, their great damp eyes peering over rolled lawns mint-green as Irish travel posters. To top it all, ten boys, faces scrubbed, hair brilliantined, shirts, pants and tennis shoes clean as chunks of snow, raced by.

"The town," said Willy, watching them run, "has gone mad. Mystery. Mystery everywhere. Samuel, what kind of tyrant's come to power? What law has passed that keeps boys clean, drives people to paint every toothpick, every geranium pot? Smell that smell? There's fresh wallpaper in all those houses! Doom in some horrible shape has tried and tested these people. Human nature doesn't just get this picky perfect overnight. I'll bet all the gold I planned last month those attics, those cellars are cleaned out, all shipshape. I'll bet you a real Thing fell on this town."

"Why, I can almost hear the cherubim singing in the Garden," Samuel protested. "How you figure Doom? Shake my hand, put 'er there. I'll bet and take your money!"

The jalopy swerved around a corner through a wind that smelled of turpentine and whitewash. Samuel threw out a gum wrapper, snorting. He was somewhat surprised at what happened next. An old man in new overalls, with mirror-bright shoes, ran out into the street, grabbed the crumpled gum wrapper and shook his fist after the departing jalopy.

"Doom . . ." Samuel Fitts looked back, his voice fading. "Well, . . . the bet *still* stands."

They opened the door upon a barbershop teeming with customers whose hair had already been cut and oiled, whose faces were shaved close and pink, yet who sat waiting to vault back into the chairs where three barbers flourished their shears and combs. A stock-market uproar filled the room as customers and barbers all talked at once.

When Willy and Samuel entered, the uproar ceased instantly. It was if they had fired a shotgun blast through the door.

"Sam . . . Willy . . ."

In the silence some of the sitting men stood up and some of the standing men sat down, slowly, staring.

"Samuel," said Willy out of the corner of his mouth, "I feel like the Red Death standing here." Aloud he said, "Howdy! Here I am to finish my lecture on the Interesting Flora and Fauna of the Great American Desert, and—"

"No!"

Antonelli, the head barber, rushed frantically at Willy, seized his arm, clapped his hand over Willy's mouth like a snuffer on a candle. "Willy," he whispered, looking apprehensively over his shoulder at his customers. "Promise me one thing: buy a needle and thread, sew up your lips. Silence, man, if you value your life!"

Willy and Samuel felt themselves hurried forward. Two

already neat customers leaped out of the barber chairs without being asked. As they stepped into the chairs, the two miners glimpsed their own images in the flyspecked mirror.

"Samuel, there we are! Look! Compare!"

"Why," said Samuel, blinking, "we're the only men in all Rock Junction who really *need* a shave and a haircut."

"Strangers!" Antonelli laid them out in the chairs as if to anesthetize them quickly. "You don't know what strangers you are!"

"Why, we've only been gone a couple of months—" A steaming towel inundated Willy's face; he subsided with muffled cries. In steaming darkness he heard Antonelli's low and urgent voice.

"We'll fix you to look like everyone else. Not that the way you look is dangerous, no, but the kind of talk you miners talk might upset folks at a time like this."

"Time like this, hell!" Willy lifted the seething towel. One bleary eye fixed Antonelli. "What's wrong with Rock Junction?"

"Not just Rock Junction." Antonelli gazed off at some incredible dream beyond the horizon. "Phoenix, Tucson, Denver. All the cities in America! My wife and I are going as tourists to Chicago next week. Imagine Chicago all painted and clean and new. The Pearl of the Orient, they call it! Pittsburgh, Cincinnati, Buffalo, the same! All because—well, get up now, walk over and switch on that television set against the wall."

Willy handed Antonelli the steaming towel, walked over, switched on the television set, listened to it hum, fiddled with the dials and waited. White snow drifted down the screen.

"Try the radio now," said Antonelli.

Willy felt everyone watch as he twisted the radio dial from station to station.

"Hell," he said at last, "both your television and radio are broken."

"No," said Antonelli simply.

Willy lay back down in the chair and closed his eyes.

Antonelli leaned forward, breathing hard.

"Listen," he said.

"Imagine four weeks ago, a late Saturday morning, women and children staring at clowns and magicians on TV. In beauty shops, women staring at TV fashions. In the barbershop and hardware stores, men staring at baseball or trout fishing. Everybody everywhere in the civilized world staring. No sound, no motion, except on the little black-and-white screens.

"And then, in the middle of all that staring . . ."

Antonelli paused to lift up one corner of the broiling cloth. "Sunspots on the sun," he said.

Willy stiffened.

"Biggest damn sunspots in the history of mortal man," said Antonelli. "Whole damn world flooded with electricity. Wiped every TV screen clean as a whistle, leaving nothing, and, after that, more nothing."

His voice was remote as the voice of a man describing an arctic landscape. He lathered Willy's face, not looking at what he was doing. Willy peered across the barbershop at the soft snow falling down and down that humming screen in an eternal winter. He could almost hear the rabbit thumping of all the hearts in the shop.

Antonelli continued his funeral oration.

"It took us all that first day to realize what had happened. Two hours after that first sunspot storm hit, every TV repairman in the United States was on the road. Everyone figured it was just their own set. With the radios conked out, too, it was only that night, when newsboys, like in the old days, ran headlines through the streets, that we got the shock about the sunspots maybe going on—for the rest of our lives!"

The customers murmured.

Antonelli's hand, holding the razor, shook. He had to wait.

"All that blankness, that empty stuff falling down, falling down inside our television sets, oh, I tell you, it gave everyone the willies. It was like a good friend who talks to you in your front room and suddenly shuts up and lies there, pale, and you know he's dead and you begin to turn cold yourself.

"That first night, there was a run on the town's movie houses. Films weren't much, but it was like the Oddfellows' Ball downtown till midnight. Drugstores fizzed up two hundred vanilla, three hundred chocolate sodas that first night of the Calamity. But you can't buy movies and sodas every night. What then? Phone your in-laws for canasta or parchesi?"

"Might as well," observed Willy, "blow your brains out."

"Sure, but people had to get out of their haunted houses.

Walking through their parlors was like whistling past a graveyard. All that silence . . ."

Willy sat up a little. "Speaking of silence—"

"On the third night," said Antonelli quickly, "we were all still in shock. We were saved from outright lunacy by one woman. Somewhere in this town this woman strolled out of the house, and came back a minute later. In one hand she held a paintbrush. And in the other—"

"A bucket of paint," said Willy.

Everyone smiled, seeing how well he understood.

"If those psychologists ever strike off gold medals, they should pin one on that woman and every woman like her in every little town who saved our world from coming to an end. Those women who instinctively wandered in at twilight and brought us the miracle cure."

Willy imagined it. There were the glaring fathers and the scowling sons slumped by their dead TV sets waiting for the damn things to shout Ball One, or Strike Two! And then they looked up from their wake and there in the twilight saw the fair women of great purpose and dignity standing and waiting with brushes and paint. And a glorious light kindled their cheeks and eyes. . . .

"Lord, it spread like wildfire!" said Antonelli. "House to house, city to city. Jigsaw-puzzle craze, 1932, yoyo craze, 1928, were nothing compared with the Everybody Do Everything Craze that blew this town to smithereens and glued it back again. Men everywhere slapped paint on anything that stood still ten seconds; men everywhere climbed steeples, straddled fences, fell off roofs and ladders by the hundreds. Women painted cupboards, closets; kids painted Tinkertoys, wagons, kites. If they hadn't kept busy, you could have built a wall around this town, renamed it Babbling Brooks. All towns, everywhere, the same, where people had forgotten how to waggle their jaws, make their own talk. I tell you, men were moving in mindless circles, dazed, until their wives shoved a brush into their hands and pointed them toward the nearest unpainted wall!"

"Looks like you finished the job," said Willy.

"Paint stores ran out of paint three times the first week." Antonelli surveyed the town with pride. "The painting could only last so long, of course, unless you start painting hedges and spraying grass blades one by one. Now that the attics and cellars are cleaned out, too, our fire is seeping off into, well, women canning fruit again, making tomato pickles, raspberry, strawberry preserves. Basement shelves are loaded. Big church doings, too. Organized bowling, night donkey baseball, box socials, beer busts. Music shop sold five hundred ukeleles, two hundred and twelve steel guitars, four hundred and sixty ocarinas and kazoos in four weeks. I'm studying trombone. Mac, there, the flute. Band Concerts Thursday and Sunday nights. Hand-crank ice-cream machines? Bert Tyson's sold two hundred last week alone. Twenty-eight days, Willy, Twenty-eight Days That Shook the World!"

Willy Bersinger and Samuel Fitts sat there, trying to imagine and feel the shock, the crushing blow.

"Twenty-eight days, the barbershop jammed with men getting shaved twice a day so they can sit and stare at customers like they might *say* something," said Antonelli, shaving Willy now. "Once, remember, before TV, barbers were supposed to be great talkers. Well, this month it took us one whole week to warm up, get the rust out. Now we're spouting fourteen to the dozen. No quality, but our quantity is ferocious. When you came in you heard the commotion. Oh, it'll simmer down when we get used to the great Oblivion."

"Is *that* what everyone calls it?"

"It sure looked that way to most of us, there for a while."

Willy Bersinger laughed quietly and shook his head. "Now I know why you didn't want me to start lecturing when I walked in that door."

Of course, thought Willy, why didn't I see it right off? Four short weeks ago the wilderness fell on this town and shook it good and scared it plenty. Because of the sunspots, all the towns in all the Western world have had enough silence to last them ten years. And here I come by with another dose of silence, my easy talk about deserts and nights with no moon and only stars and just the little sound of the sand blowing along the empty river bottoms. No telling what might have happened if Antonelli hadn't shut me up. I see me, tarred and feathered, leaving town.

"Antonelli," he said aloud. "Thanks."

"For nothing," said Antonelli. He picked up his comb and shears. "Now, short on the sides, long in back?"

"Long on the sides," said Willy Bersinger, closing his eyes again, "short in back."

• • •

An hour later Willy and Samuel climbed back into their jalopy, which someone, they never knew who, had washed and polished while they were in the barbershop.

"Doom." Samuel handed over a small sack of gold dust. "With a capital D."

"Keep it." Willy sat, thoughtful, behind the wheel. "Let's take this money and hit out for Phoenix, Tucson, Kansas City, why not? Right now we're a surplus commodity around here. We won't be welcome again until those little sets begin to herringbone and dance and sing. Sure as hell, if we stay, we'll open our traps and the gila monsters and chicken hawks and the wilderness will slip out and make us trouble."

Willy squinted at the highway straight ahead.

"Pearl of the Orient, that's what he said. Can you imagine that dirty old town, Chicago, all painted up fresh and new as a babe in the morning light? We just got to go see Chicago, by God!"

He started the car, let it idle, and looked at the town.

"Man survives," he murmured. "Man endures. Too bad we missed the big change. It must have been a fierce thing, a time of trials and testings. Samuel, I don't recall, do you? What have *we* ever seen on TV?"

"Saw a woman wrestle a bear two falls out of three, one night."

"Who won?"

"Damned if I know. She—"

But then the jalopy moved and took Willy Bersinger and Samuel Fitts with it, their hair cut, oiled and neat on their sweet-smelling skulls, their cheeks pink-shaven, their fingernails flashing in the sun. They sailed under clipped green, fresh-watered trees, through flowered lanes, past daffodil-, lilac-, violet-, rose- and peppermint-colored houses on the dustless road.

"Pearl of the Orient, here we come!"

A perfumed dog with permanented hair ran out, nipped their tires and barked, until they were gone away and completely out of sight.

PERHAPS WE ARE GOING AWAY

It was a strange thing that could not be told. It touched along the hairs on his neck as he lay wakening. Eyes shut, he pressed his hands to the dirt.

Was the earth, shaking old fires under its crust, turning over in its sleep?

Were buffalo on the dust prairies, in the whistling grass, drumming the sod, moving this way like a dark weather?

No.

What? What, then?

He opened his eyes and was the boy Ho-Awi, of a tribe named for a bird, by the hills named for the shadows of owls, near the great ocean itself, on a day that was evil for no reason.

Ho-Awi stared at the tent flaps, which shivered like a great beast remembering winter.

Tell me, he thought, the terrible thing, where does it come from? Whom will it kill?

He lifted the flap and stepped out into his village.

He turned slowly, a boy with bones in his dark cheeks like the keels of small birds flying. His brown eyes saw god-filled, cloud-filled sky, his cupped ear heard thistles ticking the war drums, but still the greater mystery drew him to the edge of the village.

Here, legend said, the land went on like a tide to another sea. Between here and there was as much earth as there were stars across the night sky. Somewhere in all that land, storms of black buffalo harvested the grass. And here stood Ho-Awi, his stomach a fist, wondering, searching, waiting, afraid.

You too? said the shadow of a hawk.

Ho-Awi turned.

It was the shadow of his grandfather's hand that wrote on the wind.

71

No. The grandfather made the sign for silence. His tongue moved soft in a toothless mouth. His eyes were small creeks running behind the sunken flesh beds, the cracked sand washes of his face.

Now they stood on the edge of the day, drawn close by the unknown.

And Old Man did as the boy had done. His mummified ear turned, his nostril twitched. Old Man too ached for some answering growl from any direction that would tell them only a great timberfall of weather had dropped from a distant sky. But the wind gave no answer, spoke only to itself.

The Old Man made the sign which said they must go on the Great Hunt. This, said his hands like mouths, was a day for the rabbit young and the featherless old. Let no warrior come with them. The hare and the dying vulture must track together. For only the very young saw life ahead, and only the very old saw life behind; the others between were so busy with life they saw nothing.

The Old Man wheeled slowly in all directions.

Yes! He knew, he was certain, he was sure! To find this thing of darkness would take the innocence of the newborn and the innocence of the blind to see very clear.

Come! said the trembling fingers.

And snuffling rabbit and earthbound hawk shadowed out of the village into changing weather.

They searched the high hills to see if the stones lay atop each other, and they were so arranged. They scanned the prairies, but found only the winds which played there like tribal children all day. And found arrowheads from old wars.

No, the Old Man's hand drew on the sky, the men of this nation and that beyond smoke by the summer fires while the squaws cut wood. It is not arrows flying that we almost hear.

At last, when the sun sank into the nation of buffalo hunters, the Old Man looked up.

The birds, his hands cried suddenly, are flying south! Summer is over!

No, the boy's hands said, summer has just begun! I see no birds!

They are so high, said the Old Man's fingers, that only the blind can feel their passage. They shadow the heart more than the earth. I feel them pass south in my blood. Summer goes. We may go with it. Perhaps we are going away.

No! cried the boy aloud, suddenly afraid. Go where? Why? For what?

Who knows? said the Old Man, and perhaps we will not move. Still, even without moving, perhaps we are going away.

No! Go back! cried the boy, to the empty sky, the birds unseen, the unshadowed air. Summer, stay!

No use, said the Old One's single hand, moving by itself. Not you cr me or our people can stay this weather. It is a season changed, come to live on the land for all time.

But from where does it come?

This way, said the Old Man at last.

And in the dusk they looked down at the great waters of the east that went over the edge of the world, where no one had ever gone.

There. The Old Man's hand clenched and thrust out. There *it* is.

Far ahead, a single light burned on the shore.

With the moon rising, the Old Man and the rabbit boy padded on the sands, heard strange voices in the sea, smelled wild burnings from the now suddenly close fire.

They crawled on their bellies. They lay looking in at the light.

And the more he looked, the colder Ho-Awi became, and he knew that all the Old Man had said was true.

For drawn to this fire built of sticks and moss, which flickered brightly in the soft evening wind which was cooler now, at the heart of summer, were such creatures as he had never seen.

These were men with faces like white-hot coals, with some eyes in these faces as blue as sky. All these men had glossy hair on their cheeks and chins, which grew to a point. One man stood with raised lightning in his hand and a great moon of sharp stuff on his head like the face of a fish. The others had bright round tinkling crusts of material cleaved to their chests which gonged slightly when they moved. As Ho-Awi watched, some men lifted the gonging bright things from their heads, unskinned the eye-blinding crab shells, the turtle casings from their chests, their arms, their legs, and tossed these discarded sheaths to the sand. Doing this, the creatures laughed, while out in the bay stood a black shape on the waters, a great dark canoe with things like torn clouds hung on poles over it.

After a long while of holding their breath, the Old Man and the boy went away.

From a hill, they watched the fire that was no bigger than a star now. You could wink it out with an eyelash. If you closed your eyes, it was destroyed.

Still, it remained.

Is this, asked the boy, the great happening?

The Old One's face was that of a fallen eagle, filled with dreadful years and unwanted wisdom. The eyes were resplendently bright, as if they welled with a rise of cold clear water in which all could be seen, like a river that drank the sky and earth and knew it, accepted silently and would not deny the accumulation of dust, time, shape, sound and destiny.

The Old Man nodded, once.

This was the terrible weather. This was how summer would end. This made the birds wheel south, shadowless, through a grieving land.

The worn hands stopped moving. The time of questions was done.

Far away, the fire leaped. One of the creatures moved. The bright stuff on his tortoise-shell body flashed. It was like an arrow cutting a wound in the night.

Then the boy vanished in darkness, following the eagle and the hawk that lived in the stone body of his grandfather.

Below, the sea reared up and poured another great salt wave in billions of pieces which crashed and hissed like knives swarming along the continental shores.

AND THE SAILOR, HOME FROM THE SEA

"Good morning, Captain."

"Good morning, Hanks."

"Coffee's ready, sir, sit down."

"Thank you, Hanks."

The old man sat by the galley table, his hands in his lap. He looked at them and they were like speckled trout idling beneath frosty waters, the exhalations of his faint breath on the air. He had seen such trout as these surfacing in the mountain streams when he was ten. He became fascinated with their trembling motion there below, for as he watched they seemed to grow paler.

"Captain," said Hanks, "you all right?"

The captain jerked his head up and flashed his old burning glance.

"Of course! What do you mean, am I all right?"

The cook put down the coffee from which rose warm vapors of women so far gone in his past they were only dark musk and rubbed incense to his nose. Quite suddenly he sneezed, and Hanks was there with a cloth.

"Thank you, Hanks." He blew his nose and then tremblingly drank the brew.

"Hanks?"

"Yes, sir, Captain?"

"The barometer is falling."

Hanks turned to stare at the wall.

"No, sir, it's fair and mild, that's what it says, fair and mild!"

"The storm is rising and it will be a long time and a hard pull before another calm."

"I won't have that kind of talk!" said Hanks, circling him.

"I must say what I feel. The calm had to end one day. The storm had to come. I've been ready now a long time."

A long time, yes. How many years? The sand fell through

75

the glass beyond counting. The snows fell through the glass, too, applying and reapplying whiteness to whiteness, burying deeper and yet deeper winters beyond recall.

He got up, swaying, moved to the galley door, opened it, and stepped forth . . .

. . . onto the porch of a house built like the prow of a ship, onto a porch whose deck was tarred ship's timbers. He looked down upon not water but the summer-baked dirt of his front yard. Moving to the rail, he gazed upon gently rolling hills that spread forever in any direction you wheeled to strike your eye.

What am I doing here, he thought with sudden wildness, on a strange ship-house stranded without canvas in the midst of lonesome prairies where the only sound is bird shadow one way in autumn, another way come spring!

What indeed!

He quieted, raising the binoculars which hung from the rail, to survey the emptiness of land as well as life.

Kate Katherine Katie, where are you?

He was always forgetting by night, drowned deep in his bed, remembering by day when he came forth from memory. He was alone and had been alone for twenty years now, save for Hanks, the first face at dawn, the last at sundown.

And Kate?

A thousand storms and a thousand calms ago there had been a calm and a storm that had stayed on the rest of his life.

"There she is, Kate!" He heard his early-morning voice, running along the dock. "There's the ship will take us wherever we want to go!"

And again they moved, incredible pair, Kate miraculously what? twenty-five at most: and himself leaned far into his forties, but no more than a child holding her hand, drawing her up the gangplank.

Then, hesitant, Kate turned to face the Alexandrian hills of San Francisco and said half aloud to herself or no one, "I shall never touch land again."

"The trip's not that long!"

"Oh, yes," she said quietly. "It will be a very long journey."

And for a moment all he heard was the immense creaking of the ship like a Fate turning in its sleep.

"Now, why did I say that?" she asked. "Silly."

She put her foot out and down and stepped aboard the ship.

They sailed that night for the Southern Isles, a groom with the skin of a tortoise and a bride lithe as a salamander dancing on the fiery hearth of the afterdeck on August afternoons.

Then, midway in the voyage, a calm fell upon the ship like a great warm breath, an exhalation that collapsed the sails in a mournful yet a peaceful sigh.

Perhaps this sigh wakened him, or perhaps it was Katie, rising up to listen.

Not a rat-scurry of rope, not a whisper of canvas, not a rustle of naked feet on the deck. The ship was spelled for certain. It was as if the moon rising had said a single silver word: Peace.

The men, fastened to their stations by the incantation of the word, did not turn when the captain moved to the rail with his wife and sensed that Now had become Eternity.

And then, as if she could read the future in the mirror that held the ship fast, she said, fervently, "There's never been a finer night, nor two happier people on a better ship. Oh, I wish we could stay here a thousand years, this is perfect, our own world where we make our own laws and live by them. Promise you'll never let me die."

"Never," he said. "Shall I tell you why?"

"Yes, and make me believe it."

He remembered then, and told her, of a story he had heard once of a woman so lovely the gods were jealous of Time and put her to sea and said she might never touch shore again where the earth might burden her with gravity and weaken her with vain encounters, senseless excursions, and wild alarms that would cause her death. If she stayed on the water she would live forever and be beautiful. So she sailed many years, passing the island where her lover grew old. Time and again she called to him, demanding that he summon her ashore. But, fearful of her destruction, he refused, and one day she took it on herself to land and run to him. And they had one night together, a night of beauties and wonder, before he found her, when the sun rose, a very old woman, a withered leaf, at his side.

"Did I hear the story once?" he asked. "Or will someone tell it later, and are we part of it? Is that why I've carried you off from the land, so the noise and traffic and millions of people and things can't wear you away?"

But Kate was laughing at him now. She threw her head back and let the sound out, for every man's head turned and every mouth smiled.

"Tom, Tom, remember what I said before we sailed? I'd never touch land again? I must have guessed your reason for running off with me. All right, then, I'll stay on board wherever we go, around the world. Then I'll never change, and you won't either, will you?"

"I'll always be forty-eight!"

And he laughed, too, glad he had got the darkness out of himself, holding her shoulders and kissing her throat which was like bending to winter at the heart of August. And that night, in the blazing calm that would last forever, she was a fall of snow in his bed. . . .

"Hanks, do you remember the calm in August ninety-seven?" The old man examined his faraway hands. "How long did it last?"

"Nine, ten days, sir."

"No, Hanks. I swear it, we lived nine full *years* in those days of the calm."

Nine days, nine years. And in the midst of those days and years he thought, Oh, Kate, I'm glad I brought you, I'm glad I didn't let the others joke me out of making myself younger by touching you. Love is everywhere, they said, waiting on the docks, underneath the trees, like warm coconuts to be fondled, nuzzled, drunk. But, God, they wrong. Poor drunken souls, let them wrestle apes in Borneo, melons in Sumatra, what could they build with dancing monkeys and dark rooms? Sailing home, those captains slept with themselves. Themselves! Such sinful company, ten thousand miles! No, Kate, no matter what, there's us!

And the great deep breathing calm went on at the center of the ocean world beyond which lay nothing, the dreadnought continents foundered and sunk by time.

But on the ninth day the men themselves let down the boats and sat in them waiting for orders, and there was nothing for it but to row for a wind, the captain joining his men.

Toward the end of the tenth day, an island came slowly up over the horizon.

He called to his wife, "Kate, we'll row in for provisions. Will you come along?"

She stared at the island as if she had seen it somewhere long before she was born, and shook her head, slowly, no.

"Go on! I won't touch land until we're home!"

And looking up at her he knew that she was, by instinct, living the legend he had so lightly spun and told. Like the golden woman in the myth, she sensed some secret evil on a lonely swelter of sand and coral that might diminish or, more, destroy her.

"God bless you, Kate! Three hours!"

And he rowed away to the island with his men.

Late in the day they rowed back with five kegs of fresh sweet water and the boats odorous with warm fruit and flowers.

And waiting for him was Kate who would not go ashore, who would not, she said, touch ground.

She was first to drink the clear cool water.

Brushing her hair, looking out at the unmoved tides that night, she said, "It's almost over. There'll be a change by morning. Oh, Tom, hold me. After its being so warm, it'll be so cold."

In the night he woke. Kate, breathing in the dark, murmured. Her hand fell upon his, white hot. She cried out in her sleep. He felt her wrist and there first heard the rising of the storm.

As he sat by her, the ship lifted high on a great slow breast of water, and the spell was broken.

The slack canvas shuddered against the sky. Every rope hummed as if a huge hand had passed down the ship as over a silent harp, calling forth fresh sounds of voyaging.

The calm over, one storm began.

Another followed.

Of the two storms, one ended abruptly—the fever that raged in Kate and burned her to a white dust. A great silence moved in her body and then did not move at all.

The sail mender was brought to dress her for the sea. The motion of his needle flickering in the underwater light of the cabin was like a tropic fish, sharp, thin, infinitely patient, nibbling away at the shroud, skirting the dark, sealing the silence in.

In the final hours of the vast storm above, they brought the white calm from below and let her free in a fall that tore the sea only a moment. Then, without trace, Kate and life were gone.

"Kate, Kate, oh, Kate!"

He could not leave her here, lost to the tidal flows between the Japan Sea and the Golden Gate. Weeping that night, he stormed himself out of the storm. Gripped to the wheel, he circled the ship again and again around that wound that had healed with untimely swiftness. Then he knew a calm that lasted the rest of his days. He never raised his voice or clenched his fist again to any man. And with that pale voice and unclenched fist, he turned the ship away at last from the unscarred ground, circled the earth, delivered his goods, then turned his face from the sea for all time. Leaving his ship to nudge the green-mantled dock, he walked and rode inland twelve hundred miles. Blindly, he bought land, blindly he built, with Hanks, not knowing for a long while what he had bought or built. Only knowing that he had always been too old, and had been young for a short hour with Kate, and now was very old indeed and would never chance such an hour again.

So, in mid-continent, a thousand miles from the sea on the east, a thousand miles from the hateful sea on the west, he damned the life and the water he had known, remembering not what had been given but what had been so swiftly taken away.

On this land, then, he walked out and cast forth seed, prepared himself for his first harvest and called himself farmer.

But one night in that first summer of living as far from the sea as any man could get, he was waked by an incredible, a familiar, sound. Trembling in his bed, he whispered, No, no, it can't be—I'm mad! But . . . *listen!*

He opened the farmhouse door to look upon the land. He stepped out on the porch, spelled by this thing he had done without knowing it. He held to the porch rail and blinked, wet-eyed, out beyond his house.

There, in the moonlight, hill after slow-rising hill of wheat blew in tidal winds with the motion of waves. An immense Pacific of grain shimmered off beyond seeing, with his house, his now-recognized ship, becalmed in its midst.

He stayed out half the night, striding here, standing there, stunned with the discovery, lost in the deeps of this inland sea. And with the following years, tackle by tackle, timber by timber, the house shaped itself to the size, feel, and thrust of ships he had sailed in crueler winds and deeper waters.

"How long, Hanks, since we last saw water?"

"Twenty years, Captain."

"No, yesterday morning."

Coming back through the door, his heart pounded. The wall barometer clouded over, flickered with a faint lightning that played along the rims of his eyelids.

"No coffee, Hanks. Just—a cup of clear water."

Hanks went away and came back.

"Hanks? Promise. Bury me where she is."

"But, Captain, she's—" Hanks stopped. He nodded. "Where she is. Yes, sir."

"Good. Now give me the cup."

The water was fresh. It came from the islands beneath the earth. It tasted of sleep.

"One cup. She was right, Hanks, you know. Not to touch land, ever again. She was right. But I brought her one cup of water from the land, and the land was in water that touched her lips. One cup. Oh, if *only* . . . !"

He shifted it in his rusted hands. A typhoon swarmed from nowhere, filling the cup. It was a black storm raging in a small place.

He raised the cup and drank the typhoon.

"Hanks!" someone cried.

But not he. The typhoon, storming, had gone, and he with it.

The cup fell empty to the floor.

It was a mild morning. The air was sweet and the wind steady. Hanks had worked half the night digging and half the morning filling. Now the work was done. The town minister helped, and then stood back as Hanks jigsawed the final square of sod into place. Piece after piece, he fitted neatly and tamped and joined. And on each piece, as Hanks had made certain, was the golden, the full rich ripe-grained wheat, as high as a ten-year-old boy.

Hanks bent and put the last piece to rest.

"No marker?" asked the minister.

"Oh, no, sir, and never will be one."

The minister started to protest, when Hanks took his arm, and walked him up the hill a way, then turned and pointed back.

They stood a long moment. The minister nodded at last, smiled quietly and said, "I see. I understand."

For there was just the ocean of wheat going on and on

forever, vast tides of it blowing in the wind, moving east and ever east beyond, and not a line or seam or ripple to show where the old man sank from sight.

"It was a sea burial," said the minister.

"It was," said Hanks. "As I promised. It was, indeed."

Then they turned and walked off along the hilly shore, saying nothing again until they reached and entered the creaking house.

EL DÍA DE MUERTE

Morning.

The little boy, Raimundo, ran across the Avenida Madero. He ran through the early smell of incense from many churches and in the smell of charcoal from ten thousand breakfast cookings. He moved in the thoughts of death. For Mexico City was cool with death thoughts in the morning. There were shadows of churches and always women in black, in mourning black, and the smoke from the church candles and charcoal braziers made a smell of sweet death in his nostrils as he ran. And he did not think it strange, for all thoughts were death thoughts on this day.

This was El Día de Muerte, the Day of Death.

On this day in all the far places of the country, the women sat by little wooden slat stands and from these sold the white sugar skulls and candy corpses to be chewed and swallowed. In all of the churches services would be said, and in graveyards tonight candles would be illumined, much wine drunk, and many high man-soprano songs cried forth.

Raimundo ran with a sense of the entire universe in him; all the things his Tío Jorge had told him, all the things he had himself seen in his years. On this day events would be happening in such far places as Guanajuato and Lake Pátzcuaro. Here in the great bull ring of Mexico City even now the *trabajandos* were raking and smoothing the sands, tickets were selling and the bulls were nervously eliminating themselves, their eyes swiveling, fixing, in their hidden stalls, waiting for death.

In the graveyard at Guanajuato the great iron gates were swinging wide to let the *turistas* step down the spiral cool staircase into the deep earth, there to walk in the dry echoing catacombs and gaze upon mummies rigid as toys, stood against the wall. One hundred and ten mummies stiffly wired

83

to the stones, faces horror-mouthed and shrivel-eyed; bodies that rustled if you touched them.

At Lake Pátzcuaro, on the island of Janitzio, the great fishing seines flew down in butterfly swoops to gather silverine fish. The island, with Father Morelos' huge stone statue on top of it, had already begun the tequila drinking that started the celebratory Día de Muerte.

In Lenares, a small town, a truck ran over a dog and did not stop to come back and see.

Christ himself was in each church, with blood upon him, and agony in him.

And Raimundo ran in the November light across the Avenida Madero.

Ah, the sweet terrors! In the windows, the sugar skulls with names on their snowy brows: JOSÉ, CARLOTTA, RAMONA, LUISA! All the names on chocolate death's-heads and frosted bones.

The sky was glazed blue pottery over him and the grass flamed green as he ran past the *glorietas*. In his hand he held very tightly fifty centavos, much money for much sweets, for surely he must purchase legs, sockets and ribs to chew. The day of eating of Death. They would show Death, ah, yes, they would! He and *madrecita mia*, and his brothers, aye, and his sisters!

In his mind he saw a skull with candy lettering: RAIMUNDO. I shall eat my own skull, he thought. And in this way cheat Death who always drips at the window in the rain or squeaks in that hinge of the old door or hangs in our urine like a little pale cloud. Cheat Death who is rolled into tamales by the sick tamale maker, Death wrapped in a fine corn-tortilla shroud.

In his mind, Raimundo heard his old Tío Jorge talking all this. His ancient, adobe-faced uncle who gestured his fingers to each small word and said, "Death is in your nostrils like clock-spring hairs, Death grows in your stomach like a child. Death shines on your eyelids like a lacquer."

From a rickety stand an old woman with a sour mouth and tiny beards in her ears sold shingles on which miniature funerals were conducted. There was a little cardboard coffin and a crepe-paper priest with an infinitesimal Bible, and crepe-paper altar boys with small nuts for heads, and there were attendants holding holy flags, and a candy-white corpse with tiny black eyes inside the tiny coffin, and on the altar behind the coffin was a movie star's picture. These little shingle funerals could be taken home, where you threw away the movie star's picture and pasted in a photograph of your own dead in its place on the altar. So you had a small funeral of your loved one over again.

Raimundo put out a twenty-centavo piece. "One," he said. And he bought a shingle with a funeral on it.

Tío Jorge said, "Life is a wanting of things, Raimundito. You must always be wanting things in life. You will want *frijoles*, you will want water, you will desire women, you will desire sleep; most especially sleep. You will want a burro, you will want a new roof on your house, you will want fine shoes from the glass windows of the *zapatería*, and, again, you will want sleep. You will want rain, you will want jungle fruits, you will want good meat; you will, once more, desire sleep. You will seek a horse, you will seek children, you will seek the jewels in the great shining stores on the *avenida* and, ah, yes, remember? You will lastly seek sleep. Remember, Raimundo, you will want things. Life is this wanting. You will want things until you no longer want them, and then it is time to be wanting only sleep and sleep. There is a time for all of us, when sleep is the great and the beautiful thing. And when nothing is wanted but only sleep, then it is one thinks of the Day of the Dead and the happy sleeping ones. Remember, Raimundo?"

"Sí, Tío Jorge."

"What do *you* want, Raimundo?"

"I don't know."

"What do all men want, Raimundo?"

"What?"

"What is there to want, Raimundo?"

"Maybe I know. Ah, but I don't know, I don't!"

"*I* know what you want, Raimundo."

"What?"

"I know what all men in this land want; there is much of it and it is wanted far over and above all other wantings and it is worshiped and wanted, for it is rest and a peacefulness of limb and body. . . ."

Raimundo entered the store and picked up a sugar skull with his name frosted upon it.

"You hold it in your hand, Raimundo," whispered Tío Jorge. "Even at your age you hold it delicately and nibble, swallow it into your blood. In your hands, Raimundo; look!"

The sugar skull.

"Ah!"

"In the street I see a dog. I drive my car. Do I pause? Do I unpress my foot from the pedal? No! More speed! Bom! So! The dog is happier, is he not? Out of this world, forever gone?"

Raimundo paid money and proudly inserted his dirty fingers within the sugar skull, giving it a brain of five wriggling parts.

He walked from the store and looked upon the wide, sun-filled boulevard with the cars rushing and roaring through it. He squinted his eyes and ...

The *barreras* were full. In *la sombra* and *el sol*, in shadow or in sun, the great round seats of the bull ring were filled to the sky. The band exploded in brass! The gates flung wide! The matadors, the *banderilleros*, the picadors, all of them came walking or riding across the fresh, smooth sand in the warm sunlight. The band crashed and banged and the crowd stirred and stirred and murmured and cried aloud.

The music finished with a cymbal.

Behind the *barrera* walls the men in the tight glittery costumes adjusted their birettas upon their greasy black hair-dos and felt of their capes and swords and talked, and a man bent over the wall above with a camera to whirr and click at them.

The band whammed proudly again. A door burst open, the first black giant of a bull rushed out, loins jolting, little fluttery ribbons tacked to his neck. The bull!

Raimundo ran forward, lightly, lightly, on the Avenida Madero. Lightly lightly he ran between the fast black huge bull cars. One gigantic car roared and horned at him. Lightly lightly ran Raimundito.

The *banderillero* ran forward lightly, lightly, like a blue feather blown over the dimpled bull-ring sands—the bull a black cliff rising. The *banderillero* stood now, poised, and stamped his foot. The *banderillas* are raised, ah! so! Softly softly ran the blue ballet slippers in the quiet sand and the bull ran and the *banderillero* rose softly in an arc upon the air and the two poles struck down and the bull slammed to a halt, grunting-shrieking as the pikes bit deep in his withers! Now the *banderillero*, the source of this pain, was gone. The crowd roared!

The Guanajuato cemetery gates swung open.

Raimundo stood frozen and quiet and the car bore down upon him. All of the land smelled of ancient death and dust and everywhere things ran toward death or were in death.

The *turistas* filed into the cemetery of Guanajuato. A huge wooden door was opened and they walked down the twisting steps into the catacombs where the one hundred and ten dead shrunken people stood horrible against the walls. The jutting teeth of them, the wide eyes staring into spaces of nothing. The naked bodies of women like so many wire frames with clay clinging all askew to them. "We stand them in the catacombs because their relatives cannot afford the rent on their graves," whispered the little caretaker.

Below the cemetery hill, a juggling act, a man balancing something on his head, a crowd following past the coffin-carpenter's shop, to the music of the carpenter, nails fringing his mouth, bent to beat the coffin like a drum. Balanced delicately upon his proud dark head the juggler carries a silvery satin-skinned box, which he touches lightly now and again to give it balance. He walks with solemn dignity, his bare feet gliding over the cobbles, behind him the women in black *rebozos* toothing tangerines. And in the box, hidden away, safe and unseen, is the small child body of his daughter, newly dead.

The procession passes the open coffin shops and the banging of nails and sawing of boards is heard through the land. In the catacomb, the standing dead await the procession.

Raimundo held his body so, like a *torero*, to make a *veronica*, for the great hurtling car to pass and the crowd to cry *"Ole!"* He smiled wildly.

The black car rose over and blotted light from his eyes as it touched him. Blackness ran through him. It was night. . . .

In the churchyard on the island of Janitzio, under the great dark statue of Father Morelos, it is blackness, it is midnight. You hear the high voices of men grown shrill on wine, men with voices like women, but not soft women, no, high, hard and drunken women, quick, savage and melancholy women. On the dark lake little fires glow on Indian boats coming from the mainland, bringing tourists from Mexico City to see the ceremony of El Día de Muerte, sliding across the dark foggy lake, all bundled and wrapped against the cold.

Sunlight.

Christ moved.

From the crucifix he took down a hand, lifted it, suddenly —waved it.

The hot sun shone in golden explosions from the high church tower in Guadalajara, and in blasts from the high, swaying crucifix. In the street below, if Christ looked down with mellow warm eyes, and he did so now in this moment, he saw two thousand upturned faces: the spectators like so many melons scattered about the market, so many hands raised to shield the uptilted and curious eyes. A little wind blew and the tower cross sighed very gently and pressed forward under it.

Christ waved his hand. Those in the market below waved back. A small shout trickled through the crowd. Traffic did not move in the street. It was eleven of a hot green Sunday morning. You could smell the fresh clipped grass from the plaza, and the incense from the church doors.

Christ took his other hand down also and waved it and suddenly jerked away from the cross and hung by his feet, face down, a small silver medallion jingling in his face, suspended from about his dark neck.

"*Olé! Olé!*" cried one small boy far below, pointing up at him and then at himself. "You see him, you see? That is Gómez, my brother! Gómez who is my brother!" And the small boy walked through the crowd with a hat, collecting money.

Movement. Raimundo, in the street, covered his eyes and screamed. Darkness again.

The tourists from the boats moved in the dream of the island of Janitzio at midnight. In the dim street the great nets hung like fog from the lake, and rivers of today's silver minnows lay glittering in cascades upon the slopes. Moonlight struck them like a cymbal striking another cymbal; they gave off a silent reverberation.

In the crumbling church at the top of the rough hill is a Christ much drilled by termites, but the blood still congeals thickly from his artistic wounds and it will be years before the agony is insect-eaten from his suffering mask.

Outside the church, a woman with Tarascan blood lifting and falling in her throat sits fluttering ripped morning-glories through the flames of six candles. The flowers, passing through the flames like moths, give off a gentle sexual odor. Already the moving tourists come and stand about her, looking down, wanting to ask, but not asking, what she is doing, seated there upon her husband's grave.

In the church, like resin from a great beautiful tree, the limbs of Christ, themselves hewn from beautiful limbs of imported trees, give off a sweet sacred resin in little raining droplets that hang but never fall, blood that gives a garment for his nakedness.

"*Olé!*" roared the crowd.

Bright sunlight again. A pressure on Raimundo's flung body. The car, the daylight, the pain!

The picador jousted his horse forward, the horse with thick mattresses tied to it, and kicked the bull in the shoulder with his boot and at the same time penetrated that shoulder with the long stick and the nail on the end of it. The picador withdrew. Music played. The matador moved slowly forward.

The bull stood with one foot forward in the center of the sun-held ring, his organs nervous. The eyes were dull glazed hypnotic eyes of fear-hate. He kept eliminating nervously, nervously, until he was streaked and foul with a nervous casting out. The greenish matter pulsed from his buttocks and the blood pulsed from his gored shoulder and the six *banderillas* bindled and clattered on his spine.

The matador took time to rearrange his red cloth over his blade, just so carefully, while the crowd and the pulsing bull waited.

The bull can see nothing, know nothing. The bull desires not to see of this or that. The world is pain and shadows and light and weariness. The bull stands only to be dispatched. It will welcome an end to confusion, to the racing shapes, the traitorous capes, the lying flourishes and false fronts. The bull plants out its feet in feeble stances and remains in one position, slowly moving its head back and forth, eyes glazed, the excrement still unfelt rivuleting from its flanks, the blood tiredly pumping from the neck. Somewhere off in the glazed distance a man holds out a bright sword. The bull does not move. The sword, held by the smiling man, now cuts three short gashes down the nose of the empty-eyed bull—*so*!

The crowd shouts.

The bull takes the cutting and does not even flinch. Blood flushes from the snuffling, cut nostrils.

The matador stamps his foot.

The bull runs with feeble obedience toward the enemy. The sword pierces his neck. The bull falls, thuds, kicks, is silent.

"Olé!" shouts the crowd. The band blows out a brass finale!

Raimundo felt the car hit. There were swift intervals of light and darkness.

In the Janitzio churchyard two hundred candles burned atop two hundred rocky graves, men sang, tourists watched, fog poured up from the lake.

In Guanajuato, sunlight! Striking down through a slot in the catacomb, sunlight showed the brown eyes of a woman, mouth wide in rictus, cross-armed. Tourists touched and thumped her like a drum.

"Olé!" The matador circled the ring, his small black biretta in his fingers, high. It rained. Centavo pieces, purses, shoes, hats. The matador stood in this rain with his tiny biretta raised for an umbrella!

A man ran up with a cut-off ear of the slain bull. The matador held it up to the crowd. Everywhere he walked the crowd threw up their hats and money. But thumbs jerked down and though the shouts were glad they were not so glad that he keep the cut-off ear. Thumbs went down. Without a look behind him, shrugging, the matador gave the ear a cracking toss. The bloody ear lay on the sand, while the crowd, glad that he had thrown it away, because he was not *that* good, cheered. The bucklers came out, chained the slumped bull to a team of high-stamping horses, who whistled fearful sirens in their nostrils at the hot blood odor and bolted like white explosions across the arena when released, yanking, bounding the dead slumped bull behind, leaving a harrowing of the horns in sand and amulets of blood.

Raimundo felt the sugar skull jolt from his fingers. The funeral on the wooden slat was torn from his other wide-flung hand.

Bang! The bull hit, rebounded from the *barrera* wall as the horses vanished, jangling, screaming, in the tunnel.

A man ran to the *barrera* of Señor Villalta, poking upward the *banderillas*, their sharp prongs choked with bull blood and flesh. *"Gracias!"* Villalta threw down a peso and took the *banderillas* proudly, the little orange and blue crepe papers fluttering, to hand about like musical instruments to his wife, to cigar-smoking friends.

Christ moved.

The crowd looked up at the swaying cross on the cathedral. Christ balanced on two hands, legs up in the sky!

The small boy ran through the crowd. "You see my brother? Pay! My brother! Pay!"

Christ now hung by one hand on the swaying cross. Below him was all the city of Guadalajara, very sweet and very quiet with Sunday. I will make much money today, he thought.

The cross jolted. His hand slipped. The crowd screamed. Christ fell.

Christ dies each hour. You see him in carven postures in ten thousand agonized places, eyes lifted to high dusty heavens of ten thousand small churches, and always there is much blood, ah, much blood.

"See!" said Señor Villalta. "See!" He wagged the *banderillas* in the face of his friends, red and wet.

With children chasing, snatching at him, laughing, the matador circles the ring again to the ever-increasing shower of hats, running and not stopping.

And now the tourist boats cross the dawn-pale lake of Pátzcuaro, leaving Janitzio behind, the candles snuffed, the graveyard deserted, the torn flowers strewn and shriveling. The boats pull up and the tourists step out in the new light, and in the hotel on the mainland shore a great silver urn waits, bubbling with fresh coffee; a little whisper of steam, like the last part of the fog from the lake, goes up into the warm air of the hotel dining room, and there is a good sound of chattered plates and tining forks and low converse, and a gentle lidding of eyes and a mouthing of coffee in dreams already begun before the pillow. Doors close. The tourists sleep on fog-damp pillows, in fog-damp sheets, like earth-spittled winding clothes. The coffee smell is as rich as the skin of a Tarascan.

In Guanajuato the gates close, the rigid nightmares are turned from. The spiral stair is taken up in hot November light. A dog barks. A wind stirs the dead morning-glories on the pastry-cake monuments. The big door whams down on the catacomb opening. The withered people are hidden.

The band hoots out its last triumphant hooting and the *barreras* are empty. Outside, the people walk away between ranks of phlegm-eyed beggers who sing high high songs, and the blood spoor of the last bull is raked and wiped and raked and wiped by the men with the rakes down in the wide shadowed ring. In the shower, the matador is slapped upon his wet buttocks by a man who has won money because of him this day.

Raimundo fell, Christ fell, in glaring light. A bull rushed, a car rushed, opening a great vault of blackness in the air which slammed, thundered shut and said nothing but sleep. Raimundo touched the earth, Christ touched the earth but did not know.

The cardboard funeral was shattered to bits. The sugar skull broke in the far gutter in three dozen fragments of blind snow.

The boy, the Christ, lay quiet.

The night bull went away to give other people darkness, to teach other people sleep.

Ah, said the crowd.

RAIMUNDO, said the bits of the sugar skull strewn on the earth.

People ran to surround the silence. They looked at the sleep.

And the sugar skull with the letters R and A and I and M and U and N and D and O was snatched up and eaten by children who fought over the name.

THE ILLUSTRATED WOMAN

When a new patient wanders into the office and stretches out to stutter forth a compendious ticker tape of free association, it is up to the psychiatrist immediately beyond, behind and above to decide at just which points of the anatomy the client is in touch with the couch.

In other words, where does the patient make contact with reality?

Some people seem to float half an inch above any surface whatsoever. They have not seen earth in so long, they have become somewhat airsick.

Still others so firmly weight themselves down, clutch, thrust, heave their bodies toward reality, that long after they are gone you find their tiger shapes and claw marks in the upholstery.

In the case of Emma Fleet, Dr. George C. George was a long time deciding which was furniture and which was woman and where what touched which.

For, to begin with, Emma Fleet resembled a couch.

"Mrs. Emma Fleet, Doctor," announced his receptionist.

Dr. George C. George gasped.

For it was a traumatic experience, seeing this woman shunt herself through the door without benefit of railroad switchman or the ground crews who rush about under Macy's Easter balloons, heaving on lines, guiding the massive images to some eternal hangar off beyond.

In came Emma Fleet, as quick as her name, the floor shifting like a huge scales under her weight.

Dr. George must have gasped again, guessing her at four hundred on the hoof, for Emma Fleet smiled as if reading his mind.

"Four hundred two and a half pounds, to be exact," she said.

He found himself staring at his furniture.

"Oh, it'll hold all right," said Mrs. Fleet intuitively.

She sat down.

The couch yelped like a cur.

Dr. George cleared his throat. "Before you make yourself comfortable," he said. "I feel I should say immediately and honestly that we in the psychiatrical field have had little success in inhibiting appetites. The whole problem of weight and food has so far eluded our ability for coping. A strange admission, perhaps, but unless we put our frailties forth, we might be in danger of fooling ourselves and thus taking money under false pretenses. So, if you are here seeking help for your figure, I must list myself among the nonplussed."

"Thank you for your honesty, Doctor," said Emma Fleet. "However, I don't wish to lose. I'd prefer your helping me *gain* another one hundred or two hundred pounds."

"Oh, no!" Dr. George exclaimed.

"Oh, yes. But my heart will not allow what my deep dear soul would most gladly endure. My physical heart might fail at what my loving heart and mind would ask of it."

She sighed. The couch sighed.

"Well, let me brief you. I'm married to Willy Fleet. We work for the Dillbeck-Horsemann Traveling Shows. I'm known as Lady Bountiful. And Willy . . ."

She swooned up out of the couch and glided or rather escorted her shadow across the floor. She opened the door.

Beyond, in the waiting room, a cane in one hand, a straw hat in the other, seated rigidly, staring at the wall, was a tiny man with tiny feet and tiny hands and tiny bright-blue eyes in a tiny head. He was, at the most, one would guess, three feet high, and probably weighed sixty pounds in the rain. But there was a proud, gloomy, almost violent look of genius blazing in that small but craggy face.

"That's Willy Fleet," said Emma lovingly, and shut the door.

The couch, sat on, cried again.

Emma beamed at the psychiatrist, who was still staring, in shock, at the door.

"No children, of course," he heard himself say.

"No children." Her smile lingered. "But that's not my problem, either. Willy, in a way, is my child. And I, in a way, besides being his wife, am his mother. It all has to do with size, I imagine, and we're happy with the way we've balanced things off."

"Well, if your problem isn't children, or your size or his, or controlling weight, then what . . . ?"

Emma Fleet laughed lightly, tolerantly. It was a nice laugh, like a girl's somehow caught in that great body and throat.

"Patience, Doctor. Mustn't we go back down the road to where Willy and I first met?"

The doctor shrugged, laughed quietly himself and relaxed, nodding. "You must."

"During high school," said Emma Fleet. "I weighed one-eighty and tipped the scales at two-fifty when I was twenty-one. Needless to say, I went on few summer excursions. Most of the time I was left in drydock. I had many girl friends, however, who liked to be seen with me. They weighed one-fifty, most of them, and I made them feel svelte. But that's a long time ago. I don't worry over it any more. Willy changed all that."

"Willy sounds like a remarkable man," Dr. George found himself saying, against all the rules.

"Oh, he is, he is! He *smoulders*—with ability, with talent as yet undiscovered, untapped!" she said, quickening warmly. "God bless him, he leaped into my life like summer lightning! Eight years ago I went with my girl friends to the visiting Labor Day carnival. By the end of the evening, the girls had all been seized away from me by the running boys who, rushing by, grabbed and took them off into the night. There I was alone with three Kewpie Dolls, a fake alligator handbag and nothing to do but make the Guess Your Weight man nervous by looking at him every time I went by and pretending like at any moment I might pay my money and dare him to guess.

"But the Guess Your Weight man *wasn't* nervous! After I had passed three times I saw him staring at me. With awe, yes, with admiration! And who was this Guess Your Weight man? Willy Fleet, of course. The fourth time I passed he called to me and said I could get a prize free if only I'd let him guess my weight. He was all feverish and excited. He danced around. I'd never been made over so much in my life. I blushed. I felt good. So I sat in the scales chair. I heard the pointer whizz up around and I heard Willy whistle with honest delight.

" 'Two hundred and eighty-nine pounds!' he cried. 'Oh boy oh boy, you're lovely!'

" 'I'm *what?*' I said.

" 'You're the loveliest woman in the whole world,' said Willy, looking me right in the eye.

"I blushed again. I laughed. We both laughed. Then I must have cried, for the next thing, sitting there, I felt him touch my elbow with concern. He was gazing into my face, faintly alarmed.

" 'I haven't said the wrong thing?' he asked.

" 'No,' I sobbed, and then grew quiet. 'The right thing, only the right thing. It's the first time anyone ever . . .'

" 'What?' he said.

" 'Ever put up with my fat,' I said.

" 'You're not fat,' he said. 'You're large, you're big, you're wonderful. Michelangelo would have loved you. Titian would have loved you. Da Vinci would have loved you. They knew what they were doing in those days. Size. Size is everything. I should know. Look at me. I traveled with Singer's Midgets for six seasons, known as Jack Thimble. And oh my God, dear lady, you're right out of the most glorious part of the Renaissance. Bernini, who built those colonnades around the front of St. Peter's and inside at the altar, would have lost his everlasting soul just to know someone like you.'

" 'Don't!' I cried. 'I wasn't meant to feel this happy. It'll hurt so much when you stop.'

" 'I won't stop, then,' he said. 'Miss . . . ?'

" 'Emma Gertz.'

" 'Emma,' he said, 'are you married?'

" 'Are you kidding?' I said.

" 'Emma, do you like to travel?'

" 'I've never traveled.'

" 'Emma,' he said, 'this old carnival's going to be in your town one more week. Come down every night, every day, why not? Talk to me, know me. At the end of the week, who can tell, maybe you'll travel with me.'

" 'What are you suggesting?' I said, not really angry or irritated or anything, but fascinated and intrigued that anyone would offer anything to Moby Dick's daughter.

" 'I mean marriage!' Willy Fleet looked at me, breathing hard, and I had the feeling that he was dressed in a mountaineer's rig, alpine hat, climbing boots, spikes, and a rope slung over his baby shoulder. And if I should ask him, 'Why are you saying this?' he might well answer, 'Because you're *there.*'

"But I didn't ask, so he didn't answer. We stood there in the night, at the center of the carnival, until at last I started off down the midway, swaying. 'I'm drunk!' I cried. 'Oh, so very drunk, and I've had nothing to drink.'

" 'Now that I've found you,' called Willy Fleet after me, 'you'll never escape me, remember!'

"Stunned and reeling, blinded by his large man's words sung out in his soprano voice, I somehow blundered from the carnival grounds and trekked home.

"The next week we were married."

Emma Fleet paused and looked at her hands.

"Would it bother you if I told about the honeymoon?" she asked shyly.

"No," said the doctor, then lowered his voice, for he was responding all too quickly to the details. "Please *do* go on."

"The honeymoon." Emma sounded her *vox humana.* The response from all the chambers of her body vibrated the touch, the room, the doctor, the dear bones within the doctor.

"The honeymoon . . . was not usual."

The doctor's eyebrows lifted the faintest touch. He looked from the woman to the door beyond which, in miniature, sat the image of Edmund Hillary, he of Everest.

"You have never seen such a rush as Willy spirited me off to his home, a lovely dollhouse, really, with one large normal-sized room that was to be mine, or, rather, ours. There, very politely, always the kind, the thoughtful, the quiet gentleman, he asked for my blouse, which I gave him, my skirt, which I gave him. Right down the list, I handed him the garments that he named, until at last . . . Can one blush from head to foot? One can. One did. I stood like a veritable hearthfire stoked by a blush of all-encompassing and ever-moving color that surged and resurged up and down my body in tints of pink and rose and then pink again.

" 'My God!' cried Willy, 'you're the loveliest grand camellia that ever did unfurl!' Whereupon new tides of blush moved in hidden avalanches within, showing only to color the tent of my body, the outermost and, to Willy anyway, most precious skin.

"What did Willy do then? Guess."

"I daren't," said the doctor, flustered himself.

"He walked around and around me."

"*Circled* you?"

"Around and around, like a sculptor gazing at a huge block of snow-white granite. He said to himself. Granite or marble from which he might shape images of beauty as yet unguessed. Around and around he walked, sighing and shaking his head happily at his fortune, his little hands clasped, his little eyes bright. Where to begin, he seemed to be thinking, where, where to begin!?

"He spoke at last. 'Emma,' he asked, 'why, why do you think I've worked for years as the Guess Your Weight man at the carnival? Why? Because I have been searching my lifetime through for such as you. Night after night, summer after summer, I've watched those scales jump and twitter! And now at last I've the means, the way, the wall, the canvas, whereby to express my genius!'

"He stopped walking and looked at me, his eyes brimming over.

"'Emma,' he said softly, 'may I have permission to do anything absolutely whatsoever at all with you?'

"'Oh, Willy, Willy,' I cried. 'Anything!'"

Emma Fleet paused.

The doctor found himself out at the edge of his chair. "Yes, yes, and *then?*"

"And then," said Emma Fleet, "he brought out all his boxes and bottles of inks and stencils and his bright silver tattoo needles."

"Tattoo needles?"

The doctor fell back in his chair. "He . . . tattooed you?"

"He tattooed me."

"He was a tattoo artist?"

"He was, he is, an artist. It only happens that the form his art takes happens to be the tattoo."

"And you," said the doctor slowly, "were the canvas for which he had been searching much of his adult life?"

"I was the canvas for which he had searched *all* of his life."

She let it sink, and *did* sink, and kept on sinking, into the doctor. Then when she saw it had struck bottom and stirred up vast quantities of mud, she went serenely on.

"So our grand life began! I loved Willy and Willy loved me and we both loved this thing that was larger than ourselves that we were doing together. Nothing less than creating the greatest picture the world has ever seen! 'Nothing less than perfection!' cried Willy. 'Nothing less than perfection!' cried myself in response.

"Oh, it was a happy time. Ten thousand cozy busy hours we spent together. You can't imagine how proud it made me to be the vast shore along which the genius of Willy Fleet ebbed and flowed in a tide of colors.

"One year alone we spent on my right arm and my left, half a year on my right leg, eight months on my left, in preparation for the grand explosion of bright detail which erupted out along my collarbone and shoulderblades, which fountained upward from my hips to meet in a glorious July celebration of pinwheels, Titian nudes, Giorgione landscapes and El Greco cross-indexes of lightning on my façade, prickling with vast electric fires up and down my spine.

"Dear me, there never has been, there never will be, a love like ours again, a love where two people so sincerely dedicated themselves to one task, of giving beauty to the world in equal portions. We flew to each other day after day, and I ate more, grew larger, with the years, Willy approved, Willy applauded. Just that much more room, more space for his configurations to flower in. We could not bear to be apart, for we both felt, were certain, that once the Masterpiece was finished we could leave circus, carnival, or vaudeville forever. It was grandiose, yes, but we knew that once finished, I could be toured through the Art Institute in Chicago, the Kress Collection in Washington, the Tate Gallery in London, the Louvre, the Uffizi, the Vatican Museum! For the rest of our lives we would travel with the sun!

"So it went, year on year. We didn't need the world or the people of the world, we had each other. We worked at our ordinary jobs by day, and then, till after midnight, there was Willy at my ankle, there was Willy at my elbow, there was Willy exploring up the incredible slope of my back toward the snowy-talcumed crest. Willy wouldn't let me see, most of the time. He didn't like me looking over his shoulder, he didn't like me looking over *my* shoulder, for that matter. Months passed before, curious beyond madness, I would be allowed to see his progress slow inch by inch as the brilliant inks inundated me and I drowned in the rainbow of his inspirations. Eight years, eight glorious wondrous years. And then at last it was done, it was finished. And Willy threw himself down and slept for forty-eight hours straight. And I slept near him, the mammoth bedded with the black lamb. That was just four weeks ago. Four short weeks back, our happiness came to an end."

"Ah, yes," said the doctor. "You and your husband are suffering from the creative equivalent of the 'baby blues,' the depression a mother feels after her child is born. Your work is finished. A listless and somewhat sad period invariably follows. But, now, consider, you will reap the rewards of your long labor, surely? You *will* tour the world?"

"No," cried Emma Fleet, and a tear sprang to her eye. "At any moment, Willy will run off and never return. He has begun to wander about the city. Yesterday I caught him brushing off the carnival scales. Today I found him working, for the first time in eight years, back at his Guess Your Weight booth!"

"Dear me," said the psychiatrist. "He's . . . ?"

"Weighing new women, yes! Shopping for new canvas! He hasn't said, but I know, I know! This time he'll find a heavier woman yet, five hundred, six hundred pounds! I guessed this would happen, a month ago, when we finished the Masterpiece. So I ate still more, and stretched my skin still more, so that little places appeared here and there, little open patches that Willy had to repair, fill in with fresh detail. But now I'm done, exhausted, I've stuffed to distraction, the last fill-in work is done. There's not a millionth of an inch of space left between my ankles and my Adam's apple where we can squeeze in one last demon, dervish or baroque angel. I am, to Willy, work over and done. Now he wants to move on. He will marry, I fear, four more times in his life, each time to a larger woman, a greater extension for a greater mural, and the grand finale of his talent. Then, too, in the last week, he has become critical."

"Of the Masterpiece with a capital *M*?" asked the doctor.

"Like all artists, he is a superb perfectionist. Now he finds little flaws, a face here done slightly in the wrong tint or texture, a hand there twisted slightly askew by my hurried diet to gain more weight and thus give him new space and renew his attentions. To him, above all, I was a beginning. Now he must move on from his apprenticeship to his true masterworks. On, Doctor, I am about to be abandoned. What is there for a woman who weighs four hundred pounds and is laved with illustrations? If he leaves, what shall I do, where go, who would want me now? Will I be lost again in the world as I was lost before my wild happiness?"

"A psychiatrist," said the psychiatrist, "is not supposed to give advice. But . . ."

"But, but, but?" she cried, eagerly.

"A psychiatrist is supposed to let the patient discover and cure himself. Yet, in this case . . ."

"This case, yes, go on!"

"It seems so simple. To keep your husband's love . . ."

"To keep his love, yes?"

The doctor smiled. "You must destroy the Masterpiece."

"What?"

"Erase it, get rid of it. Those tattoos *will* come off, won't they? I read somewhere once that—"

"Oh, Doctor!" Emma Fleet leaped up. "That's *it!* It can be done! And, best of all, Willy can do it! It will take three months alone to wash me clean, rid me of the very Masterpiece that irks him now. Then, virgin white again, we can start another eight years, after that another eight and another. Oh, Doctor, I know he'll do it! Perhaps he was only waiting for me to suggest—and I too stupid to guess! Oh, Doctor, Doctor!"

And she crushed him in her arms.

When the doctor broke happily free, she stood off, turning in a circle.

"How strange," she said. "In half an hour you solve the next three thousand days and beyond of my life. You're very wise. I'll pay you anything!"

"My usual modest fee is sufficient," said the doctor.

"I can hardly wait to tell Willy! But first," she said, "since you've been so wise, you deserve to see the Masterpiece before it is destroyed."

"That's hardly necessary, Mrs.—"

"You must discover for yourself the rare mind, eye and artistic hand of Willy Fleet, before it is gone forever and we start anew!" she cried, unbuttoning her voluminous coat.

"It isn't really—"

"There!" she said, and flung her coat wide.

The doctor was somehow not surprised to see that she was stark naked beneath her coat.

He gasped. His eyes grew large. His mouth fell open. He sat down slowly, though in reality he somehow wished to

stand, as he had in the fifth grade as a boy, during the salute
to the flag, following which three dozen voices broke into
an awed and tremulous song:

> *"O beautiful for spacious skies*
> *For amber waves of grain,*
> *For purple mountain majesties*
> *Above the fruited plain . . ."*

But, still seated, overwhelmed, he gazed at the continental vastness of the woman.

Upon which nothing whatsoever was stitched, painted,
watercolored or in any way tattooed.

Naked, unadorned, untouched, unlined, unillustrated.

He gasped again.

Now she had whipped her coat back about her with a
winsome acrobat's smile, as if she had just performed a tow-
ering feat. Now she was sailing toward the door.

"Wait—" said the doctor.

But she was out the door, in the reception room, babbling,
whispering, "Willy, Willy!" and bending to her husband, hiss-
ing in his tiny ear until *his* eyes flexed wide, and his mouth
firm and passionate dropped open and he cried aloud and
clapped his hands with elation.

"Doctor, Doctor, thank you, thank you!"

He darted forward and seized the doctor's hand and shook
it, hard. The doctor was surprised at the fire and rock hard-
ness of that grip. It was the hand of a dedicated artist, as
were the eyes burning up at him darkly from the wildly il-
luminated face.

"Everything's going to be fine!" cried Willy.

The doctor hesitated, glancing from Willy to the great
shadowing balloon that tugged at him wanting to fly off
away.

"We won't have to come back again, ever?"

Good Lord, the doctor thought, does *he* think that *he* has
illustrated her from stem to stern, and does she humor him
about it? Is *he* mad?

Or does *she* imagine that he has tattooed her from neck
to toebone, and does he humor her? Is *she* mad?

Or, most strange of all, do they *both* believe that he has
swarmed as across the Sistine Chapel ceiling, covering her
with rare and significant beauties? Do they both believe,

know, humor each other in their specially dimensioned world?

"Will we have to come back again?" asked Willy Fleet a second time.

"No." The doctor breathed a prayer. "I think not."

Why? Because, by some idiot grace, he had done the right thing, hadn't he? By prescribing for a half-seen cause he had made a full cure, yes? Regardless if she believed or he believed or both believed in the Masterpiece, by suggesting the pictures be erased, destroyed, the doctor had made her a clean, lovely and inviting canvas again, if *she* needed to be. And if he, on the other hand, wished a new woman to scribble, scrawl and pretend to tattoo on, well, that worked, too. For new and untouched she would be.

"Thank you, Doctor, oh thank you, thank you!"

"Don't thank me," said the doctor. "I've done nothing." He almost said, It was all a fluke, a joke, a surprise! I fell downstairs and landed on my feet!

"Goodbye, goodbye!"

And the elevator slid down, the big woman and the little man sinking from sight into the now suddenly not-too-solid earth, where the atoms opened to let them pass.

"Goodbye, thanks, thanks . . . thanks . . ."

Their voices faded, calling his name and praising his intellect long after they had passed the fourth floor.

The doctor looked around and moved unsteadily back into his office. He shut the door and leaned against it.

"Doctor," he murmured, "heal thyself."

He stepped forward. He did not feel real. He must lie down, if but for a moment.

Where?

On the couch, of course, on the couch.

SOME LIVE LIKE LAZARUS

You won't believe it when I tell you I waited more than sixty years for a murder, hoped as only a woman can hope that it might happen, and didn't move a finger to stop it when it finally drew near. Anna Marie, I thought, you can't stand guard forever. Murder, when ten thousand days have passed, is more than a surprise, it is a miracle.

"Hold on! Don't let me fall!"

Mrs. Harrison's voice.

Did I ever, in half a century, hear it whisper? Was it always screaming, shrieking, demanding, threatening?

Yes, always.

"Come along, Mother. There you are, Mother."

Her son Roger's voice.

Did I ever in all the years hear it rise above a murmur, protest, or, even faintly birdlike, argue?

No. Always the loving monotone.

This morning, no different than any other of their first mornings, they arrived in their great black hearse for their annual Green Bay summer. There he was, thrusting his hand in to hoist the window dummy after him, an ancient sachet of bones and talcum dust that was named, surely for some terrible practical joke, Mother.

"Easy does it, Mother."

"You're bruising my arm!"

"Sorry, Mother."

I watched from a window of the lake pavilion as he trundled her off down the path in her wheel chair, she pushing her cane like a musket ahead to blast any Fates or Furies they might meet out of the way.

"Careful, don't run me into the flowers, thank God we'd sense not to go to Paris after all. You'd've had me in that nasty traffic. You're not disappointed?"

"No, Mother."

"We'll see Paris next year."

Next year . . . next year . . . no year at all, I heard someone murmur. Myself, gripping the window sill. For almost seventy years I had heard her promise this to the boy, boy-man, man, man-grasshopper and the now livid male praying mantis that he was, pushing his eternally cold and fur-wrapped woman past the hotel verandas where, in another age, paper fans had fluttered like Oriental butterflies in the hands of basking ladies.

"There, Mother, inside the cottage . . ." his faint voice fading still more, forever young when he was old, forever old when he was very young.

How old is she now? I wondered. Ninety-eight, yes, ninety-nine wicked years old. She seemed like a horror film repeated each year because the hotel entertainment fund could not afford to buy a new one to run in the moth-flaked evenings.

So, through all the repetitions of arrivals and departures, my mind ran back to when the foundations of the Green Bay Hotel were freshly poured and the parasols were new leaf green and lemon gold, that summer of 1890 when I first saw Roger, who was five, but whose eyes already were old and wise and tired.

He stood on the pavilion grass looking at the sun and the bright pennants as I came up to him.

"Hello," I said.

He simply looked at me.

I hesitated, tagged him and ran.

He did not move.

I came back and tagged him again.

He looked at the place where I had touched him, on the shoulder, and was about to run after me when her voice came from a distance.

"Roger, don't dirty your clothes!"

And he walked slowly away toward his cottage, not looking back.

That was the day I started to hate him.

Parasols have come and gone in a thousand summer colors, whole flights of butterfly fans have blown away on August winds, the pavilion has burned and been built again in the selfsame size and shape, the lake has dried like a plum in its basin, and my hatred, like these things, came and went, grew very large, stopped still for love, returned, then diminished with the years.

I remember when he was seven, them driving by in their horse carriage, his hair long, brushing his poutish, shrugging shoulders. They were holding hands and she was saying, "If you're very good this summer, next year we'll go to London. Or the year after that, at the latest."

And my watching their faces, comparing their eyes, their ears, their mouths, so when he came in for a soda pop one noon that summer I walked straight up to him and cried, "She's not your mother!"

"What!" He looked around in panic, as if she might be near.

"She's not your aunt or your grandma, either!" I cried. "She's a witch that stole you when you were a baby. You don't know who your mama is or your pa. You don't look anything like her. She's holding you for a million ransom which comes due when you're twenty-one from some duke or king!"

"Don't say that!" he shouted, jumping up.

"Why not?" I said angrily. "Why do you come around here? You can't play this, can't play that, can't do nothing, what good are you? She says, she does. I know *her!* She hangs upside down from the ceiling in her black clothes in her bedroom at midnight!"

"Don't say that!" His face was frightened and pale.

"Why not say it?"

"Because," he bleated, "it's true."

And he was out the door and running.

I didn't see him again until the next summer. And then only once, briefly, when I took some clean linen down to their cottage.

The summer when we were both twelve was the summer that for a time I didn't hate him.

He called my name outside the pavilion screen door and when I looked out he said, very quietly, "Anna Marie, when I am twenty and you are twenty, I'm going to marry you."

"Who's going to let you?" I asked.

"I'm going to let you," he said. "You just remember, Anna Marie. You wait for me. Promise?"

I could only nod. "But what about—"

"She'll be dead by then," he said, very gravely. "She's old. She's *old.*"

And then he turned and went away.

The next summer they did not come to the resort at all. I heard she was sick. I prayed every night that she would die.

But two years later they were back, and the year after the year after that until Roger was nineteen and I was nineteen, and then at last we had reached and touched twenty, and for one of the few times in all the years, they came into the pavilion together, she in her wheel chair now, deeper in her furs than ever before, her face a gathering of white dust and folded parchment.

She eyed me as I set her ice-cream sundae down before her, and eyed Roger as he said, "Mother, I want you to meet—"

"I do not meet girls who wait on public tables," she said. "I acknowledge they exist, work, and are paid. I immediately forget their names."

She touched and nibbled her ice cream, touched and nibbled her ice cream, while Roger sat not touching his at all.

They left a day earlier than usual that year. I saw Roger as he paid the bill, in the hotel lobby. He shook my hand to say goodbye and I could not help but say, "You've forgotten."

He took a half step back, then turned around, patting his coat pockets.

"Luggage, bills paid, wallet, no, I seem to have everything," he said.

"A long time ago," I said, "you made a promise."

He was silent.

"Roger," I said, "I'm twenty now. And so are you."

He seized my hand again, swiftly, as if he were falling over the side of a ship and it was me going away, leaving him to drown forever beyond help.

"One more year, Anna! Two, three, at the most!"

"Oh, no," I said, forlornly.

"Four years at the outside! The doctors say—"

"The doctors don't know what I know, Roger. She'll live forever. She'll bury you and me and drink wine at our funerals."

"She's a sick woman, Anna! My God, she *can't* survive!"

"She will, because we give her strength. She knows we want her dead. That really gives her the power to go on."

"I can't talk this way, I can't!" Seizing his luggage, he started down the hall.

"I won't wait, Roger," I said.

He turned at the door and looked at me so helplessly, so palely, like a moth pinned to the wall, that I could not say it again.

The door slammed shut.

The summer was over.

The next year Roger came directly to the soda fountain, where he said, "Is it true? Who is he?"

"Paul," I said. "You know Paul. He'll manage the hotel someday. We'll marry this fall."

"That doesn't give me much time," said Roger.

"It's too late," I said. "I've already promised."

"Promised, hell! You don't love him!"

"I think I do."

"Think, hell! Thinking's one thing, knowing's another. You *know* you love me!"

"Do I, Roger?"

"Stop relishing the damn business so much! You know you do! Oh, Anna, you'll be miserable!"

"I'm miserable now," I said.

"Oh, Anna, Anna, wait!"

"I have waited, most of my life. But I know what will happen."

"Anna!" He blurted it out as if it had come to him suddenly. "What if—what if she died *this* summer?"

"She won't."

"But if she did, if she took a turn for the worse, I mean, in the next two months—" He searched my face. He shortened it. "The next month, Anna, two weeks, listen, if she died in two short weeks, would you wait that long, would you marry me then?!"

I began to cry. "Oh, Roger, we've never even kissed. This is ridiculous."

"Answer me, if she died one week, seven days from now . . ." He grabbed my arms.

"But how can you be sure?"

"I'll *make* myself sure! I swear she'll be dead a week from now, or I'll never bother you again with this!"

And he flung the screen doors wide, hurrying off into the day that was suddenly too bright.

"Roger, don't—" I cried.

But my mind thought, Roger *do,* do something, anything, to start it all or end it all.

That night in bed I thought, what ways are there for murder that no one could know? Is Roger, a hundred yards away this moment, thinking the same? Will he search the woods tomorrow for toadstools resembling mushrooms, or drive the car too fast and fling her door wide on a curve? I saw the wax dummy witch fly through the air in a lovely soaring arc, to break like ridiculous peanut brittle on an oak, an elm, a maple. I sat up in bed. I laughed until I wept. I wept until I laughed again. No, no, I thought, he'll find a better way. A night burglar will shock her heart into her throat. Once in her throat, he will not let it go down again, she'll choke on her own panic.

And then the oldest, the darkest, most childish thought of all. There's only one way to finish a woman whose mouth is the color of blood. Being what she is, no relative, not an aunt or a great grandmother, surprise her with a stake driven through her heart!

I heard her scream. It was so loud, all the night birds jumped from the trees to cover the stars.

I lay back down. Dear Christian Anna Marie, I thought, what's this? Do you want to kill? Yes, for why not kill a killer, a woman who strangled her child in his crib and has not loosened the throttling cord since? He is so pale, poor man, because he has not breathed free air, all of his life.

And then, unbidden, the lines of an old poem stood up in my head. Where I had read them or who had put them down, or if I had written them myself, within my head over the years, I could not say. But the lines were there and I read them in the dark:

> *Some live like Lazarus*
> *In a tomb of life*
> *And come forth curious late to twilight hospitals*
> *And mortuary rooms.*

The lines vanished. For a while I could recall no more, and then, unable to fend it off, for it came of itself, a last fragment appeared in the dark:

> *Better cold skies seen bitter to the North*
> *Than stillborn stay, all blind and gone to ghost.*

If Rio is lost, well, love the Arctic Coast!
O ancient Lazarus
Come ye forth.

There the poem stopped and let me be. At last I slept, restless, hoping for dawn, and good and final news.

The next day I saw him pushing her along the pier and thought, Yes, that's it! She'll vanish and be found a week from now, on the shore, like a sea monster floating, all face and no body.

That day passed. Well, surely, I thought, tomorrow . . .

The second day of the week, the third, the fourth and then the fifth and sixth passed, and on the seventh day one of the maids came running up the path, shrieking.

"Oh, it's terrible, terrible!"

"Mrs. Harrison?" I cried. I felt a terrible and quite uncontrollable smile on my face.

"No, no, her *son!* He's hung himself!"

"Hung himself?" I said ridiculously, and found myself, stunned, explaining to her. "Oh, no, it wasn't *him* was going to die, it was—" I babbled. I stopped, for the maid was clutching, pulling my arm.

"We cut him down, oh, God, he's still alive, quick!"

Still alive? He still breathed, yes, and walked around through the other years, yes, but alive? No.

It was she who gained strength and lived through his attempt to escape her. She never forgave his trying to run off.

"What do you mean by that, what do you mean?" I remember her screaming at him as he lay feeling his throat, in the cottage, his eyes shut, wilted, and I hurried in the door. "What do you mean doing that, what, what?"

And looking at him there I knew he had tried to run away from both of us, we were both impossible to him. I did not forgive him that either, for a while. But I did feel my old hatred of him become something else, a kind of dull pain, as I turned and went back for a doctor.

"What do you mean, you silly boy?" she cried.

I married Paul that autumn.

After that, the years poured through the glass swiftly. Once each year, Roger led himself into the pavilion to sit eating mint ice with his limp empty-gloved hands, but he never called me by my name again, nor did he mention the old promise.

Here and there in the hundreds of months that passed I thought, for his own sake now, for no one else, sometime, somehow he must simply up and destroy the dragon with the hideous bellows face and the rust-scaled hands. For Roger and only for Roger, Roger must do it.

Surely *this* year, I thought, when he was fifty, fifty-one, fifty-two. Between seasons I caught myself examining occasional Chicago papers, hoping to find a picture of her lying slit like a monstrous yellow chicken. But no, but no, but no. . . .

I'd almost forgotten them when they returned this morning. He's very old now, more like a doddering husband than a son. Baked gray clay he is, with milky blue eyes, a toothless mouth, and manicured fingernails which seem stronger because the flesh has baked away.

At noon today, after a moment of standing out, a lone gray wingless hawk staring at a sky in which he had never soared or flown, he came inside and spoke to me, his voice rising.

"Why didn't you tell me?"

"Tell you what?" I said, scooping out his ice cream before he asked for it.

"One of the maids just mentioned, your husband died five years ago! You should have told me!"

"Well, now you know," I said.

He sat down slowly. "Lord," he said, tasting the ice cream and savoring it, eyes shut, "this is bitter." Then, a long time later, he said, "Anna, I never asked. Were there ever any children?"

"No," I said. "And I don't know why. I guess I'll never know why."

I left him sitting there and went to wash the dishes.

At nine tonight I heard someone laughing by the lake. I hadn't heard Roger laugh since he was a child, so I didn't think it was him until the doors burst wide and he entered, flinging his arms about, unable to control his almost weeping hilarity.

"Roger!" I asked. "What's wrong?"

"Nothing! Oh, nothing!" he cried. "Everything's lovely! A root beer, Anna! Take one yourself! Drink with me!"

We drank together, he laughed, winked, then got immensely calm. Still smiling, though, he looked suddenly, beautifully young.

"Anna," he whispered intensely, leaning forward, "guess what? I'm flying to China tomorrow! Then India! Then London, Madrid, Paris, Berlin, Rome, Mexico City!"

"*You* are, Roger?"

"I am," he said. "I, I, I, not we, we, we, but I, Roger Bidwell Harrison, I I, *I!*"

I stared at him and he gazed quietly back at me, and I must have gasped. For then I knew what he had finally done tonight, this hour, within the last few minutes.

"Oh, no," my lips must have murmured.

Oh, but yes, yes, his eyes upon me replied, incredible miracle of miracles, after all these waiting years. Tonight at last. Tonight.

I let him talk. After Rome it was Vienna and Stockholm, he'd saved thousands of schedules, flight charts and hotel bulletins for forty years; he knew the moons and tides, the goings and comings of everything on the sea and in the sky.

"But best of all," he said at last, "Anna, Anna, will you come along with me? I've lots of money put away, don't let me run on! Anna, tell me, *will* you?"

I came around the counter slowly and saw myself in the mirror, a woman in her seventieth year going to a party half a century late.

I sat down beside him and shook my head.

"Oh, but, Anna, why not, there's no reason why!"

"There is a reason," I said. "You."

"Me, but I don't count!"

"That's just it, Roger, you do."

"Anna, we could have a wonderful time—"

"I daresay. But, Roger, you've *been* married for seventy years. Now, for the first time, you're not married. You don't want to turn around and get married again right off, do you?"

"*Don't* I?" he asked, blinking.

"You don't, you really don't. You deserve a little while, at least, off by yourself, to see the world, to know who Roger Harrison is. A little while away from women. Then, when you've gone around the world and come back, is time to think of other things."

"If you *say* so—"

"No. It mustn't be anything I say or know or tell you to do. Right now it must be you telling yourself what to know and see and do. Go have a grand time. If you can, be happy."

"Will you be here waiting for me when I come back?"

"I haven't it in me any more to wait, but I'll be here."

He moved toward the door, then stopped and looked at me as if surprised by some new question that had come into his mind.

"Anna," he said, "if all this had happened forty, fifty years ago, would you have gone away with me then? Would you really have me?"

I did not answer.

"Anna?" he asked.

After a long while I said, "There are some questions that should never be asked."

Because, I went on, thinking, there can be no answers. Looking down the years toward the lake, I could not remember, so I could not say, whether we could have ever been happy. Perhaps even as a child, sensing the impossible in Roger, I had clenched the impossible, and therefore the rare, to my heart, simply because it was impossible and rare. He was a sprig of farewell summer pressed in an old book, to be taken out, turned over, admired, once a year, but more than that? Who could say? Surely not I, so long, so late in the day. Life is questions, not answers.

Roger had come very close to read my face, my mind, while I thought all this. What he saw there made him look away, close his eyes, then take my hand and press it to his cheek.

"I'll be back. I swear I will!"

Outside the door he stood bewildered for a moment in the moonlight, looking at the world and all its directions, east, west, north, south, like a child out of school for his first summer not knowing which way to go first, just breathing, just listening, just seeing.

"Don't hurry!" I said fervently. "Oh, God, whatever you do, please, enjoy yourself, don't hurry!"

I saw him run off toward the limousine near the cottage where I was supposed to rap in the morning and where I would get no answer. But I knew that I would not go to the cottage and that I'd keep the maids from going there because the old lady had given orders not to be bothered.

That would give Roger the chance, the start he needed. In a week or two or three, I might call the police. Then if they met Roger coming back on the boat from all those wild places, it wouldn't matter.

Police? Perhaps not even them. Perhaps she died of a heart attack and poor Roger only thinks he killed her and now proudly sails off into the world, his pride not allowing him to know that only her own self-made death released him.

But then again, if at last all the murder he had put away for seventy years had forced him tonight to lay hands on and kill the hideous turkey, I could not find it in my heart to weep for her but only for the great time it had taken to act out the sentence.

The road is silent. An hour has passed since the limousine roared away down the road.

Now I have just put out the lights and stand alone in the pavilion looking out at the shining lake where in another century, under another sun, a small boy with an old face was first touched to play tag with me and now, very late, had tagged me back, had kissed my hand and run away, and this time myself, stunned, not following.

Many things I do not know, tonight.

But one thing I'm sure of.

I do not hate Roger Harrison any more.

A MIRACLE OF RARE DEVICE

On a day neither too mellow nor too tart, too hot nor too cold, the ancient tin lizzie came over the desert hill traveling at commotion speed. The vibration of the various armored parts of the car caused road-runners to spurt up in floury bursts of dust. Gila monsters, lazy displays of Indian jewelry, took themselves out of the way. Like an infestation, the Ford clamored and dinned away into the deeps of the wilderness.

In the front seat, squinting back, Old Will Bantlin shouted, "Turn off!"

Bob Greenhill spun-swung the lizzie off behind a billboard. Instantly both men turned. Both peered over the crumpled top of their car, praying to the dust they had wheeled up on the air.

"Lay down! Lay low! Please . . ."

And the dust blew slowly down. Just in time.

"Duck!"

A motorcycle, looking as if it had burned through all nine rings of hell, thundered by. Hunched over its oily handlebars, a hurricane figure, a man with a creased and most unpleasant face, goggled and sun-deviled, leaned on the wind. Roaring bike and man flung away down the road.

The two old men sat up in their lizzie, exhaling.

"So long, Ned Hopper," said Bob Greenhill.

"Why?" said Will Bantlin. "Why's he always tailing us?"

"Willy-William, talk sense," said Greenhill. "We're his luck, his Judas goats. Why should he let us go, when trailing us around the land makes him rich and happy and us poor and wise?"

The two men looked at each other, half in, half out of their smiles. What the world hadn't done to them, thinking about it had. They had enjoyed thirty years of nonviolence together, in their case meaning nonwork. "I feel a harvest coming on," Will would say, and they'd clear out of town be-

115

fore the wheat ripened. Or, "Those apples are ready to fall!" So they'd stand back about three hundred miles so as not to get hit on the head.

Now Bob Greenhill slowly let the car, in a magnificent controlled detonation, drift back out on the road.

"Willy, friend, don't be discouraged."

"I've been through 'discouraged,' " said Will. "I'm knee deep in 'accepting.' "

"Accepting what?"

"Finding a treasure chest of canned fish one day and no can opener. Finding a thousand can openers next day and no fish."

Bob Greenhill listened to the motor talking to itself like an old man under the hood, sounding like sleepless nights and rusty bones and well-worn dreams.

"Our bad luck can't last forever, Willy."

"No, but it sure tries. You and me sell ties and who's across the street ten cents cheaper?"

"Ned Hopper."

"We strike gold in Tonopah and who registers the claim first?"

"Old Ned."

"Haven't we done him a lifetime of favors? Aren't we overdue for something just ours, that never winds up his?"

"Time's ripe, Willy," said Robert, driving calmly. "Trouble is, you, me, Ned never really decided what we wanted. We've run through all the ghost towns, see something, grab. Ned sees and grabs, too. He don't want it, he just wants it because *we* want it. He keeps it 'till we're out of sight, then tears it up and hang-dogs after us for more litter. The day we really know what we want is the day Ned gets scared of us and runs off forever. Ah, hell." Bob Greenhill breathed the clear fresh-water air running in morning streams over the windshield. "It's good anyway. That sky. Those hills. The desert and . . ."

His voice faded.

Will Bantlin glanced over. "What's wrong?"

"For some reason . . ." Bob Greenhill's eyes rolled, his leathery hands turned the wheel slow, "we got to . . . pull off . . . the road."

The lizzie bumped on the dirt shoulder. They drove down in a dusty wash and up out and suddenly along a dry peninsula of land overlooking the desert. Bob Greenhill, looking hypnotized, put out his hand to turn the ignition key. The old man under the hood stopped complaining about the insomnia and slept.

"Now, why did you do *that?*" asked Will Bantlin.

Bob Greenhill gazed at the wheel in his suddenly intuitive hands. "Seemed as if I had to. Why?" He blinked up. He let his bones settle and his eyes grow lazy. "Maybe only to look at the land out there. Good. All of it been here a billion years."

"Except for that city," said Will Bantlin.

"City?" said Bob.

He turned to look and the desert was there and the distant hills the color of lions, and far out beyond, suspended in a sea of warm morning sand and light, was a kind of floating image, a hasty sketch of a city.

"That can't be Phoenix," said Bob Greenhill. "Phoenix is ninety miles off. No other big place around."

Will Bantlin rumpled the map on his knees, searching. "No. No other town."

"It's coming clearer!" cried Bob Greenhill, suddenly.

They both stood absolutely straight up in the car and stared over the dusty windshield, the wind whining softly over their craggy faces.

"Why, you know what that is, Bob? A mirage! Sure, that's it! Light rays just right, atmosphere, sky, temperature. City's the other side of the horizon somewhere. Look how it jumps, fades in and out. It's reflected against that sky up there like a mirror and comes down here where we can see it! A mirage, by Gosh!"

"That *big?*"

Bob Greenhill measured the city as it grew taller, clearer in a shift of wind, a soft far whirlabout of sand.

"The granddaddy of them all! That's not Phoenix. Not Santa Fe or Alamagordo, no. Let's see. It's not Kansas City—"

"That's too far off, anyway."

"Yeah, but look at those buildings. Big! Tallest in the country. Only one place like that in the world."

"You don't mean—New York?"

Will Bantlin nodded slowly and they both stood in the silence looking out at the mirage. And the city was tall and shining now and almost perfect in the early-morning light.

"Oh, my," said Bob, after a long while. "That's fine."

"It is," said Will.

"But," said Will, a moment later, whispering, as if afraid the city might hear, "what's it doing three thousand miles from home, here in the middle of Nowhere, Arizona?"

Bob Greenhill gazed and spoke. "Willy, friend, never question nature. It just sits there and minds its knitting. Radio waves, rainbows, northern lights, all that, heck, let's just say a great big picture got took of New York City and is being developed here, three thousand miles away on a morn when we need cheering, just for us."

"Not just us." Will peered over the side of the car. "Look!"

There in the floury dust lay innumerable crosshatchings, diagonals, fascinating symbols printed out in a quiet tapestry.

"Tire marks," said Bob Greenhill. "Hundreds of them. Thousands. Lots of cars pulled off here."

"For what, Bob?" Will Bantlin leaped from the car, landed on the earth, tromped it, turned on it, knelt to touch it with a swift and suddenly trembling hand. "For what, for what? To see the mirage? Yes, sir! To see the mirage!"

"So?"

"Boy, howdy!" Will stood up, thrummed his voice like a motor. "Brrrummm!" He turned an imaginary wheel. He ran along a tire track. "Brrrummm! Eeeee! Brakes on! Robert-Bob, you know what we got here?! Look east! Look west. This is the only point in miles you can pull off the highway and sit and stare your eyes out!"

"Sure, it's nice people have an eye for beauty—"

"Beauty, my socks! Who owns this land?"

"The state, I reckon."

"You reckon wrong! You and me! We set up camp, register a claim, improve the property, and the law reads it's ours. Right?"

"Hold on!" Bob Greenhill was staring out at the desert and the strange city there. "You mean you want to . . . *homestead a mirage?*"

"Right, by zingo! Homestead a mirage!"

Robert Greenhill stood down and wandered around the car looking at the tire-treaded earth.

"Can we *do* that?"

"*Do* it? Excuse my dust!"

In an instant Will Bantlin was pounding tent pegs into the soil, stringing twine.

"From here to here, and here to here, it's a gold mine, we

pan it, it's a cow, we milk it, it's a lakeful of money, we swim in it!"

Rummaging in the car, he heaved out cases and brought forth a large cardboard which had once advertised cheap cravats. This, reversed, he painted over with a brush and began lettering.

"Willy," said his friend, "nobody's going to pay to see any darned old—"

"Mirage? Put up a fence, tell folks they can't see a thing, and that's just their itch. There!"

He held up the sign.

> SECRET VIEW MIRAGE—THE MYSTERIOUS CITY
> *25¢ per car. Motorbikes a dime.*

"Here comes a car. Watch!"

"William—"

But Will, running, lifted the sign.

"Hey! Look! Hey!"

The car roared past, a bull ignoring the matador.

Bob shut his eyes so as not to see Will's smile wiped away.

But then—a marvelous sound.

The squeal of brakes.

The car was backing up! Will was leaping forward, waving, pointing.

"Yes, sir! Yes, ma'am! Secret View Mirage! The Mysterious City! Drive right in!"

The treadmarks in the simple dust became numerous, and then, quite suddenly, innumerable.

A great boll of heat-wafted dust hung over the dry peninsula where in a vast sound of arrivals, with braked tires, slammed doors, stilled engines, the cars of many kinds from many places came and took their places in a line. And the people in the cars were as different as people can be who come from four directions but are drawn in a single moment by a single thing, all talking at first, but growing still at last at what they saw out in the desert. The wind blew softly about their faces, fluttering the hair of the women, the open shirt collars of the men. They sat in their cars for a long time or they stood out on the rim of the earth, saying nothing, and at last one by one turned to go.

As the first car drove back out past Bob and Will, the woman in it nodded happily.

"Thanks! Why, it *is* just like Rome!"

"Did she say Rome or home?" asked Will.

Another car wheeled toward the exit.

"Yes, sir!" The driver reached out to shake Bob's hand. "Just looking made me feel I could speak French!"

"French!" cried Bob.

Both stepped forward swiftly as the third car made to leave. An old man sat at the wheel, shaking his head.

"Never seen the like. I mean to say, fog and all, Westminster Bridge, better than a postcard, and Big Ben off there in the distance. How do you do it? God bless. Much obliged."

Both men, disquieted, let the old man drive away, then slowly wheeled to look out along their small thrust of land toward the growing simmer of noon.

"Big Ben?" said Will Bantlin. "Westminster Bridge? Fog?"

Faintly, faintly, they thought they heard, they could not be sure, they cupped their ears, wasn't that a vast clock striking three times off there beyond land's rim? Weren't foghorns calling after boats and boat horns calling down on some lost river?

"Almost speak French?" whispered Robert. "Big Ben? Home? Rome? *Is* that Rome out there, Will?"

The wind shifted. A broiling surge of warm air tumbled up, plucking changes on an invisible harp. The fog almost solidified into gray stone monuments. The sun almost built a golden statue on top of a breasted mount of fresh-cut snow marble.

"How—" said William Bantlin, "how could it change? How could it be four, five cities? Did we tell anyone what city they'd see? No. Well, then, Bob, *well!*"

Now they fixed their gaze on their last customer, who stood alone at the rim of the dry peninsula. Gesturing his friend to silence, Robert moved silently to stand to one side and behind their paying visitor.

He was a man in his late forties with a vital, sunburned face, good, warm, clearwater eyes, fine cheekbones, a receptive mouth. He looked as if he had traveled a long way around in his life, over many deserts, in search of a particular oasis. He resembled those architects found wandering the rubbled streets below their buildings as the iron, steel and glass go soaring up to block out, fill in an empty piece of sky. His face was that of such builders who suddenly see reared up before them on the instant, from horizon to horizon, the perfect implementation of an old, old dream. Now, only half aware of William and Robert beside him, the stranger spoke at last in a quiet, an easy, a wondrous voice, saying what he saw, telling what he felt:

" 'In Xanadu . . .' "

"What?" asked William.

The stranger half smiled, kept his eyes on the mirage and quietly, from memory, recited.

> *"In Xanadu did Kubla Khan*
> *A stately pleasure-dome decree:*
> *Where Alph, the sacred river, ran*
> *Through caverns measureless to man,*
> *Down to a sunless sea."*

His voice spelled the weather and the weather blew about the other two men and made them more still.

> *"So twice five miles of fertile ground*
> *With walls and towers were girdled round:*
> *And here were gardens bright with sinuous rills,*
> *Where blossomed many an incense-bearing tree.*
> *And here were forests ancient as the hills,*
> *Enfolding sunny spots of greenery."*

William and Robert looked off at the mirage, and what the stranger said was there, in the golden dust, some fabled Middle East or Far East clustering of minarets, domes, frail towers risen up in a magnificent sift of pollen from the Gobi, a spread of river stone baked bright by the fertile Euphrates, Palmyra not yet ruins, only just begun, newly minted, then abandoned by the departing years, now shimmered by heat, now threatening to blow away forever.

The stranger, his face transformed, beautified by his vision, finished it out:

> *"It was a miracle of rare device,*
> *A sunny pleasure-dome with caves of ice!"*

And the stranger grew silent.

Which made the silence in Bob and Will all the deeper.

The stranger fumbled with his wallet, his eyes wet.

"Thank you, thank you."

"You already paid us," said William.

"If I had more, you'd get it all."

He gripped William's hand, left a five-dollar bill in it, got into his car, looked for a last time out at the mirage, then sat down, started the car, idled it with wonderful ease and, face glowing, eyes peaceful, drove away.

Robert walked a few steps after the car, stunned.

Then William suddenly exploded, flung his arms up, whooped, kicked his feet, wheeled around.

"Hallelujah! Fat of the land! Full dinner pails! New squeaky shoes! Look at my fistfuls!"

But Robert said, "I don't think we should take it."

William stopped dancing. "What?"

Robert looked steadily at the desert.

"We can't ever really own it. It's 'way out there. Sure, we can homestead the land, but . . . We don't even know what that thing is."

"Why, it's New York and—"

"Ever *been* to New York?"

"Always wanted. Never did."

"Always wanted, never did." Robert nodded slowly. "Same as them. You heard: Paris. Rome. London. And this last man. Xanadu. Willy, Willy, we got hold of something strange and big here. I'm scared we don't do right by it."

"Well, we're not keeping anyone out, are we?"

"Who knows? Might be a quarter's too much for some. It don't seem right, a natural thing handled by unnatural rules. Look and tell me I'm wrong."

William looked.

And the city was there like the first city he had seen as a boy when his mother took him on a train across a long meadow of grass early one morning and the city rose up head by head, tower by tower to look at him, to watch him coming near. It was that fresh, that new, that old, that frightening, that wonderful.

"I think," said Robert, "we should take just enough to buy gas for a week, put the rest of the money in the first poorbox we come to. That mirage is a clear river running, and people coming by thirsty. If we're wise, we dip one cup, drink it cool in the heat of the day and go. If we stop, build dams, try to own the whole river . . ."

William, peering out through the whispering dust wind, tried to relax, accept.

"If you say so."

"I don't. The wilderness all around says."

"Well, I say *different!*"

Both men jumped and spun about.

Half up the slope stood a motorcycle. Sitting it, rainbowed with oil, eyes goggled, grease masking his stubbly cheeks, was a man of familiar arrogance and free-running contempt.

"Ned Hopper!"

Ned Hopper smiled his most evilly benevolent smile, unbraked the cycle and glided the rest of the way down to halt by his old friends.

"You—" said Robert.

"Me! Me! Me!" Ned Hopper honked his cycle horn four times, laughing loud, head back. "Me!"

"Shut up!" cried Robert. "Bust it like a mirror."

"Bust *what* like a mirror?"

William, catching Robert's concern, glanced apprehensively out beyond at the desert.

The mirage flurried, trembled, misted away, then hung itself like a tapestry once more on the air.

"Nothing out there! What you guys up to?" Ned peered down at the treadmarked earth. "I was twenty miles on today when I realized you boys was hiding back behind. Says to myself, that ain't like my buddies who led me to that gold mine in 'forty-seven, lent me this cycle with a dice roll in 'fifty-five. All those years we help each other and now you got secrets from friend Ned. So I come back. Been up on that hill half the day, spying." Ned lifted binoculars from his greasy jacket front. "You know I can read lips. Sure! Saw all the cars run in here, the cash. Quite a show you're running!"

"Keep your voice down," warned Robert. "So long."

Ned smiled sweetly. "Sorry to see you go. But I surely respect your getting off my property."

"Yours!" Robert and William caught themselves and said in a trembling whisper, "Yours?"

Ned laughed. "When I saw what you was up to, I just cycled into Phoenix. See this little bitty government paper sticking out my back pocket?"

The paper was there, neatly folded.

William put out his hand.

"Don't give him the pleasure," said Robert.

William pulled his hand back. "You want us to believe you filed a homestead claim?"

Ned shut up the smile inside his eyes. "I do. I don't. Even if I was lying, I could still make Phoneix on my bike quicker'n your jalopy." Ned surveyed the land with his binoculars. "So just put down all the money you earned from two this afternoon, when I filed my claim, from which time on you was trespassing my land."

Robert flung the coins into the dust. Ned Hopper glanced casually at the bright litter.

"The U.S. Government Mint! Hot dog, nothing out there, but dumb bunnies willing to pay for it!"

Robert turned slowly to look at the desert.

"You don't see nothing?"

Ned snorted. "Nothing, and you *know* it!"

"But we do!" cried William. "We—"

"William," said Robert.

"But, Bob!"

"Nothing out there. Like he said."

More cars were driving up now in a great thrum of engines.

"Excuse, gents, got to mind the box office!" Ned strode off, waving. "Yes, sir, ma'am! This way! Cash in advance!"

"Why?" William watched Ned Hopper run off, yelling. "Why are we letting him do this?"

"Wait," said Robert, almost serenely. "You'll see."

They got out of the way as a Ford, a Buick and an ancient Moon motored in.

Twilight. On a hill about two hundred yards above the Mysterious City Mirage viewpoint, William Bantlin and Robert Greenhill fried and picked at a small supper, hardly bacon, mostly beans. From time to time, Robert used some battered opera glasses on the scene below.

"Had thirty customers since we left this afternoon," he observed. "Got to shut down soon, though. Only ten minutes of sun left."

William stared at a single bean on the end of his fork. "Tell me again: Why? Why every time our luck is good, Ned Hopper jumps out of the earth."

Robert sighed on the opera-glass lenses and wiped them on his cuff. "Because, friend Will, we are the pure in heart. We shine with a light. And the villains of the world, they see that light beyond the hills and say, 'Why, now, there's some innocent, some sweet all-day sucker.' And the villains come to warm their hands at us. I don't know what we can do about it, except maybe put out the light."

"I wouldn't want to do that." William brooded gently, his palms to the fire. "It's just I was hoping this time was comeuppance time. A man like Ned Hopper, living his white underbelly life, ain't he about due for a bolt of lightning?"

"Due?" Robert screwed the opera glasses tighter into his eyes. "Why, it just struck! Oh, ye of little faith!" William jumped up beside him. They shared the glasses, one lens each, peering down. "Look!"

And William, looking, cried, "Peduncle Q. Mackinaw!"

"Also, Gullable M. Crackers!"

For, far below, Ned Hopper was stomping around outside a car. People gesticulated at him. He handed them some money. The car drove off. Faintly you could hear Ned's anguished cries.

William gasped. "He's giving money back! Now he almost hit that man there. The man shook his fist at him! Ned's paid him back, too! Look—more fond farewells!"

"Yah-hee" whooped Robert, happy with his half of the glasses.

Below, all the cars were dusting away now. Old Ned did a violent kicking dance, threw his goggles into the dust, tore down the sign, let forth a terrible oath.

"Dear me," mused Robert. "I'm glad I can't hear them words. Come on, Willy!"

As William Bantlin and Robert Greenhill drove back up to the Mysterious City turn-off, Ned Hopper rocketed out in a screaming fury. Braying, roaring on his cycle, he hurled the painted cardboard through the air. The sign whistled up, a boomerang. It hissed, narrowly missing Bob. Long after Ned was gone in his banging thunder, the sign sank down and lay on the earth, where William picked it up and brushed it off.

It was twilight indeed now and the sun touching the far hills and the land quiet and hushed and Ned Hopper gone away, and the two men alone in the abandoned territory in the thousand-treaded dust, looking out at the sand and the strange air.

"Oh, no. . . . Yes," said Robert.

The desert was empty in the pink-gold light of the setting sun. The mirage was gone. A few dust devils whirled and fell apart, 'way out on the horizon, but that was all.

William let out a huge groan of bereavement. "*He* did it! Ned! Ned Hopper, come back, you! Oh, damn it, Ned, you spoiled it all! Blast you to perdition!" He stopped. "Bob, how can you *stand* there!?"

Robert smiled sadly. "Right now I'm feeling sorry for Ned Hopper."

"Sorry!"

"He never saw what we saw. He never saw what anybody saw. He never believed for one second. And you know what? Disbelief is catching. It rubs off on people."

William searched the disinhabited land. "Is *that* what happened?"

"Who knows?" Robert shook his head. "One thing sure: when folks drove in here, the city, the cities, the mirage, whatever, was there. But it's awful hard to see when people stand in your way. Without so much as moving, Ned Hopper put his big hand across the sun. First thing you know, theater's closed for good."

"Can't we—" William hesitated. "Can't we open it up again?"

"How? How do you bring a thing like that back?"

They let their eyes play over the sand, the hills, the few long clouds, the sky emptied of wind and very still.

"Maybe if we just look out the sides of our eyes, not direct at it, relax, take it easy . . ."

They both looked down at their shoes, their hands, the rocks at their feet, anything. But at last William mourned, "*Are* we? Are we the pure in heart?"

Robert laughed just a little bit. "Oh, not like the kids who came through here today and saw anything they wanted to see, and not like the big simple people born in the wheat fields and by God's grace wandering the world and will never grow up. We're neither the little children nor the big children of the world, Willy, but we are one thing: glad to be alive. We know the air mornings on the road, how the stars go up and then down the sky. That villain, he stopped being glad a long time ago. I hate to think of him driving his cycle on the road the rest of the night, the rest of the year."

As he finished this, Robert noticed that William was sliding his eyes carefully to one side, toward the desert.

Robert whispered carefully, *"See* anything?"

A single car came down the highway.

The two men glanced at each other. A wild look of hope flashed in their eyes. But they could not quite bring themselves to fling up their hands and yell. They simply stood with the painted sign held in their arms.

The car roared by.

The two men followed it with their wistful eyes.

The car braked. It backed up. In it were a man, a woman, a boy, a girl. The man called out, "You closed for the night?!"

William said, "It's no use—"

Robert cut in. "He means, no use giving us money! Last customer of the day, and family, free! On the house!"

"Thank you, neighbor, thank you!"

The car roared out onto the viewpoint.

William seized Robert's elbow. "Bob, what ails you? Disappoint those kids, that nice family?"

"Hush up," said Robert, gently. "Come on."

The kids piled out of the car. The man and his wife climbed slowly out into the sunset. The sky was all gold and blue now, and a bird sang somewhere in the fields of sand and lion-pollen.

"Watch," said Robert.

And they moved up to stand behind the family where it lined up now to look out over the desert.

William held his breath.

The man and wife squinted into the twilight uneasily.

The kids said nothing. Their eyes flexed and filled with a distillation of late sunlight.

William cleared his throat. "It's late. Uh—can't see too well."

The man was going to reply, when the boy said, "Oh, we can see fine!"

"Sure!" The girl pointed. "There!"

The mother and father followed her gesture, as if it might help, and it did.

"Lord," said the woman, "for a moment I thought . . . But now—Yes, there it is!"

The man read his wife's face, saw a thing there, borrowed it and placed it on the land and in the air.

"Yes," he said, at last. "Oh, yes."

William stared at them, at the desert and then at Robert, who smiled and nodded.

The faces of the father, the mother, the daughter, the son were glowing now, looking off at the desert.

"Oh," murmured the girl, "is it *really* there?"

And the father nodded, his face bright with what he saw that was just within seeing and just beyond knowing. He spoke as if he stood alone in a great forest church.

"Yes. And, Lord, it's beautiful."

William started to lift his head, but Robert whispered, "Easy. It's coming. Don't try. Easy, Will."

And then William knew what to do.

"I," he said, "am going to go stand with the kids."

And he walked slowly over and stood right behind the boy and the girl. He stood for a long time there, like a man between two warm fires on a cool evening, and they warmed him and he breathed easy and at last let his eyes drift up, let his attention wander easy out toward the twilight desert and the hoped-for city in the dusk.

And there in the dust softly blown high from the land, reassembled on the wind into half-shapes of towers and spires and minarets, was the mirage.

He felt Robert's breath on his neck, close, whispering, half talking to himself.

"It was a miracle of rare device,
A sunny pleasure-dome with caves of ice!"

And the city was there.

And the sun set and the first stars came out.

And the city was very clear, as William heard himself repeat, aloud or perhaps for only his secret pleasure, " 'It was a miracle of rare device . . .' "

And they stood in the dark until they could not see.

AND SO DIED RIABOUCHINSKA

The cellar was cold cement and the dead man was cold stone and the air was filled with an invisible fall of rain, while the people gathered to look at the body as if it had been washed in on an empty shore at morning. The gravity of the earth was drawn to a focus here in this single basement room—a gravity so immense that it pulled their faces down, bent their mouths at the corners and drained their cheeks. Their hands hung weighted and their feet were planted so they could not move without seeming to walk under water.

A voice was calling, but nobody listened.

The voice called again and only after a long time did the people turn and look, momentarily, into the air. They were at the seashore in November and this was a gull crying over their heads in the gray color of dawn. It was a sad crying, like the birds going south for the steel winter to come. It was an ocean sounding the shore so far away that it was only a whisper of sand and wind in a seashell.

The people in the basement room shifted their gaze to a table and a golden box resting there, no more than twenty-four inches long, inscribed with the name RIABOUCHINSKA. Under the lid of this small coffin the voice at last settled with finality, and the people stared at the box, and the dead man lay on the floor, not hearing the soft cry.

"Let me out, let me out, oh, please, please, someone let me out."

And finally Mr. Fabian, the ventriloquist, bent and whispered to the golden box, "No, Ria, this is serious business. Later. Be quiet, now, that's a good girl." He shut his eyes and tried to laugh.

From under the polished lid her calm voice said, "Please don't laugh. You should be much kinder now after what's happened."

Detective Lieutenant Krovitch touched Fabian's arm. "If

you don't mind we'll save your dummy act for later. Right now there's all *this* to clean up." He glanced at the woman, who had now taken a folding chair. "Mrs. Fabian." He nodded to the young man sitting next to her. "Mr. Douglas, you're Mr. Fabian's press agent and manager?"

The young man said he was. Krovitch looked at the face of the man on the floor. "Fabian, Mrs. Fabian, Mr. Douglas— all of you say you don't know this man who was murdered here last night, never heard the name Ockham before. Yet Ockham earlier told the stage manager he knew Fabian and had to see him about something vitally important."

The voice in the box began again quietly.

Krovitch shouted. *"Damn* it, Fabian!"

Under the lid, the voice laughed. It was like a muffled bell ringing.

"Pay no attention to her, Lieutenant," said Fabian.

"Her? Or *you,* damn it! What is this? Get together, you two!"

"We'll never be together," said the quiet voice, "never again after tonight."

Krovitch put out his hand. "Give me the key, Fabian."

In the silence there was the rattle of the key in the small lock, the squeal of the miniature hinges as the lid was opened and laid back against the table top.

"Thank you," said Riabouchinska.

Krovitch stood motionless, just looking down and seeing Riabouchinska in her box and not quite believing what he saw.

The face was white and it was cut from marble or from the whitest wood he had ever seen. It might have been cut from snow. And the neck that held the head which was as dainty as a porcelain cup with the sun shining through the thinness of it, the neck was also white. And the hands could have been ivory and they were thin small things with tiny fingernails and whorls on the pads of the fingers, little delicate spirals and lines.

She was all white stone, with light pouring through the stone and light coming out of the dark eyes with blue tones beneath like fresh mulberries. He was reminded of milk glass and of cream poured into a crystal tumbler. The brows were arched and black and thin and the cheeks were hollowed and there was a faint pink vein in each temple and a faint blue vein barely visible above the slender bridge of the nose, between the shining dark eyes.

Her lips were half parted and it looked as if they might be slightly damp, and the nostrils were arched and modeled perfectly, as were the ears. The hair was black and it was parted in the middle and drawn back of the ears and it was real—he could see every single strand of hair. Her gown was as black as her hair and draped in such a fashion as to show her shoulders, which were carved wood as white as a stone that has lain a long time in the sun. She was very beautiful. Krovitch felt his throat move and then he stopped and did not say anything.

Fabian took Riabouchinska from her box. "My lovely lady" he said. "Carved from the rarest imported woods. She's appeared in Paris, Rome, Istanbul. Everyone in the world loves her and thinks she's really human, some sort of incredibly delicate midget creature. They won't accept that she was once part of many forests growing far away from cities and idiotic people."

Fabian's wife, Alyce, watched her husband, not taking her eyes from his mouth. Her eyes did not blink once in all the time he was telling of the doll he held in his arms. He in turn seemed aware of no one but the doll; the cellar and its people were lost in a mist that settled everywhere.

But finally the small figure stirred and quivered. "Please, don't talk about me! You know Alyce doesn't like it."

"Alyce never has liked it."

"Shh, don't!" cried Riabouchinska. "Not here, not now." And then, swiftly, she turned to Krovitch and her tiny lips moved. "How did it all happen? Mr. Ockham, I mean, Mr. Ockham."

Fabian said, "You'd better go to sleep now, Ria."

"But I don't want to," she replied. "I've as much right to listen and talk, I'm as much a part of this murder as Alyce or—or Mr. Douglas even!"

The press agent threw down his cigarette. "Don't drag me into this, you—" And he looked at the doll as if it had suddenly become six feet tall and were breathing there before him.

"It's just that I want the truth to be told." Riabouchinska turned her head to see all of the room. "And if I'm locked in my coffin there'll be no truth, for John's a consummate liar and I must watch after him, isn't that right, John?"

"Yes," he said, his eyes shut, "I suppose it is."

"John loves me best of all the women in the world and I love him and try to understand his wrong way of thinking."

Krovitch hit the table with his fist. "God damn, oh, God *damn* it, Fabian! If you think you can—"

"I'm helpless," said Fabian.

"But she's—"

"I know, I know what you want to say," said Fabian quietly, looking at the detective. "She's in my throat, is that it? No, no. She's not in my throat. She's somewhere else. I don't know. Here, or here." He touched his chest, his head.

"She's quick to hide. Sometimes there's nothing I can do. Sometimes she is only herself, nothing of me at all. Sometimes she tells me what to do and I must do it. She stands guard, she reprimands me, is honest where I am dishonest, good when I am wicked as all the sins that ever were. She lives a life apart. She's raised a wall in my head and lives there, ignoring me if I try to make her say improper things, co-operating if I suggest the right words and pantomime." Fabian sighed. "So if you intend going on I'm afraid Ria must be present. Locking her up will do no good, no good at all."

Lieutenant Krovitch sat silently for the better part of a minute, then made his decision. "All right. Let her stay. It just may be, by God, that before the night's over I'll be tired enough to ask even a ventriloquist's dummy questions."

Krovitch unwrapped a fresh cigar, lit it and puffed smoke. "So you don't recognize the dead man, Mr. Douglas?"

"He looks vaguely familiar. Could be an actor."

Krovitch swore. "Let's all stop lying, what do you say? Look at Ockham's shoes, his clothing. It's obvious he needed money and came here tonight to beg, borrow or steal some. Let me ask you this, Douglas. Are you in love with Mrs. Fabian?"

"Now, wait just a moment!" cried Alyce Fabian.

Krovitch motioned her down. "You sit there, side by side, the two of you. I'm not exactly blind. When a press agent sits where the husband should be sitting, consoling the wife, well! The way you look at the marionette's coffin, Mrs. Fabian, holding your breath when she appears. You make fists when she talks. Hell, you're obvious."

"If you think for one moment I'm jealous of a stick of wood!"

"Aren't you?"

"No, no, I'm not!"

Fabian moved. "You needn't tell him anything, Alyce."

"Let her!"

They all jerked their heads and stared at the small figurine, whose mouth was now slowly shutting. Even Fabian looked at the marionette as if it had struck him a blow.

After a long while Alyce Fabian began to speak.

"I married John seven years ago because he said he loved me and because I loved him and I loved Riabouchinska. At first, anyway. But then I began to see that he really lived all of his life and paid most of his attentions to her and I was a shadow waiting in the wings every night.

"He spent fifty thousand dollars a year on her wardrobe —a hundred thousand dollars for a dollhouse with gold and silver and platinum furniture. He tucked her in a small satin bed each night and talked to her. I thought it was all an elaborate joke at first and I was wonderfully amused. But when it finally came to me that I was indeed merely an assistant in his act I began to feel a vague sort of hatred and distrust—not for the marionette, because after all it wasn't her doing, but I felt a terrible growing dislike and hatred for John, because it *was* his fault. He, after all, was the control, and all of his cleverness and natural sadism came out through his relationship with the wooden doll.

"And when I finally became very jealous, how silly of me! It was the greatest tribute I could have paid him and the way he had gone about perfecting the art of throwing his voice. It was all so idiotic, it was all so strange. And yet I knew that something had hold of John, just as people who drink have a hungry animal somewhere in them, starving to death.

"So I moved back and forth from anger to pity, from jealousy to understanding. There were long periods when I didn't hate him at all, and I never hated the thing that Ria was in him, for she was the best half, the good part, the honest and the lovely part of him. She was everything that he never let himself try to be."

Alyce Fabian stopped talking and the basement room was silent.

"Tell about Mr. Douglas," said a voice, whispering.

Mrs. Fabian did not look up at the marionette. With an effort she finished it out. "When the years passed and there was so little love and understanding from John, I guess it was natural I turned to—Mr. Douglas."

Krovitch nodded. "Everything begins to fall into place. Mr. Ockham was a very poor man, down on his luck, and he came to this theater tonight because he knew something about you and Mr. Douglas. Perhaps he threatened to speak to Mr. Fabian if you didn't buy him off. That would give you the best of reasons to get rid of him."

"That's even sillier than all the rest," said Alyce Fabian tiredly. "I didn't kill him."

"Mr. Douglas might have and not told you."

"Why kill a man?" said Douglas. "John knew all about us."

"I did indeed," said John Fabian, and laughed.

He stopped laughing and his hand twitched, hidden in the snowflake interior of the tiny doll, and her mouth opened and shut, opened and shut. He was trying to make her carry the laughter on after he had stopped, but there was no sound, save the little empty whisper of her lips moving and gasping, while Fabian stared down at the little face and perspiration came out, shining, upon his cheeks.

The next afternoon Lieutenant Krovitch moved through the theater darkness backstage, found the iron stairs and climbed with great thought, taking as much time as he deemed necessary on each step, up to the second-level dressing rooms. He rapped on one of the thin-paneled doors.

"Come in," said Fabian's voice from what seemed a great distance.

Krovitch entered and closed the door and stood looking at the man who was slumped before his dressing mirror. "I have something I'd like to show you," Krovitch said. His face showing no emotion whatever, he opened a manila folder and pulled out a glossy photograph which he placed on the dressing table.

John Fabian raised his eyebrows, glanced quickly up at Krovitch and then settled slowly back in his chair. He put his fingers to the bridge of his nose and massaged his face carefully, as if he had a headache. Krovitch turned the picture over and began to read from the typewritten data on the back. "Name, Miss Ilyana Riamonova. One hundred pounds. Blue eyes. Black hair. Oval face. Born 1914, New York City. Disappeared 1934. Believed a victim of amnesia. Of Russo-Slav parentage. Et cetera, Et cetera."

Fabian's lip twitched.

Krovitch laid the photograph down, shaking his head thoughtfully. "It was pretty silly of me to go through police files for a picture of a marionette. You should have heard the laughter at headquarters. *God*. Still, here she is—Riabouchinska. *Not* papier-mâché, *not* wood, *not* a puppet, but a woman who once lived and moved around and—disappeared." He looked steadily at Fabian. "Suppose you take it from there?"

Fabian half smiled. "There's nothing to it at all. I saw this woman's picture a long time ago, liked her looks and copied my marionette after her."

"Nothing to it at all." Krovitch took a deep breath and exhaled, wiping his face with a huge handkerchief. "Fabian, this very morning I shuffled through a stack of *Billboard* magazines that high. In the year 1934 I found an interesting article concerning an act which played on a second-rate circuit, known as Fabian and Sweet William. Sweet William was a little boy dummy. There was a girl assistant—Ilyana Riamonova. No picture of her in the article, but I at least had a name, the name of a real person, to go on. It was simple to check police files then and dig up this picture. The resemblance, needless to say, between the live woman on one hand and the puppet on the other is nothing short of incredible. Suppose you go back and tell your story over again, Fabian."

"She was my assistant, that's all. I simply used her as a model."

"You're making me sweat," said the detective. "Do you think I'm a fool? Do you think I don't know love when I see it? I've watched you handle the marionette, I've seen you talk to it, I've seen how you make it react to you. You're in love with the puppet naturally, because you loved the original woman very, very much. I've lived too long not to sense that. Hell, Fabian, stop fencing around."

Fabian lifted his pale slender hands, turned them over, examined them and let them fall.

"All right. In 1934 I was billed as Fabian and Sweet William. Sweet William was a small bulb-nosed boy dummy I carved a long time ago. I was in Los Angeles when this girl appeared at the stage door one night. She'd followed my work for years. She was desperate for a job and she hoped to be my assistant. . . ."

He remembered her in the half-light of the alley behind the theater and how startled he was at her freshness and eagerness to work with and for him and the way the cool rain touched softly down through the narrow alleyway and caught in small spangles through her hair, melting in dark warmness, and the rain beaded upon her white porcelain hand holding her coat together at her neck.

He saw her lips' motion in the dark and her voice, separated off on another sound track, it seemed, speaking to him in the autumn wind, and he remembered that without his saying yes or no or perhaps she was suddenly on the stage with him, in the great pouring bright light, and in two months he, who had always prided himself on his cynicism and disbelief, had stepped off the rim of the world after her, plunging down a bottomless place of no limit and no light anywhere.

Arguments followed, and more than arguments—things said and done that lacked all sense and sanity and fairness. She had edged away from him at last, causing his rages and remarkable hysterias. Once he burned her entire wardrobe in a fit of jealousy. She had taken this quietly. But then one night he handed her a week's notice, accused her of monstrous disloyalty, shouted at her, seized her, slapped her again and again across the face, bullied her about and thrust her out the door, slamming it!

She disappeared that night.

When he found the next day that she was really gone and there was nowhere to find her, it was like standing in the center of a titanic explosion. All the world was smashed flat and all the echoes of the explosion came back to reverberate at midnight, at four in the morning, at dawn, and he was up early, stunned with the sound of coffee simmering and the sound of matches being struck and cigarettes lit and himself trying to shave and looking at mirrors that were sickening in their distortion.

He clipped out all the advertisements that he took in the papers and pasted them in neat rows in a scrapbook—all the ads describing her and telling about her and asking for her back. He even put a private detective on the case. People talked. The police dropped by to question him. There was more talk.

But she was gone like a piece of white incredibly fragile tissue paper, blown over the sky and down. A record of her was sent to the largest cities, and that was the end of it for the police. But not for Fabian. She might be dead or just running away, but wherever she was he knew that somehow and in some way he would have her back.

One night he came home, bringing his own darkness with him, and collapsed upon a chair, and before he knew it he found himself speaking to Sweet William in the totally black room

"William, it's all over and done. I can't keep it up!"

And William cried, "Coward! Coward!" from the air above his head, out of the emptiness. "You can get her back if you want!"

Sweet William squeaked and clappered at him in the night. "Yes, you can! *Think!*" he insisted. "Think of a way. You can do it. Put me aside, lock me up. Start all over."

"Start all over?"

"Yes," whispered Sweet William, and darkness moved within darkness. "Yes. Buy wood. Buy fine new wood. Buy hard-grained wood. Buy beautiful fresh new wood. And carve. Carve slowly and carve carefully. Whittle away. Cut delicately. Make the little nostrils so. And cut her thin black eyebrows round and high, so, and make her cheeks in small hollows. Carve, carve . . ."

"No! It's foolish. I could never do it!"

"Yes you could. Yes you could, could, could, could . . ."

The voice faded, a ripple of water in an underground stream. The stream rose up and swallowed him. His head fell forward. Sweet William sighed. And then the two of them lay like stones buried under a waterfall.

The next morning, John Fabian bought the hardest, finest-grained piece of wood that he could find and brought it home and laid it on the table, but could not touch it. He sat for hours staring at it. It was impossible to think that out of this cold chunk of material he expected his hands and his memory to re-create something warm and pliable and familiar. There was no way even faintly to approximate that quality of rain and summer and the first powderings of snow upon a clear pane of glass in the middle of a December night. No way, no way at all to catch the snowflake without having it melt swiftly in your clumsy fingers.

And yet Sweet William spoke out, sighing and whispering, after midnight, "You can do it. Oh, yes, yes, you can do it!"

And so he began. It took him an entire month to carve her hands into things as natural and beautiful as shells lying in the sun. Another month and the skeleton, like a fossil imprint he was searching out, stamped and hidden in the wood, was revealed, all febrile and so infinitely delicate as to suggest the veins in the white flesh of an apple.

And all the while Sweet William lay mantled in dust in his box that was fast becoming a very real coffin. Sweet William croaking and wheezing some feeble sarcasm, some sour criticism, some hint, some help but dying all the time, fading, soon to be untouched, soon to be like a sheath molted in summer and left behind to blow in the wind.

As the weeks passed and Fabian molded and scraped and polished the new wood, Sweet William lay longer and longer in stricken silence, and one day as Fabian held the puppet in his hand Sweet William seemed to look at him a moment with puzzled eyes and then there was a death rattle in his throat.

And Sweet William was gone.

Now as he worked, a fluttering, a faint motion of speech began far back in his throat, echoing and re-echoing, speaking silently like a breeze among dry leaves. And then for the first time he held the doll in a certain way in his hands and memory moved down his arms and into his fingers and from his fingers into the hollowed wood and the tiny hands flickered and the body became suddenly soft and pliable and her eyes opened and looked up at him.

And the small mouth opened the merest fraction of an inch and she was ready to speak and he knew all of the things that she must say to him, he knew the first and the second and the third things he would have her say. There was a whisper, a whisper, a whisper.

The tiny head turned this way gently, that way gently. The mouth half opened again and began to speak. And as it spoke he bent his head and he could feel the warm breath—of *course* it was there!—coming from her mouth, and when he listened very carefully, holding her to his head, his eyes shut, wasn't *it* there, too, softly, *gently*—the beating of her heart?

Krovitch sat in a chair for a full minute after Fabian stopped talking. Finally he said, "I *see*. And your wife?"

"Alyce? She was my second assistant, of course. She worked very hard and, God help her, she loved me. It's hard now to know why I ever married her. It was unfair of me."

"What about the dead man—Ockham?"

"I never saw him before you showed me his body in the theater basement yesterday."

"Fabian," said the detective.

"It's the truth!"

"Fabian."

"The truth, the truth, damn it, I swear it's the truth!"

"The truth." There was a whisper like the sea coming in on the gray shore at early morning. The water was ebbing in a fine lace on the sand. The sky was cold and empty. There were no people on the shore. The sun was gone. And the whisper said again, "The truth."

Fabian sat up straight and took hold of his knees with his thin hands. His face was rigid. Krovitch found himself making the same motion he had made the day before—looking at the gray ceiling as if it were a November sky and a lonely bird going over and away, gray within the cold grayness.

"The truth." Fading. "The truth."

Krovitch lifted himself and moved as carefully as he could to the far side of the dressing room where the golden box lay open and inside the box the thing that whispered and talked and could laugh sometimes and could sometimes sing. He carried the golden box over and set it down in front of Fabian and waited for him to put his living hand within the gloved delicate hollowness, waited for the fine small mouth to quiver and the eyes to focus. He did not have to wait long.

"The first letter came a month ago."

"No."

"The first letter came a month ago."

"No, *no!*"

"The letter said, 'Riabouchinska, born 1914, died 1934. Born again in 1935.' Mr. Ockham was a juggler. He'd been on the same bill with John and Sweet William years before. He remembered that once there had been a woman, before there was a puppet."

"No, that's not true!"

"Yes," said the voice.

Snow was falling in silences and even deeper silences through the dressing room. Fabian's mouth trembled. He stared at the blank walls as if seeking some new door by which to escape. He half rose from his chair. "Please . . ."

"Ockham threatened to tell about us to everyone in the world."

Krovitch saw the doll quiver, saw the fluttering of the lips, saw Fabian's eyes widen and fix and his throat convulse and tighten as if to stop the whispering.

"I—I was in the room when Mr. Ockham came. I lay in my box and I listened and heard, and I *know*." The voice blurred, then recovered and went on. "Mr. Ockham threatened to tear me up, burn me into ashes if John didn't pay him a thousand dollars. Then suddenly there was a falling sound. A cry. Mr. Ockham's head must have struck the floor. I heard John cry out and I heard him swearing, I heard him sobbing. I heard a gasping and a choking sound."

"You heard nothing! You're deaf, you're blind! You're wood!" cried Fabian.

"But I *hear!*" she said, and stopped as if someone had put a hand to her mouth.

Fabian had leaped to his feet now and stood with the doll in his hand. The mouth clapped twice, three times, then finally made words. "The choking sound stopped. I heard John drag Mr. Ockham down the stairs under the theater to the old dressing rooms that haven't been used in years. Down, down, down I heard them going away and away—down . . ."

Krovitch stepped back as if he were watching a motion picture that had suddenly grown monstrously tall. The figures terrified and frightened him, they were immense, they towered! They threatened to inundate him with size. Someone had turned up the sound so that it screamed.

He saw Fabian's teeth, a grimace, a whisper, a clenching. He saw the man's eyes squeeze shut.

Now the soft voice was so high and faint it trembled toward nothingness.

"I'm not made to live this way. This way. There's nothing for us now. Everyone will know, everyone will. Even when you killed him and I lay asleep last night, I dreamed. I knew, I realized. We both knew, we both realized that these would be our last days, our last hours. Because while I've lived with your weakness and I've lived with your lies, I can't live with something that kills and hurts in killing. There's no way to go on from here. How *can* I live alongside such knowledge? . . ."

Fabian held her into the sunlight which shone dimly though the small dressing-room window. She looked at him and there was nothing in her eyes. His hand shook and in shaking made the marionette tremble, too. Her mouth closed and opened, closed and opened, closed and opened, again and again and again. Silence.

Fabian moved his fingers unbelievingly to his own mouth. A film slid across his eyes. He looked like a man lost in the street, trying to remember the number of a certain house, trying to find a certain window with a certain light. He swayed about, staring at the walls, at Krovitch, at the doll, at his free hand, turning the fingers over, touching his throat, opening his mouth. He listened.

Miles away in a cave, a single wave came in from the sea and whispered down in foam. A gull moved soundlessly, not beating its wings—a shadow.

"She's gone. She's gone. I can't find her. She's run off. I can't find her. I can't find her. I try, I try, but she's run away off far. Will you help me? Will you help me find her? Will you help me find her? Will you please help me find her?"

Riabouchinska slipped bonelessly from his limp hand, folded over and glided noiselessly down to lie upon the cold floor, her eyes closed, her mouth shut.

Fabian did not look at her as Krovitch led him out the door.

THE BEGGAR ON O'CONNELL BRIDGE

"A fool," I said. "That's what I am."

"Why?" asked my wife. "What for?"

I brooded by our third-floor hotel window. On the Dublin street below, a man passed, his face to the lamplight.

"Him," I muttered. "Two days ago . . ."

Two days ago, as I was walking along, someone had hissed at me from the hotel alley. "Sir, it's important! Sir!"

I turned into the shadow. This little man, in the direst tones, said, "I've a job in Belfast if I just had a pound for the train fare!"

I hesitated.

"A most important job!" he went on swiftly. "Pays well! I'll—I'll mail you back the loan! Just give me your name and hotel."

He knew me for a tourist. It was too late, his promise to pay had moved me. The pound note crackled in my hand, being worked free from several others.

The man's eyes skimmed like a shadowing hawk.

"And if I had *two* pounds, why, I could eat on the way."

I uncrumpled two bills.

"And three pounds would bring the wife, not leave her here alone."

I unleafed a third.

"Ah, hell!" cried the man. "Five, just five poor pounds, would find us a hotel in that brutal city, and let me get to the job, for sure!"

What a dancing fighter he was, light on his toes, in and out, weaving, tapping with his hands, flickering with his eyes, smiling with his mouth, jabbing with his tongue.

"Lord thank you, bless you, sir!"

He ran, my five pounds with him.

I was half in the hotel before I realized that, for all his vows, he had not recorded my name.

"Gah!" I cried then.

"Gah!" I cried now, my wife behind me, at the window.

For there, passing below, was the very fellow who should have been in Belfast two nights ago.

"Oh, I know *him*," said my wife. "He stopped me this noon. Wanted train fare to Galway."

"Did you give it to him?"

"No," said my wife simply.

Then the worst thing happened. The demon far down on the sidewalk glanced up, saw us and damn if he didn't *wave!*

I had to stop myself from waving back. A sickly grin played on my lips.

"It's got so I hate to leave the hotel," I said.

"It's cold out, all right." My wife was putting on her coat.

"No," I said. "Not the cold. *Them.*"

And we looked again from the window.

There was the cobbled Dublin street with the night wind blowing in a fine soot along one way to Trinity College, another to St. Stephen's Green. Across by the sweetshop two men stood mummified in the shadows. On the corner a single man, hands deep in his pockets, felt for his entombed bones, a muzzle of ice for a beard. Farther up, in a doorway, was a bundle of old newspapers that would stir like a pack of mice and wish you the time of evening if you walked by. Below, by the hotel entrance, stood a feverish hothouse rose of a woman with a mysterious bundle.

"Oh, the beggars," said my wife.

"No, not just 'oh, the beggars,' " I said, "but oh, the people in the streets, who somehow became beggars."

"It looks like a motion picture. All of them waiting down there in the dark for the hero to come out."

"The hero," I said. "That's me, damn it."

My wife peered at me. "You're not afraid of them?"

"Yes, no. Hell. It's that woman with the bundle who's worst. She's a force of nature, she is. Assaults you with her poverty. As for the others—well, it's a big chess game for me now. We've been in Dublin what, eight weeks? Eight weeks I've sat up here with my typewriter, studying their off hours and on. When they take a coffee break I take one, run for the sweetshop, the bookstore, the Oympia Theatre. If I time it right, there's no handout, no my wanting to trot them into the barbershop or the kitchen. I know every secret exit in the hotel."

"Lord," said my wife, "you sound driven."

"I am. But most of all by that beggar on O'Connell Bridge!"

"Which one?"

"Which one indeed. He's a wonder, a terror. I hate him, I love him. To see is to disbelieve him. Come on."

The elevator, which had haunted its untidy shaft for a hundred years, came wafting skyward, dragging its ungodly chains and dread intestines after. The door exhaled open. The lift groaned as if we had trod its stomach. In a great protestation of ennui, the ghost sank back toward earth, us in it.

On the way my wife said, "If you held your face right, the beggars wouldn't bother you."

"My face," I explained patiently, "is my face. It's from Apple Dumpling, Wisconsin, Sarsaparilla, Maine. 'Kind to Dogs' is writ on my brow for all to read. Let the street be empty, then let me step out and there's a strikers' march of freeloaders leaping out of manholes for miles around."

"If," my wife went on, "you could just learn to look over, around or through those people, stare them *down*." She mused. "Shall I show you how to handle them?"

"All right, show me! We're here!"

I flung the elevator door wide and we advanced through the Royal Hibernian Hotel lobby to squint out at the sooty night.

"Jesus come and get me," I murmured. "There they are, their heads up, their eyes on fire. They smell apple pie already."

'Meet me down by the bookstore in two minutes," said my wife. "Watch."

"Wait!" I cried.

But she was out the door, down the steps and on the sidewalk.

I watched, nose pressed to the glass pane.

The beggars on one corner, the other, across from, in front of, the hotel, *leaned* toward my wife. Their eyes glowed.

My wife looked calmly at them all for a long moment.

The beggars hesitated, creaking, I was sure, in their shoes. Then their bones settled. Their mouths collapsed. Their eyes snuffed out. Their heads sank down.

The wind blew.

With a tat-tat like a small drum, my wife's shoes went briskly away, fading.

From below, in the Buttery, I heard music and laughter. I'll run down, I thought, and slug in a quick one. Then, bravery resurgent . . .

Hell, I thought, and swung the door wide.

The effect was much as if someone had struck a great Mongolian bronze gong once.

I thought I heard a tremendous insuck of breath.

Then I heard shoe leather flinting the cobbles in sparks. The men came running, fireflies sprinkling the bricks under their hobnailed shoes. I saw hands waving. Mouths opened on smiles like old pianos.

Far down the street, at the bookshop, my wife waited, her back turned. But that third eye in the back of her head must have caught the scene: Columbus greeted by Indians, Saint Francis amidst his squirrel friends with a bag of nuts. For a terrific moment I felt like a pope on St. Peter's balcony with a tumult, or at the very least the Timultys, below.

I was not half down the steps when the woman charged up, thrusting the unwrapped bundle at me.

"Ah, see the poor child!" she wailed.

I stared at the baby.

The baby stared back.

God in heaven, did or did not the shrewd thing *wink* at me?

I've gone mad, I thought; the babe's eyes are shut. She's filled it with beer to keep it warm and on display.

My hands, my coins, blurred among them.

"Praise be!"

"The *child* thanks you, sir!"

"Ah, sure. There's only a few of us left!"

I broke through them and beyond, still running. Defeated, I could have scuffed slowly the rest of the way, my resolve so much putty in my mouth, but no, on I rushed, thinking, The baby *is* real, *isn't* it? Not a prop? No. I had heard it cry, often. Blast her, I thought, she pinches it when she sees Okeemogo, Iowa, coming. Cynic, I cried silently, and answered, No—coward.

My wife, without turning, saw my reflection in the bookshop window and nodded.

I stood getting my breath, brooding at my own image: the summer eyes, the ebullient and defenseless mouth.

"All right, say it." I sighed. "It's the way I hold my face."

"I love the way you hold your face." She took my arm. "I wish I could do it, too."

I looked back as one of the beggars strolled off in the blowing dark with my shillings.

" 'There's only a few of us left,' " I said aloud. "What did he mean, saying that?"

" 'There's only a few of us left.' " My wife stared into the shadows. "Is that what he said?"

"It's something to think about. A few of what? Left where?"

The street was empty now. It was starting to rain.

"Well," I said at last, "let me show you the even bigger mystery, the man who provokes me to strange wild rages, then calms me to delight. Solve him and you solve all the beggars that ever were."

"On O'Connell Bridge?" asked my wife.

"On O'Connell Bridge," I said.

And we walked on down in the gently misting rain.

Halfway to the bridge, as we were examining some fine Irish crystal in a window, a woman with a shawl over her head plucked at my elbow.

"Destroyed!" The woman sobbed. "My poor sister. Cancer, the doctor said, her dead in a month! And me with mouths to feed! Ah, God, if you had just a penny!"

I felt my wife's arm tighten to mine.

I looked at the woman, split as always, one half saying, "A penny is all she asks!," the other half doubting: "Clever woman, she knows that by her underasking you'll overpay!," and hating myself for the battle of halves.

I gasped. "You're . . ."

"I'm what, sir?"

Why, I thought, you're the woman who was just back by the hotel with the bundled baby!

"I'm sick!" She hid in shadow. "Sick with crying for the half dead!"

You've stashed the baby somewhere, I thought, and put on a green instead of a gray shawl and run the long way around to cut us off here.

"Cancer . . ." One bell in her tower, and she knew how to toll it. "Cancer . . ."

My wife cut across it. "Beg pardon, but aren't you the same woman we just met at our hotel?"

The woman and I were both shocked at this rank insubordination. It wasn't done!

The woman's face crumpled. I peered close. And yes, by God, it was a different face. I could not but admire her. She knew, sensed, and learned what actors know, sense, learn: that by thrusting, yelling, all fiery-lipped arrogance one moment, you are one character; and by sinking, giving way, crumpling the mouth and eyes, in pitiful collapse, you are another. The same woman, yes, but the same face and role? Quite obviously no.

She gave me a last blow beneath the belt. "Cancer."

I flinched.

It was a brief tussle then, a kind of disengagement from one woman and an engagement with the other. The wife lost my arm and the woman found my cash. As if she were on roller skates, she whisked around the corner, sobbing happily.

"Lord!" In awe, I watched her go. "She's studied Stanislavsky. In one book he says that squinting one eye and twitching one lip to the side will disguise you. I wonder if she has nerve enough to be at the hotel when we go back?"

"I wonder," said my wife, "when my husband will stop admiring and start criticising such Abbey Theatre acting as that."

"But what if it were true? Everything she said? And she's lived with it so long she can't cry any more, and so has to play-act in order to survive? What if?"

"It can't be true," said my wife slowly. "I just won't believe it."

But that single bell was still tolling somewhere in the chimney-smoking dark.

"Now," said my wife, "here's where we turn for O'Connell Bridge, isn't it?"

"It is."

The corner was probably empty in the falling rain for a long time after we were gone.

There stood the graystone bridge bearing the great O'Connell's name, and there the River Liffey rolling cold gray waters under, and even from a block off I heard faint singing. My mind spun in a great leap back to December.

"Christmas," I murmured, "is the best time of all in Dublin."

For beggars, I meant, but left it unsaid.

For in the week before Christmas the Dublin streets teem

with raven flocks of children herded by schoolmasters or nuns. They cluster in doorways, peer from theater lobbies, jostle in alleys, "God Rest You Merry, Gentlemen" on their lips, "It Came Upon a Midnight Clear" in their eyes, tambourines in hand, snowflakes shaping a collar of grace about their tender necks. It is singing everywhere and anywhere in Dublin on such nights, and there was no night my wife and I did not walk down along Grafton Street to hear "Away in a Manger" being sung to the queue outside the cinema or "Deck the Halls" in front of the Four Provinces pub. In all, we counted in Christ's season one night half a hundred bands of convent girls or public-school boys lacing the cold air and weaving great treadles of song up, down, over and across from end to end of Dublin. Like walking in snowfall, you could not walk among them and not be touched. The sweet beggars, I called them, who gave in turn for what you gave as you went your way.

Given such example, even the most dilapidated beggars of Dublin washed their hands, mended their torn smiles, borrowed banjos or bought a fiddle and killed a cat. They even gathered for four-part harmonies. How could they stay silent when half the world was singing and the other half, idled on the tuneful river, was paying dearly, gladly, for just another chorus?

So Christmas was best for all; the beggars *worked*—off key, it's true, but there they were, one time in the year, *busy*.

But Christmas was over, the licorice-suited children back in their aviaries, and the beggers of the town, shut and glad for the silence, returned to their workless ways. All save the beggars on O'Connell Bridge, who, all through the year, most of them, tried to give as good as they got.

"They have their self-respect," I said, walking my wife. "I'm glad this first man here strums a guitar, the next one a fiddle. And there, now, by God, in the very center of the bridge!"

"The man we're looking for?"

"That's him. Squeezing the concertina. It's all right to look. Or I *think* it is."

"What do you mean, you think it is? He's blind, isn't he?"

These raw words shocked me, as if my wife had said something indecent.

The rain fell gently, softly upon graystoned Dublin, graystoned riverbank, gray lava-flowing river.

"That's the trouble," I said at last. "I don't know."

And we both, in passing, looked at the man standing there in the very middle of O'Connell Bridge.

He was a man of no great height, a bandy statue swiped from some country garden perhaps, and his clothes, like the clothes of most in Ireland, too often laundered by the weather, and his hair too often grayed by the smoking air, and his cheeks sooted with beard, and a nest or two of witless hair in each cupped ear, and the blushing cheeks of a man who has stood too long in the cold and drunk too much in the pub so as to stand too long in the cold again. Dark glasses covered his eyes, and there was no telling what lay behind. I had begun to wonder, weeks back, if his sight prowled me along, damming my guilty speed, or if only his ears caught the passing of a harried conscience. There was that awful fear I might seize, in passing, the glasses from his nose. But I feared much more the abyss I might find, into which my senses, in one terrible roar, might tumble. Best not to know if civet's orb or interstellar space gaped behind the smoked panes.

But, even more, there was a special reason why I could not let the man be.

In the rain and wind and snow, for two solid months, I had seen him standing here with no cap or hat on his head.

He was the only man in all of Dublin I saw in the downpours and drizzles who stood by the hour alone with the drench mizzling his ears, threading his ash-red hair, plastering it over his skull, rivuleting his eyebrows, and purling over the coal-black insect lenses of the glasses on his rain-pearled nose.

Down through the greaves of his cheeks, the lines about his mouth, and off his chin, like a storm on a gargoyle's flint, the weather ran. His sharp chin shot the guzzle in a steady fauceting off in the air, down his tweed scarf and locomotive-colored coat.

"Why doesn't he wear a hat?" I said suddenly.

"Why," said my wife, "maybe he hasn't got one."

"He must have one," I said.

"Keep your voice down."

"He's *got* to have one," I said, quieter.

"Maybe he can't afford one."

"Nobody's *that* poor, even in Dublin. Everyone has a cap at least!"

"Well, maybe he has bills to pay, someone sick."

"But to stand for weeks, months, in the rain, and not so much as flinch or turn his head, ignore the rain, it's beyond understanding." I shook my head. "I can only think it's a trick. That must be it. Like the others, this is his way of getting sympathy, of making you cold and miserable as himself as you go by, so you'll give him more."

"I bet you're sorry you said that already," said my wife.

"I am. I am." For even under my cap the rain was running off my nose. "Sweet God in heaven, what's the answer?"

"Why don't you ask him?"

"No." I was even more afraid of that.

Then the last thing happened, the thing that went with his standing bareheaded in the cold rain.

For a moment, while we had been talking at some distance, he had been silent. Now, as if the weather had freshened him to life, he gave his concertina a great mash. From the folding, unfolding snake box he squeezed a series of asthmatic notes which were no preparation for what followed.

He opened his mouth. He sang.

The sweet clear baritone voice which rang over O'Connell Bridge, steady and sure, was beautifully shaped and controlled, not a quiver, not a flaw, anywhere in it. The man just opened his mouth, which meant that all kinds of secret doors in his body gave way. He did not sing so much as let his soul free.

"Oh," said my wife, "how lovely."

"Lovely." I nodded.

We listened while he sang the full irony of Dublin's Fair City where it rains twelve inches a month the winter through, followed by the white-wine clarity of Kathleen Mavourneen, Macushlah, and all the other tired lads, lasses, lakes, hills, past glories, present miseries, but all somehow revived and moving about young and freshly painted in the light spring, suddenly-not-winter rain. If he breathed at all, it must have been through his ears, so smooth the line, so steady the putting forth of word following round belled word.

"Why," said my wife, "he could be on the stage."

"Maybe he was once."

"Oh, he's too good to be standing here."

"I've thought that often."

My wife fumbled with her purse. I looked from her to the singing man, the rain falling on his bare head, streaming through his shellacked hair, trembling on his ear lobes. My wife had her purse open.

And then, the strange perversity. Before my wife could move toward him, I took her elbow and led her down the other side of the bridge. She pulled back for a moment, giving me a look, then came along.

As we went away along the bank of the Liffey, he started a new song, one we had heard often in Ireland. Glancing back, I saw him, head proud, black glasses taking the pour, mouth open, and the fine voice clear:

"I'll be glad when you're dead
                    in your grave, old man,
Be glad when you're dead
                    in your grave, old man.
Be glad when you're dead,
Flowers over your head,
And then I'll marry the journeyman. . . ."

It is only later, looking back, that you see that while you were doing all the other things in life, working on an article concerning one part of Ireland in your rain-battered hotel, taking your wife to dinner, wandering in the museums, you also had an eye beyond to the street and those who served themselves who only stood to wait.

The beggars of Dublin, who bothers to wonder on them, look, see, know, understand? Yet the outer shell of the eye sees and the inner shell of the mind records, and yourself, caught between, ignores the rare service these two halves of a bright sense are up to.

So I did and did not concern myself with beggars. So I did run from them or walk to meet them, by turn. So I heard but did not hear, considered but did not consider:

"There's only a few of us left!"

One day I was sure the stone gargoyle man taking his daily shower on O'Connell Bridge while he sang Irish opera was *not* blind. And the next his head to me was a cup of darkness.

One afternoon I found myself lingering before a tweed shop near O'Connell Bridge, staring in, staring in at a stack of good thick burly caps. I did not need another cap. I had a life's supply collected in a suitcase, yet in I went to pay out money for a fine warm brown-colored cap which I turned round and round in my hands, in a strange trance.

"Sir," said the clerk. "That cap is a seven. I would guess your head, sir, at a seven and one half."

"This will fit me. This will fit me." I stuffed the cap into my pocket.

"Let me get you a sack, sir——"

"No!" Hot-cheeked, suddenly suspicious of what I was up to, I fled.

There was the bridge in the soft rain. All I need do now was walk over——

In the middle of the bridge, my singing man was not there.

In his place stood an old man and woman cranking a great piano-box hurdy-gurdy which racketed and coughed like a coffee grinder eating glass and stone, giving forth no melody but a grand and melancholy sort of iron indigestion.

I waited for the tune, if tune it was, to finish. I kneaded the new tweed cap in my sweaty fist while the hurdy-gurdy prickled, spanged and thumped.

"Be damned to ya!" the old man and old woman, furious with their job, seemed to say, their faces thunderous pale, their eyes red-hot in the rain. "Pay us! Listen! But we'll give you no tune! Make up your own!" their mute lips said.

And standing there on the spot where the beggar always sang without his cap, I thought, Why don't they take one fiftieth of the money they make each month and have the thing tuned? If I were cranking the box, I'd want a tune, at least for myself! If you were cranking the box, I answered. But you're not. And it's obvious they hate the begging job, who'd blame them, and want no part of giving back a familiar song as recompense.

How different from my capless friend.

My *friend?*

I blinked with surprise, then stepped forward and nodded. "Beg pardon. The man with the concertina . . ."

The woman stopped cranking and glared at me.

"Ah?"

"The man with no cap in the rain."

"Ah, him!" snapped the woman.

"He's not here today?"

"Do you *see* him?" cried the woman.

She started cranking the infernal device.

I put a penny in the tin cup.

She peered at me as if I'd spit in the cup.

I put in another penny. She stopped.

"Do you know where he is?" I asked.

"Sick. In bed. The damn cold! We heard him go off, coughing."

"Do you know where he lives?"

"No!"

"Do you know his name?"

"Now, who would know that!"

I stood there, feeling directionless, thinking of the man somewhere off in the town, alone. I looked at the new cap foolishly.

The two old people were watching me uneasily.

I put a last shilling in the cup.

"He'll be all right," I said, not to them, but to someone, hopefully, myself.

The woman heaved the crank. The bucketing machine let loose a fall of glass and junk in its hideous interior.

"The tune," I said, numbly. "What is it?"

"You're deaf!" snapped the woman. "It's the national anthem! Do you mind removing your cap?"

I showed her the new cap in my hand.

She glared up. "Your cap, man, *your* cap!"

"Oh!" Flushing, I seized the old cap from my head.

Now I had a cap in each hand.

The woman cranked. The "music" played. The rain hit my brow, my eyelids, my mouth.

On the far side of the bridge I stopped for the hard, the slow decision: which cap to try on my drenched skull?

During the next week I passed the bridge often, but there was always just the old couple there with their pandemonium device, or no one there at all.

On the last day of our visit, my wife started to pack the new tweed cap away with my others, in the suitcase.

"Thanks, no." I took it from her. "Let's keep it out, on the mantel, please. There."

That night the hotel manager brought a farewell bottle to our room. The talk was long and good, the hour grew late, there was a fire like an orange lion on the hearth, big and lively, and the brandy in the glasses, and silence for a moment in the room, perhaps because quite suddenly we found silence falling in great soft flakes past our high windows.

The manager, glass in hand, watched the continual lace,

then looked down at the midnight stones and at last said, under his breath, " 'There's only a few of us left.' "

I glanced at my wife, and she at me.

The manager caught us.

"Do you know him, then? Has he said it to you?"

"Yes. But what does the phrase mean?"

The manager watched all those figures down there standing in the shadows and sipped his drink.

"Once I thought he meant he fought in the Troubles and there's just a few of the I.R.A. left. But no. Or maybe he means in a richer world the begging population is melting away. But no to that also. So maybe, perhaps, he means there aren't many 'human beings' left who look, see what they look at, and understand well enough for one to ask and one to give. Everyone busy, running here, jumping there, there's no time to study one another. But I guess that's bilge and hogwash, slop and sentiment."

He half turned from the window.

"So you know There's Only a Few of Us Left, do you?"

My wife and I nodded.

"Then do you know the woman with the baby?"

"Yes," I said.

"And the one with the cancer?"

"Yes," said my wife.

"And the man who needs train fare to Cork?"

"Belfast," said I.

"Galway," said my wife.

The manager smiled sadly and turned back to the window.

"What about the couple with the piano that plays no tune?"

"Has it ever?" I asked.

"Not since I was a boy."

The manager's face was shadowed now.

"Do you know the beggar on O'Connell Bridge?"

"Which one?" I said.

But I knew which one, for I was looking at the cap there on the mantel.

"Did you see the paper today?" asked the manager.

"No."

"There's just the item, bottom half of page five, *Irish Times*. It seems he just got tired. And he threw his concertina over into the River Liffey. And he jumped after it."

He was back, then, yesterday! I thought. And I didn't pass by!

"The poor bastard." The manager laughed with a hollow exhalation. "What a funny, horrid way to die. That damn silly concertina—I hate them, don't you?—wheezing on its way down, like a sick cat, and the man falling after. I laugh and I'm ashamed of laughing. Well. They didn't find the body. They're still looking."

"Oh, God!" I cried, getting up. "Oh, damn!"

The manager watched me carefully now, surprised at my concern. "You couldn't help it."

"I could! I never gave him a penny, not one, ever! Did you?"

"Come to think of it, no."

"But you're worse than I am!" I protested. "I've seen you around town, shoveling out pennies hand over fist. Why, why not to him?"

"I guess I thought he was overdoing it."

"Hell, yes!" I was at the window now, too, staring down through the falling snow. "I thought his bare head was a trick to make me feel sorry. Damn, after a while you think everything's a trick! I used to pass there winter nights with the rain thick and him there singing and he made me feel so cold I hated his guts. I wonder how many other people felt cold and hated him because he did that to them? So instead of getting money, he got nothing in his cup. I lumped him with the rest. But maybe he was one of the legitimate ones, the new poor just starting out this winter, not a beggar ever before, so you hock your clothes to feed a stomach and wind up a man in the rain without a hat."

The snow was falling fast now, erasing the lamps and the statues in the shadows of the lamps below.

"How do you tell the difference between them?" I asked. "How can you judge which is honest, which isn't?"

"The fact is," said the manager quietly, "you can't. There's no difference between them. Some have been at it longer than others, and have gone shrewd, forgotten how it all started a long time ago. On a Saturday they had food. On a Sunday they didn't. On a Monday they asked for credit. On a Tuesday they borrowed their first match. Thursday a cigarette. And a few Fridays later they found themselves, God knows how, in front of a place called the Royal Hibernian Hotel. They couldn't tell you what happened or why. One thing's sure though: they're hanging to the cliff by their fingernails. Poor bastard, someone must've stomped on that man's hands on O'Connell Bridge and he just gave up the ghost and went over. So what does it prove? You cannot stare them down or look away from them. You cannot run and hide from them. You can only give to them all. If you start drawing lines, someone gets hurt. I'm sorry now I didn't give that blind singer a shilling each time I passed. Well. Well. Let us console ourselves, hope it wasn't money but something at home or in his past did him in. There's no way to find out. The paper lists no name."

Snow fell silently across our sight. Below, the dark shapes waited. It was hard to tell whether snow was making sheep of the wolves or sheep of the sheep, gently manteling their shoulders, their backs, their hats and shawls.

A moment later, going down in the haunted night elevator, I found the new tweed cap in my hand.

Coatless, in my shirtsleeves, I stepped out into the night.

I gave the cap to the first man who came. I never knew if it fit. What money I had in my pockets was soon gone.

Then, left alone, shivering, I happened to glance up. I stood, I froze, blinking up through the drift, the drift, the silent drift of blinding snow. I saw the high hotel windows, the lights, the shadows.

What's it like up there? I thought. *Are fires lit? Is it warm as breath? Who are all those people? Are they drinking? Are they happy?*

Do they even know I'm HERE?

DEATH AND THE MAIDEN

Far out in the country beyond the woods, beyond the world, really, lived Old Mam, and she had lived there for ninety years with the door locked tight, not opening for anyone, be it wind, rain, sparrow tapping or little boy with a pailful of crayfish rapping. If you scratched at her shutters, she called through:

"Go away, Death!"

"I'm not Death!" you might say.

But she'd cry back, "Death, I know you, you come today in the shape of a girl. But I see the bones behind the freckles!"

Or someone else might knock.

"I see you, Death!" would cry Old Mam. "In the shape of a scissors-grinder! But the door is triple-locked and double-barred. I got flypaper on the cracks, tape on the keyholes, dust mops up the chimney, cobwebs in the shutters, and the electricity cut off so you can't slide in with the juice! No telephones so you can call me to my doom at three in the dark morning. And I got my ears stuffed with cotton so I can't hear your reply to what I say now. So, Death, get away!"

That's how it had been through the town's history. People in that world beyond the wood spoke of her and sometimes boys doubting the tale would heave chunks against the roof slates just to hear Old Mam wail, "Go on, goodbye, you in black with the white, white face!"

And the tale was that Old Mam, with such tactics, would live forever. After all, Death couldn't get in, could he? All the old germs in her house must have long since given up and gone to sleep. All the new germs running through the land with new names every week or ten days, if you believed the papers, couldn't get in past the bouquets of rock moss, rue, black tobacco and castor bean at every door.

157

"She'll bury us all," said the town 'way off where the train ran by.

"I'll bury them all," said Old Mam, alone and playing solitaire with Braille-marked cards, in the dark.

And that's how it was.

Years passed without another visitor, be it boy, girl, tramp or traveling man, knocking at her door. Twice a year a grocery clerk from the world beyond, seventy himself, left packages that might have been birdseed, could have been milk-bone biscuit, but were almost certainly stamped into bright steel cans with yellow lions and red devils inked on the bright wrappers, and trod off over the choppy sea of lumber on the front porch. The food might stay there for a week, baked by the sun, frozen by the moon; a proper time of antisepsis. Then, one morning, it was gone.

Old Mam's career was waiting. She did it well, with her eyes closed and her hands clasped and the hairs inside her ears trembling, listening, always ready.

So she was not surprised when, on the seventh day of August in her ninety-first year, a young man with a sunburned face walked through the wood and stood before her house.

He wore a suit like that snow which slides whispering in white linen off a winter roof to lay itself in folds on the sleeping earth. He had no car; he had walked a long way, but looked fresh and clean. He carried no cane to lean on and wore no hat to keep off the stunning blows of the sun. He did not perspire. Most important of all, he carried only one thing with him, an eight-ounce bottle with a bright-green liquid inside. Gazing deeply into this green color, he sensed he was in front of Old Mam's house, and looked up.

He didn't touch her door. He walked slowly around her house and let her feel him making the circle.

Then, with his X-ray eyes, he let her feel his steady gaze.

"Oh!" cried Old Mam, waking with a crumb of graham cracker still in her mouth. "It's you! I know who you came as this time!"

"Who?"

"A young man with a face like pink summer melon. But you got no shadow! Why's that? Why?"

"People are afraid of shadows. So I left mine back beyond the wood."

"So I see, without looking."

"Oh," said the young man with admiration. "You have Powers."

"Great Powers, to keep *you* out and *me* in!"

The young man's lips barely moved. "I won't even bother to wrestle you."

But she heard. "You'd lose, you'd lose!"

"And I like to win. So—I'll just leave this bottle on your front stoop."

He heard her heart beating fast through the walls of the house.

"Wait! What's in it? Anything left on my property, I got a right to know!"

"Well," said the young man.

"Go on!"

"In this bottle," he said, "is the first night and the first day you turned eighteen."

"What, what, what!"

"You heard me."

"The night I turned eighteen . . . the day?"

"That's it."

"In a bottle?"

He held it high and it was curved and shaped not unlike a young woman. It took the light of the world and flashed back warmth and green fire like the coals burning in a tiger's eyes. It looked now serene, now suddenly shifted and turbulent in his hands.

"I don't believe it!" cried Old Mam.

"I'll leave it and go," said the young man. "When I'm gone try a teaspoon of the green thoughts in this bottle. Then you'll know."

"It's poison!"

"No."

"You promise, mother's honor?"

"I have no mother."

"What do you swear on?"

"Myself."

"It'll kill me, that's what you want!"

"It will raise you from the dead."

"I'm not dead!"

The young man smiled at the house.

"Aren't you?" he said.

"Wait! Let me ask myself: Are you dead? *Are* you? Or *nearly,* all these years?"

"The day and the night you turned eighteen," said the young man. "Think it over."

"It's so long ago!"

Something stirred like a mouse by a coffin-sized window.

"This will bring it back."

He let the sun wash through the elixir that glowed like the crushed sap of a thousand green blades of summer grass. It looked hot and still as a green sun, it looked wild and blowing as the sea.

"This was a good day in a good year of your life."

"A good year," she murmured, hidden away.

"A vintage year. Then there was savor to your life. One swig and you'd know the taste! Why not try it, eh? Eh?"

He held the bottle higher and farther out and it was suddenly a telescope which, peered through from either end, brought to focus a time in a year long gone. A green-and-yellow time much like this year noon in which the young man offered up the past like a burning glass between his serene fingers. He tilted the bright flask, and a butterfly of white-hot illumination winged up and down the window shutters, playing them like gray piano keys, soundlessly. With hypnotic ease the burning wings frittered through the shutter slots to catch a lip, a nose, an eye, poised there. The eye snatched itself away, then, curious, relit itself from the beam of light. Now, having caught what he wanted to catch, the young man held the butterfly reflection steady, save for the breathing of its fiery wings, so that the green fire of that far-distant day poured through the shutters of not only ancient house but ancient woman. He heard her breathe out her muffled startlement, her repressed delight.

"No, no, you can't fool me!" She sounded like someone deep under water, trying not to drown in a lazy tide. "Coming back dressed in that flesh, you! Putting on that mask I can't quite see! Talking with that voice I remember from some other year. Whose voice? I don't care! My ouija board here on my lap spells who you really are and what you sell!"

"I sell just this twenty-four hours from young life."

"You sell something else!"

"No, I can't sell what I *am*."

"If I come out you'd grab and shove me six feet under. I've had you fooled, put off, for years. Now you whine back with new plans, none of which will work!"

"If you came out the door, I'd only kiss your hand, young lady."

"Don't call me what I'm not!"

"I call you what you could be an hour from now."

"An hour from now . . ." she whispered, to herself.

"How long since you been walked through this wood?"

"Some other war, or some peace," she said. "I can't see. The water's muddy."

"Young lady," he said, "it's a fine summer day. There's a tapestry of golden bees, now this design, now that, in the green church aisle of trees here. There's honey in a hollow oak flowing like a river of fire. Kick off your shoes, you can crush wild mint, wading deep. Wildflowers like clouds of yellow butterflies lie in the valley. The air under these trees is like deep well water cool and clear you drink with your nose. A summer day, young as young ever was."

"But I'm old, old as ever was."

"Not if you listen! Here's my out-and-out bargain, deal, sale—a transaction betwixt you, me and the August weather."

"What kind of deal, what do I get for my investment?"

"Twenty-four long sweet summer hours, starting now. When we've run through these woods and picked the berries and eaten the honey, we'll go on to town and buy you the finest spider-web-thin white summer dress and lift you on the train."

"The train!"

"The train to the city, an hour away, where we'll have dinner and dance all night. I'll buy you four shoes, you'll need them, wearing out one pair."

"My bones—I can't move."

"You'll run rather than walk, dance rather than run. We'll watch the stars wheel over the sky and bring the sun up, flaming. We'll string footprints along the lake shore at dawn. We'll eat the biggest breakfast in mankind's history and lie on the sand like two chicken pies warming at noon. Then, late in the day, a five-pound box of bonbons on our laps, we'll laugh back on the train, covered with the conductor's ticket-punch confetti, blue, green, orange, like we were married, and walk through town seeing nobody, no one, and wander back through the sweet dusk-smelling wood into your house . . ."

Silence.

"It's already over," murmured her voice. "And it hasn't begun."

Then: "Why are you doing this? What's in it for you?!"

The young man smiled tenderly. "Why, girl, I want to sleep with you."

She gasped. "I never slept with no one in my life!"

"You're a . . . maiden lady?"

"And proud *of* it!"

The young man sighed, shaking his head. "So it's true—you are, you really are, a maiden."

He heard nothing from the house, so listened.

Softly, as if a secret faucet had been turned somewhere with difficulty, and drop by drop an ancient system were being used for the first time in half a century, the old woman began to cry.

"Old Mam, why do you cry?"

"I don't know," she wailed.

Her weeping faded at last and he heard her rock in her chair, making a cradle rhythm to soothe herself.

"Old Mam," he whispered.

"Don't call me that!"

"All right," he said. "Clarinda."

"How did you know my name? No one knows!"

"Clarinda, why did you hide in that house, long ago?"

"I don't remember. Yes, I do. I was afraid."

"Afraid?"

"Strange. Half my years afraid of life. The other half, afraid of death. Always some kind of afraid. You! Tell the truth, now! When my twenty-four hours are up, after we walk by the lake and take the train back and come through the woods to my house, you want to . . ."

He made her say it.

". . . *sleep* with me?" she whispered.

"For ten thousand million years," he said.

"Oh." Her voice was muted. "That's a long time."

He nodded.

"A long time," she repeated. "What kind of bargain is that, young man? You give me twenty-four hours of being eighteen again and I give you ten thousand million years of my precious time."

"Don't forget, *my* time, too," he said. "I'll never go away."

"You'll lie with me?"

"I will."

"Oh, young man, young man. Your voice. So familiar."

"Look."

He saw the keyhole unplugged and her eye peer out at

him. He smiled at the sunflowers in the field and the sunflower in the sky.

"I'm blind, half blind," she cried. "But can that be Willy Winchester 'way out there?"

He said nothing.

"But, Willy, you're just twenty-one by the look of you, not a day different than you were seventy years back!"

He set the bottle by the front door and walked back out to stand in the weeds.

"Can—" She faltered. "Can you make me look like yourself?"

He nodded.

"Oh, Willy, Willy, is that really you?"

She waited, staring across the summer air to where he stood relaxed and happy and young, the sun flashing off his hair and cheeks.

A minute passed.

"Well?" he said.

"Wait!" she cried. "Let me think!"

And there in the house he could feel her letting her memories pour through her mind as sand pours through an hourglass, heaping itself at last into nothing but dust and ashes. He could hear the emptiness of those memories burning the sides of her mind as they fell down and down and made a higher and yet higher mound of sand.

All that desert, he thought, and not one oasis.

She trembled at his thought.

"Well," he said again.

And at last she answered.

"Strange," she murmured. "Now, all of a sudden, twenty-four hours, one day, traded for ten million billion years, sounds fair and good and right."

"It is, Clarinda," he said. "Oh, yes, it is."

The bolts slid back, the locks rattled, the door cracked. Her hand jerked out, seized the bottle and flicked back in.

A minute passed.

Then, as if a gun had been fired off, footsteps pelted through the halls. The back door slammed open. Upstairs, windows flew wide, as shutters fell crumbling to the grass. Downstairs, a moment later, the same. Shutters exploded to kindling as she thrust them out. The windows exhaled dust.

Then at last, from the front door, flung wide, the empty bottle sailed and smashed against a rock.

She was on the porch, quick as a bird. The sunlight struck full upon her. She stood as someone on a stage, in a single revealing motion, come from the dark. Then, down the steps, she threw her hand to catch his.

A small boy passing on the road below stopped, stared and, walking backward, moved out of sight, his eyes still wide.

"Why did he stare at me?" she said. "Am I beautiful?"

"Very beautiful."

"I need a mirror!"

"No, no, you don't."

"Will everyone in town see me beautiful? It's not just me thinking so, is it, or you pretending?"

"Beauty is what you *are*."

"Then I'm beautiful, for that's how I feel. Will everyone dance me tonight, will men fight for turns?"

"They will, one and all."

Down the path, in the sound of bees and stirring leaves, she stopped suddenly and looked into his face so like the summer sun.

"Oh, Willy, Willy, when it's all over and we come back here, will you be kind to me?"

He gazed deep into her eyes and touched her cheek with his fingers.

"Yes," he said gently. "I will be kind."

"I believe you," she said. "Oh, Willy, I believe."

And they ran down the path out of sight, leaving dust on the air and leaving the front door of the house wide and the shutters open and the windows up so the light of the sun could flash in with the birds come to build nests, raise families, and so petals of lovely summer flowers could blow like bridal showers through the long halls in a carpet and into the rooms and over the empty-but-waiting bed. And summer, with the breeze, changed the air in all the great spaces of the house so it smelled like the Beginning or the first hour after the Beginning, when the world was new and nothing would ever change and no one would ever grow old.

Somewhere rabbits ran thumping like quick hearts in the forest.

Far off, a train hooted, rushing faster, faster, faster, toward the town.

A FLIGHT OF RAVENS

He got off the bus at Washington Square and walked back half a block, glad that he had decided to come down. Right now there was no one in New York he wanted to see except Paul and Helen Pierson. He had saved them for the last, knowing that he would need them to counteract the effects of too many appointments on too many days with too many erratic, neurotic, and unhappy people. The Piersons would shake his hand, cool his brow and comfort him with friendship and good words. The evening would be loud, long and immensely happy, and he would go back to Ohio in a few days thinking well of New York simply because two amazing people had provided him with an oasis in this burning desert of panic and uncertainty.

Helen Pierson was waiting on the fourth floor of the apartment house, outside the elevator.

"Hello, hello!" she cried. "Williams, it's good to see you! Come on in! Paul will be home soon, he had to work late at the office. We're having chicken cacciatore tonight, I hope you like chicken cacciatore, I made it myself. Do you like chicken, Williams? I hope you do. How're your wife and kids? Sit down, take off your coat, take off your glasses, you're much nicer-looking without your glasses, it's been a muggy day, hasn't it? Do you want a drink?"

Somewhere in this flow he felt himself steered through a doorway, her tugging at his coat, waving her free hand, and the faint smell of strong perfume from her mouth. Good Lord, he thought, surprised, she's drunk. He looked at Helen for a long moment.

"One of those martinis," he said. "But just one. I'm not much of a drinker, you know."

"Of course, darling. Paul'll be home at six, it's five-thirty now. We're so *flattered* you're here, Williams, we're so flattered you'd spend time with us, it's been over three years!"

"Oh, hell," he snorted.

"No, but I *mean* it, Williams," she said, each word a bit slurred, each gesture a bit too careful. He felt that somehow he had got into the wrong apartment, that this was somebody's visiting sister, an aunt, or a stranger. Of course, this might have been a bad day for her, everyone had a bad day on occasion.

"I'll have one with you. I've only had one so far," she said, and he believed her. She must have started drinking, quietly and steadily, since last he had seen her. Drinking every day and every day. Until . . . He had seen it happen to other friends, time and again. One moment sober, and a minute later, after one sip, all the martinis of the last three hundred days that had taken up occupation in the blood surged from the system, rushed forward to meet the new martini like an old friend. Ten minutes ago Helen had probably been cold sober. But now her eyes had lidded a bit and her tongue was erasing the very word she was trying to say.

"I really *mean* it, Williams." She never called him by his first name. "Williams, we're so flattered you bother to come see Paulie and me. My God, you've done so well in the last three years, you've gone up in the world, you've got a reputation, you don't have to write for Paul's matinee TV show now, no more of that dreadful crap."

"It wasn't dreadful crap, it was good, Paul's a fine producer and I wrote good stuff for him."

"Dreadful crap is what it was. You're a real writer, you're top-hole now, no more dime store junk for you, how does it feel to be a successful novelist and have everyone talk about you and have money in the bank? Wait until Paul gets here, he's been waiting for you to call." Her talking poured over and about him. "You *are* nice to call us, really."

"I owe Paul everything," said Williams, breaking away from his thoughts. "I started in his shows when I was twenty-one, back in 1951, and I made ten bucks a page."

"That makes you thirty-one now, my God, only a young rooster," said Helen. "How old do you think I am, Williams, go on, guess, how old do you think I am?"

"Oh, I don't know," he said, flushing.

"No, go on, guess, guess how old I am," she asked.

A million years, he thought, suddenly a million years old. But Paul'll be all right. He'll be here soon and he'll be all right. I wonder if he'll know you, Helen, when he comes in the door?

"I'm no good at guessing ages," he said.

Your body, he thought, is built of the old bricks of this city, and in it are tars and asphalts and mortars unseen and limed with age, you breathe carbon monoxide from your lungs, and the color of your eyes is hysterical blue neon, and the color of your lips is red-fire neon, and the color of your face is white calcimine from stone buildings, with only here or there a touch of green or blue, the veins of your throat, your temples, your wrists, like the little garden squares in New York City. So much marble, so much granite, veined and lined, and so little of the sky and the grass in you now.

"Go on, Williams, guess how old I am!"

"Thirty-six?"

She gave something that was almost a scream, and he was afraid he had been overdiplomatic.

"Thirty-six!" she cried, whooping, slapping her hands on her knees. "Thirty-six, oh, you darling, you don't really *mean* thirty-six, my God, no!" she yelled. "Why, I saw thirty-six ten years ago!"

"We've never talked about age before," he protested.

"You young nice baby," she said. "It was never *important* before. But you'd be surprised how important it can get without your knowing it. My God, you're young, Williams, do you have any idea how *young* you are?"

"Fairly, I guess," he said, looking at his hands.

"You sweet young child," she said. "Wait'll I tell Paul. Thirty-six, good Lord, that's rich. But I don't look forty or forty-six, *do* I, darling?"

She had never asked such questions before, he thought, and not asking questions like that was to stay forever young.

"Paul's just turning forty this week, it's his birthday tomorrow."

"I wish I'd known."

"Forget it, he hates gifts, he never tells anyone about his birthdays, he'd be insulted if you gave him a present. We stopped having birthday parties for him last year. He threw the cake out then, I remember, it was all lit, and he threw it down the ventilator shaft, still burning."

She stopped suddenly as if she had said something she shouldn't have said. They both sat for a moment in the tall-ceilinged room, shifting uncomfortably.

"Paulie's due home any minute," she said finally. "Another drink? How does it feel to be famous, tell me? You always were full of conscience, Williams. Quality, Paulie and I said to each other, quality. You couldn't write badly if you wanted to. We're so proud of you, Paulie and me, we tell *everyone* that you're our friend."

"That's strange," said Williams. "It's a weird world. When I was twenty-one I told everyone I knew *you*. I was really proud and excited the first time I met Paul, after he bought my first script and . . ."

The door buzzer sounded and Helen ran to answer it, leaving Williams alone with his drink. He worried that perhaps he had sounded condescending, as if he wouldn't be proud to meet Paul now. He hadn't meant it that way. Everything would be all right as soon as Paul roared in. Everything was *always* all right with Paul.

There was a great echoing of voices outside, and Helen came back bringing with her a woman of some fifty-odd years. You could tell that the woman was prematurely wrinkled and gray by the bouncing way she moved.

"I hope you don't mind, Williams, I forgot to tell you, I hope you don't mind, this is Mrs. Mears from across the hall. I told her you were coming for dinner, that you were in town for a few days to see about your new book with your publisher, and she was excited to meet you, she's read all your stories, Williams, and loves your work and wanted to meet you. Mrs. Mears, this is Mr. Williams."

The woman nodded. "I've wanted to be a writer myself," she said. "I'm working on a book now."

The two women sat. Williams felt the smile on his face as if it were separate from himself, it was like those white wax teeth children buy and pop into their mouths to make them look buck-toothed; he felt it beginning to melt, that smile.

"Have you ever sold anything?" he asked Mrs. Mears.

"No, but I keep at it," she said gallantly. "Things have been a bit complicated lately, though."

"You see," said Helen, leaning forward, "her son passed away only two weeks ago."

"I'm sorry to hear it," said Williams awkwardly.

"No, that's all right, he's better off, poor boy, he was about your age, only thirty."

"What happened?" Williams asked mechanically.

"He was terribly overweight, poor boy, weighed two hundred and eighty pounds and his friends kept making fun of him. He wanted to be an artist. He sold only a few pictures on occasion. But people made fun of him, so he went on a diet six months ago. When he died early this month he weighed just ninety-three pounds."

"My God!" said Williams. "That's terrible."

"He stayed on the diet, he stayed right *on* it, no matter what I said to him. Stayed in his room, stayed on the diet, and took the weight off so nobody knew him when they saw him at the funeral. I think he was very happy those last few days, happier than he had been in years; sort of triumphant, you might say, poor boy."

Williams drank the rest of his drink. The sense of depression that had been growing for days now closed over his head. He felt himself dropping down through a great depth of black water. He had done too much, seen too much, lived too much, talked with too many people, in the past week. He had counted on tonight making him well again, but now . . .

"My, you're a handsome young man," said Mrs. Mears. "Why didn't you *tell* me he was so handsome, Helen?" She turned almost accusingly to Helen Pierson.

"Why, I thought you *knew*," said Helen.

"Oh, much nicer than his photographs, much nicer. Do you know," said Mrs. Mears, "there was a week or so there, when Richard was on his diet, that he looked quite like you? For just a short week, I'm *sure* of that."

Yesterday, Williams continued his interior monologue, he had fled into a newsreel theater for a brief respite from endless appointments at magazines, radio stations and newspapers, and on the screen he had seen a man ready to leap from the George Washington Bridge. The police had coaxed him down. And somewhere else another man, another city, on a hotel ledge, people yelling, daring him to jump. Williams had had to leave the theater. When he stepped out into the hot concussion of sunlight everything had been too real, too raw, as it always was when you came too quickly upon a world of living creatures after a dream.

"Yes, you're a *handsome* young man," said Mrs. Mears.

"Before I forget it," said Helen. "Our son Tom is here."

Of course, Tom. Williams had seen Tom one time, years ago, when Tom had come in off the street long enough to talk; a bright boy, an alert boy, well-mannered and well-read. A son to be proud of, that was Tom.

"He's seventeen now," said Helen. "He's in his room, do you want me to bring him out? You know, he got into a little trouble. He's a nice kid. We've given him everything. But he got to running with some Washington Square gang, a bunch of roughnecks, and they robbed a store and Tom was caught, this was about two months ago. There was such excitement and, my God, what a stir, but things'll work out. Tom's a good kid, you know that, don't you, Williams?" She filled his glass.

"A fine kid." Williams started on the new drink quickly.

"You know how kids are. Not much to do in a town like this, not for kids anyway."

"I've seen the play streets."

"Aren't they awful? But what can we do? We've got a surprise for you, Williams, Paul and me. Do you know what? We're buying a place in the country, after all this time, after all these years, getting out, Paul's quitting television, yes, actually quitting, don't you think that's *wonderful?* And he's going into writing just like you, Williams, just like *you*, and we're living out in Connecticut, it's a nice little place, we're going to give him a real test, give Paulie a real chance to write, you think he can write, don't you, Williams? Don't you think he's a damn sweet little writer?"

"Of course I do!" said Williams. "Of course."

"So Paul's quitting his damned job, all that crap, and we're getting out in the country."

"How soon?"

"Sometime in August. Might have to put it off until September. But the first of the year at the latest."

Of course! Williams' spirit lifted. That'll do it! If they'll only go away, get out of this town. Paul must have saved enough by now, after all these years. If they'll only go! If she'll only let him.

He glanced across at Helen with her bright face that now was bright only because she held certain muscles forever that way, she held them steady and hard, she was not letting go of this new brightness that was like a light bulb in a room after the sun had burned out.

"Your plan sounds terrific," said Williams.

"Do you really think we can do it, Williams, do you

think we can *really* do it? You think Paul's a *terrific* writer, don't you?"

"Sure I do. You've got to try."

"He can always get his job back if he has to."

"Of course."

"So this time we'll really do it. Get out, take Tom with us, the country'll do him good, do us all good, cut out the drinking, cut out the night life, and really settle in with a typewriter and ten reams of paper for Paul to fill up. You think he's a damned good writer, don't you, Williams?"

"You know I do."

"Tell me, Mr. Williams," said Mrs. Mears. "How did you get to be a writer?"

"I liked to read when I was a kid. I started writing every day when I was twelve and kept at it," he said, nervously. He tried to think of how it had really been at the start. "I just kept at it, a thousand words a day."

"Paul was the same way," said Helen quickly.

"You must have a lot of money," said Mrs. Mears.

But at that moment there was the sound of a key clicking in the door. Williams jumped up involuntarily, smiling, relieved. He smiled at the hallway and the distant door as it opened. He kept smiling when he saw Paul's shape, and Paul looked wonderful to him coming down the hall into the room. Paul was fine to look at and Williams stuck out his hand and hurried forward, calling his name, feeling happy. Paul strode across the apartment, tall, plumper than a few years ago, his face pink, the eyes abnormally bright, slightly protuberant, faintly bloodshot, and the faint smell of whiskey on his breath. He grabbed Williams' hand, pumping away and shouting.

"Williams, for God's sake, it's good to see you, man! So you called us after all, good to see you, damn it! How you been? You're getting famous! Christ, have a drink, get some more drinks, Helen, hi there, Mears. Sit down, for God's sake."

"I've got to be going, I don't want to intrude," said Mrs. Mears, edging through the room. "Thanks for letting me come over. Goodbye, Mr. Williams."

"Williams, Goddamn it, good to see you, did Helen tell you what we plan to do, about leaving town, that is? About the country?"

"She said—"

"Boy, we're really getting out of this damn town. Summer coming on. Glad to get out of that raping office. I've read ten million words of TV crap a year for ten years, don't you think it's *time* I got out, Williams, don't you think I should've gotten out *years* ago? Connecticut for us! Do you need a drink? Have you seen Tom? Is Tom in his room, Helen? Get 'im out here, let him talk to Williams here. Gee, Williams, we're glad to see you. Been telling everyone you'd come to see us. Who've you seen in town so far?"

"I saw Reynolds last night."

"Reynolds, the editor at United Features? How is he? Does he get out much?"

"A little."

"You know he's been in his apartment for twelve months, Helen? You remember Reynolds? A nice guy, but army life or something screwed him up. He was afraid to leave his apartment all last year, afraid he'd kill someone, anyone, on the street."

"He left his apartment last night with me," said Williams. "Walked me down to the bus line."

"Hey, that's all right for Reynolds, glad to hear it. Did you hear about Banks? Killed in an auto accident in Rhode Island last week."

"No!"

"Yes, sir, damn it, one of the nicest guys in the world, best photographer who ever worked for the big magazines. Really talented, young too, damned young, got drunk and was killed in a crash on his way home. Automobiles, Christ!"

Williams felt as if a great flight of ravens were beating upon the hot air of the room. This was not Paul any more. This was the husband of the strange woman who had moved in after the Piersons went away, sometime in the last three years. Nobody knew where the Piersons had gone. It would do no good to ask this man where Paul was now, this man could not have told anyone.

"Williams, you've met our son, haven't you? Go get Tom, Helen, have him come out!"

The son was fetched, seventeen, silent, into the parlor doorway, where, feeling the drinks come over him rapidly now, Williams stood with a freshly filled glass, weaving slightly.

"This is Tom, Williams, this is Tom."

"*You* remember Tom."

"You remember Williams, Tom?"

"Say hello, Tom."

"Tom's a good boy, don't *you* think so, Williams?"

Both talking at once, never stopping, always the river, always the rush and the stumbled words and the alcohol blue-flame eyes and the hurrying on. Helen said, "Tom, say a few words of gang jargon for Mr. Williams."

Silence.

"Tom's picked it up, he's got a good mind, a good memory. Tom, say a few words of gang talk for Mr. Williams. Oh, come on, Tom," said Helen.

Silence. Tom stood tall and looking at the floor in the parlor doorway.

"Come *on*, Tom," said Helen.

"Oh, leave him alone, Helen."

"Why, Paulie, I just thought Williams would like to hear some gang jargon. You *know* it, Tom, say some for us."

"If he doesn't want to he doesn't want to!" said Paul.

Silence.

"Come on out to the kitchen while I fix myself a drink," said Paul, moving Williams along by his arm, walking huge beside him.

In the kitchen they swayed together and Paul took hold of Williams' elbow, shook his hand, talked to him close and quiet, his face like a pig's that had been crying all afternoon. "Williams, tell me, you think I can make it *go*, quitting this way? I got a swell novel idea!" He hit Williams' arm, gently at first, then, with each point of his story, harder. "You *like* that idea, Williams?" Williams drew back, but his hand was trapped. The fist smashed his arm again and again. "Say, it'll be good to write again! Write, have free time, and take off some of this fat, too."

"Don't do it like Mrs. Mears' son did."

"He was a fool!" Paul crushed Williams' arm tight, tight. In all the years of their friendship they had rarely touched, but now here was Paul gripping, pressuring, petting him. He shook Williams' shoulder, slapped his back. "In the country, by God, I'll have time to think, work off this flab! Here in town you know what we do weekends? Kill a quart or two of Scotch between us. Hard to drive out of town weekends, traffic, crowds, so we stick here, get loaded and relax. But that'll be over, in the country. I want you to read a manuscript of mine, Williams."

"Oh, Paulie, wait!"

"Stop it, Helen. Williams won't mind, will you, Williams?"

I won't mind, thought Williams, but I'll mind. I'll be afraid but not afraid. If I were sure I'd find the old Paul in the story somewhere, living and walking around, sober and light and free, sure and quick in his decisions, tasteful in his choices, direct and forceful in his criticism, the good producer but most of all the good friend, my personal god for years, if I could find *that* Paul in the story, I'd read it in a second. But I'm not sure, and I wouldn't want to see the new and strange Paul on paper, ever. Paul, he thought, oh, Paul, don't you know, don't you *realize*, that you and Helen will never get out of town, never, never?

"Hell!" cried Paul. "How you like New York, Williams? Don't like it, do you? Neurotic, you said once. Well, it's no different than Sioux City or Kenosha. You just meet more people here in a shorter time. How's it feel, Williams, so high in the world, so famous all of a sudden?"

Now both husband and wife chattered. Getting drunker, their voices collided, their words rose, fell, mixed, quarreled, blended in hypnotic tides, an unending susurrus.

"Williams," she said. "Williams," *he* said. "We're going," she said. "God damn you, Williams, I love you! Oh, you bastard, I *hate* you!" He beat Williams' arm, laughing. "Where's Tom?" "*Proud* of you!" The apartment blazed. The air swarmed with black wings. His arm was beaten senseless. "It's hard to give up my job, that old check looks good . . ."

Paul clutched Williams' white shirt front. Williams felt the buttons pop. It seemed as if Paul, in his pink intensity, were going to hit him. His jowls heaved, his mouth clouded Williams' glasses with steam. "Proud of you! *Love* you!" He pumped his arm, struck his shoulder, tore at his shirt, slapped at his face. Williams' glasses flew off and hit the linoleum with a faint tinkle.

"Christ, I'm sorry, Williams!"

"That's all right, forget it." Williams picked up his glasses. The right lens was crazed like a ridiculous spider web. He looked out through it and there was Paul, stunned, apologetic, caught in the insane glass maze trying to get free.

Williams said nothing.

"Paulie, you're so clumsy!" shrieked Helen.

The telephone and doorbell both rang at once, and Paul was talking and Helen was talking, and Tom was gone somewhere, and Williams thought clearly, I'm not sick, I don't want to throw up, not really, but I will go to the bathroom now and I will be sick and I will throw up there. And without a word, in the ringing, belling, talking, yelling, in the apologetic confusion, in the panicking friendliness, in the hot rooms, he walked through and beyond what seemed a crowd of people and sedately closed the bathroom door and got down on his knees as if he were going to pray to God, and lifted the toilet seat.

There were three sickening gasps and plunges of his mouth. His eyes tight, tears running from them, he was not sure it was over, he was not certain whether he was gasping for breath or crying, whether these were tears of pain or sadness or not tears at all. He heard the waters vanish away in white porcelain to the sea, and he knelt there, still in an attitude of prayer.

Outside the door, voices. "You all right, you all right, Williams, you *okay?*"

He fumbled in his coat pocket, drew out his wallet, checked it, saw his return-trip ticket on the train, closed it up, put it in his breast pocket and held his hand tight to it. Then he climbed to his feet, wiped his mouth carefully and stood looking in the mirror at the odd man with the spider-webbed glasses.

Standing before the door, ready to open it, his hand on the brass knob, his eyes clenched shut and his body swaying, he felt that he weighed only ninety-three pounds.

THE BEST OF ALL POSSIBLE WORLDS

The two men sat swaying side by side, unspeaking for the long while it took for the train to move through cold December twilight, pausing at one country station after another. As the twelfth depot was left behind, the older of the two men muttered, "Idiot, Idiot!" under his breath.

"What?" The younger man glanced up from his *Times*.

The old man nodded bleakly. "Did you see that damn fool rush off just now, stumbling after that woman who smelled of Chanel?"

"Oh, her?" The young man looked as if he could not decide whether to laugh or be depressed. "I followed her off the train once myself."

The old man snorted and closed his eyes. "I too, five years ago."

The young man stared at his companion as if he had found a friend in a most unlikely spot.

"Did—did the same thing happen once you reached the end of the platform?"

"Perhaps. Go on."

"Well, I was twenty feet behind her and closing up fast when her husband drove into the station with a carload of kids! Bang! The car door slammed. I saw her Cheshire-cat smile as she drove away. I waited half an hour, chilled to the bone, for another train. It taught me something, by God!"

"It taught you nothing whatsoever," replied the older man drily. "Idiot bulls, that's all of us, you, me, them, silly boys jerking like laboratory frogs if someone scratches our itch."

"My grandpa once said, 'Big in the hunkus, small in the brain, that is man's fate.' "

"A wise man. But, now, what do you make of *her?*"

"That woman? Oh, she likes to keep in trim. It must pep up her liver to know that with a little mild eye-rolling

176

she can make the lemmings swarm any night on this train. She has the best of all possible worlds, don't you think? Husband, children, plus the knowledge she's neat packaging and can prove it five trips a week, hurting no one, least of all herself. And, everything considered, she's not much to look at. It's just she *smells* so good."

"Tripe," said the old man. "It won't wash. Purely and simply, she's a woman. All women are women, all men are dirty goats. Until you accept that, you will be rationalizing your glands all your life. As it is, you will know no rest until you are seventy or thereabouts. Meanwhile, self-knowledge may give you whatever solace can be had in a sticky situation. Given all these essential and inescapable truths, few men ever strike a balance. Ask a man if he is happy and he will immediately think you are asking if he is *satisfied*. Satiety is most men's Edenic dream. I have known only one man who came heir to the very best of all possible worlds, as you used the phrase."

"Good Lord," said the young man, his eyes shining, "I wouldn't mind hearing about him."

"I hope there's time. This chap is the happiest ram, the most carefree bull, in history. Wives and girl friends galore, as the sales pitch says. Yet he has no qualms, guilts, no feverish nights of lament and self-chastisement."

"Impossible," the young man put in. "You can't eat your cake and digest it, too!"

"He did, he does, he will! Not a tremor, not a trace of moral seasickness after an all-night journey over a choppy sea of innersprings! Successful businessman. Apartment in New York on the best street, the proper height above traffic, plus a long-weekend Bucks County place on a more than correct little country stream where he herds his nannies, the happy farmer. But I met him first at his New York apartment last year, when he had just married. At dinner, his wife was truly gorgeous, snow-cream arms, fruity lips, an amplitude of harvest land below the line, a plenitude above. Honey in the horn, the full apple barrel through winter, she seemed thus to me *and* her husband, who nipped her bicep in passing. Leaving, at midnight, I found myself raising a hand to slap her on the flat of her flank like a thoroughbred. Falling down in the elevator, life floated out from under me. I nickered."

"Your powers of description," said the young commuter, breathing heavily, "are incredible."

"I write advertising copy," said the older. "But to continue. I met let us call him Smith again not two weeks later. Through sheer coincidence I was invited to crash a party by a friend. When I arrived in Bucks County, whose place should it turn out to be but Smith's! And near him, in the center of the living room, stood this dark Italian beauty, all tawny panther, all midnight and moonstones, dressed in earth colors, browns, siennas, tans, umbers, all the tones of a riotously fruitful autumn. In the babble I lost her name. Later I saw Smith crush her like a great sun-warmed vine of lush October grapes in his arms. Idiot fool, I thought. Lucky dog, I thought. Wife in town, mistress in country. He is trampling out the vintage, et cetera, and all that. Glorious. But I shall not stay for the wine festival, I thought, and slipped away, unnoticed."

"I can't stand too much of this talk," said the young commuter, trying to raise the window.

"Don't interrupt," said the older man. "Where was I?"

"Trampled. Vintage."

"Oh, yes! Well, as the party broke up, I finally caught the lovely Italian's name. *Mrs.* Smith!"

"He'd married again, eh?"

"Hardly. Not enough time. Stunned, I thought quickly, He must have two sets of friends. One set knows his city wife. The other set knows this mistress whom he *calls* wife. Smith's too smart for bigamy. No other answer. Mystery."

"Go on, go on," said the young commuter feverishly.

"Smith, in high spirits, drove me to the train station that night. On the way he said, 'What do you think of my wives?'

" 'Wives, plural?' I said.

" 'Plural, hell,' he said. 'I've had twenty in the last three years, each better than the last! Twenty, count them, twenty! Here!' As we stopped at the station he pulled out a thick photo wallet. He glanced at my face as he handed it over, 'No, no,' he laughed, 'I'm not Bluebeard with a score of old theater trunks in the attic crammed full of former mates. Look!'

"I flipped the pictures. They flew by like an animated film. Blondes, brunettes, redheads, the plain, the exotic, the fabulously impertinent or the sublimely docile gazed out at me, smiling, frowning. The flutter-flicker hypnotized, then haunted me. There was something terribly familiar about each photo.

"'Smith,' I said, 'you must be very rich to afford all these wives.'

"'Not rich, no. Look again!'

"I flipped the montage in my hands. I gasped. I knew.

"'The Mrs. Smith I met tonight, the Italian beauty, is the one and only Mrs. Smith,' I said. 'But, at the same time, the woman I met in New York two weeks ago is also the one and only Mrs. Smith. It can only follow that both women are one and the same!'

"'Correct!' cried Smith, proud of my sleuthing.

"'Impossible!' I blurted out.

"'No,' said Smith, elated. 'My wife is amazing. One of the finest off-Broadway actresses when I met her. Selfishly I asked her to quit the stage on pain of severance of our mutual insanity, our rampaging up one side of a chaise-longue and down the other. A giantess made dwarf by love, she slammed the door on the theater, to run down the alley with me. The first six months of our marriage, the earth did not move, it shook. But, inevitably, fiend that I am, I began to watch various other women ticking by like wondrous pendulums. My wife caught me noting the time. Meanwhile, she had begun to cast her eyes on passing theatrical billboards. I found her nesting with the New York *Times* next-morning reviews, desperately tearful. Crisis! How to combine two violent careers, that of passion-disheveled actress and that of anxiously rambling ram?'

"'One night,' said Smith, 'I eyed a peach Melba that drifted by. Simultaneously, an old playbill blew in the wind and clung to my wife's ankle. It was as if these two events, occurring within the moment, had shot a window shade with a rattling snap clear to the top of its roll. Light *poured* in! My wife seized my arm. Was she or was she not an actress? She was! Well, then, well! She sent me packing for twenty-four hours, wouldn't let me in the apartment, as she hurried about some vast and exciting preparations. When I returned home the next afternoon at the blue hour, as the French say in their always twilight language, my wife had vanished! A dark Latin put out her hand to me. "I am a friend of your wife's," she said and threw herself upon me, to nibble my ears, crack my ribs, until I held her off and, suddenly suspicious, cried, "This is no woman I'm with—this is my *wife!*" And we both fell laughing to the floor. This *was* my wife, with a different cosmetic, different couturier, different posture and intonation. "My actress!" I said. "Your actress!" she laughed. "Tell me what I should be and I'll be it. Carmen? All right, I'm Carmen. Brunhild? Why not? I'll study, create and, when you grow bored, re-create. I'm enrolled at the Dance Academy. I'll learn to sit, stand, walk, ten thousand ways. I'm chin deep in speech lessons, I'm signed at the Berlitz! I am also a member of the Yamayuki Judo Club—" "Good Lord," I cried, "what for?" "This!" she replied, and tossed me head over heels into bed!'

" 'Well,' said Smith, 'from that day on I've lived Reilly and nine other Irishmen's lives! Unnumbered fancies have passed me in delightful shadow plays of women all colors, shapes, sizes, fevers! My wife, finding her proper stage, our parlor, and audience, me, has fulfilled her need to be the greatest actress in the land. Too small an audience? No! For I, with my ever-wandering tastes, am there to meet her, whichever part she plays. My jungle talent coincides with her wide-ranging genius. So, caged at last, yet free, loving her I love everyone. It's the best of all possible worlds, friend, the best of all possible worlds.' "

There was a moment of silence.

The train rumbled down the track in the new December darkness.

The two commuters, the young and the old, were thoughtful now, considering the story just finished.

At last the younger man swallowed and nodded in awe. "Your friend Smith solved his problem, all right."

"He did."

The young man debated a moment, then smiled quietly. "I have a friend, too. His situation was similar, but—different. Shall I call him Quillan?"

"Yes," said the old man, "but hurry. I get off soon."

"Quillan," said the young man quickly, "was in a bar one night with a fabulous redhead. The crowd parted before her like the sea before Moses. Miraculous, I thought, revivifying, beyond the senses! A week later, in Greenwich, I saw Quillan ambling along with a dumpy little woman, his own age, of course, only thirty-two, but she'd gone to seed young. Tatty, the English would say; pudgy, snouty-nosed, not enough make-up, wrinkled stockings, spider's-nest hair, and immensely quiet; she was content to walk along, it seemed, just holding Quillan's hand. Ha, I thought, here's his poor little parsnip wife who loves the earth he treads, while other nights he's out winding up that incredible robot redhead! How sad, what a shame. And I went on my way.

"A month later I met Quillan again. He was about to dart into a dark entranceway in MacDougal Street, when he saw me. 'Oh, God!' he cried, sweating. 'Don't tell on me! My wife must never know!'

"I was about to swear myself to secrecy when a woman called to Quillan from a window above.

"I glanced up. My jaw dropped.

"There in the window stood the dumpy, seedy little woman!!

"So suddenly it was clear. The beautiful redhead was his *wife!* She danced, she sang, she talked loud and long, a brilliant intellectual, the goddess Siva, thousand-limbed, the finest throw pillow ever sewn by mortal hand. Yet she was strangely—tiring.

"So my friend Quillan had taken this obscure Village room where, two nights a week, he could sit quietly in the mouse-brown silence or walk on the dim streets with this good homely dumpy comfortably mute woman who was not his wife at all, as I had quickly supposed, but his mistress!

"I looked from Quillan to his plump companion in the window above and wrung his hand with new warmth and understanding. 'Mum's the word!' I said. The last I saw of them, they were seated in a delicatessen, Quillan and his mistress, their eyes gently touching each other, saying nothing, eating pastrami sandwiches. He too had, if you think about it, the best of all possible worlds."

The train roared, shouted its whistle and slowed. Both men, rising, stopped and looked at each other in surprise. Both spoke at once:

"You get off at *this* stop?"

Both nodded, smiling.

Silently they made their way back and, as the train stopped in the chill December night, alighted and shook hands.

"Well, give my best to Mr. Smith."

"And mine to Mr. Quillan!"

Two horns honked from opposite ends of the station. Both men looked at one car. A beautiful woman was in it. Both looked at the other car. A beautiful woman was in it.

They separated, looking back at each other like two schoolboys, each stealing a glance at the car toward which the other was moving.

"I wonder," thought the old man, "if that woman down there is . . ."

"I wonder," thought the young man, "if that lady in his car could be . . ."

But both were running now. Two car doors slammed like pistol shots ending a matinee.

The cars drove off. The station platform stood empty. It being December and cold, snow soon fell like a curtain.

THE LIFEWORK OF JUAN DÍAZ

Filomena flung the plank door shut with such violence the candle blew out; she and her crying children were left in darkness. The only things to be seen were through the window—the adobe houses, the cobbled streets, where now the gravedigger stalked up the hill, his spade on his shoulder, moonlight honing the blue metal as he turned into the high cold graveyard and was gone.

"Mamacita, what's wrong?" Filepe, her oldest son, just nine, pulled at her. For the strange dark man had said nothing, just stood at the door with the spade and nodded his head and waited until she banged the door in his face. "Mamacita?"

"That gravedigger." Filomena's hands shook as she relit the candle. "The rent is long overdue on your father's grave. Your father will be dug up and placed down in the catacomb, with a wire to hold him standing against the wall, with the other mummies."

"No, Mamacita!"

"Yes." She caught the children to her. "Unless we find the money. Yes."

"I—I will kill that gravedigger!" cried Filepe.

"It is his job. Another would take his place if he died, and another and another after him."

They thought about the man and the terrible high place where he lived and moved and the catacomb he stood guard over and the strange earth into which people went to come forth dried like desert flowers and tanned like leather for shoes and hollow as drums which could be tapped and beaten, an earth which made great cigar-brown rustling dry mummies that might languish forever leaning like fence poles along the catacomb halls. And, thinking of all this familiar but unfamiliar stuff, Filomena and her children were cold in summer, and silent though their hearts made a vast stir in

183

their bodies. They huddled together for a moment longer and then:

"Filepe," said the mother, "come." She opened the door and they stood in the moonlight listening to hear any far sound of a blue metal spade biting the earth, heaping the sand and old flowers. But there was a silence of stars. "You others," said Filomena, "to bed."

The door shut. The candle flickered.

The cobbles of the town poured in a river of gleaming moonsilver stone down the hills, past green parks and little shops and the place where the coffin maker tapped and made the clock sounds of death-watch beetles all day and all night, forever in the life of these people. Up along the slide and rush of moonlight on the stones, her skirt whispering of her need, Filomena hurried with Filepe breathless at her side. They turned in at the Official Palace.

The man behind the small, littered desk in the dimly lit office glanced up in some surprise. "Filomena, my cousin!"

"Ricardo." She took his hand and dropped it. "You must help me."

"If God does not prevent. But ask."

"They—" The bitter stone lay in her mouth; she tried to get it out. "Tonight they are taking Juan from the earth."

Ricardo, who had half risen, now sat back down, his eyes growing wide and full of light, and then narrowing and going dull. "If not God, then God's creatures prevent. Has the year gone so swiftly since Juan's death? Can it truly be the rent has come due?" He opened his empty palms and showed them to the woman. "Ah, Filomena, I have no money."

"But if you spoke to the gravedigger. You are the police."

"Filomena, Filomena, the law stops at the edge of the grave."

"But if he will give me ten weeks, only ten, it is almost the end of summer. The Day of the Dead is coming. I will make, I will sell, the candy skulls, and give him the money, oh, please, Ricardo."

And here at last, because there was no longer a way to hold the coldness in and she must let it free before it froze her so she could never move again, she put her hands to her face and wept. And Filepe, seeing that it was permitted, wept, too, and said her name over and over.

"So," said Ricardo, rising. "Yes, yes. I will walk to the

mouth of the catacomb and spit into it. But, ah, Filomena, expect no answer. Not so much as an echo. Lead the way." And he put his official cap, very old, very greasy, very worn, upon his head.

The graveyard was higher than the churches, higher than all the buildings, higher than all the hills. It lay on the highest rise of all, overlooking the night valley of the town.

As they entered the vast ironwork gate and advanced among the tombs, the three were confronted by the sight of the gravedigger's back bent into an ever-increasing hole, lifting out spade after spade of dry dirt onto an ever-increasing mound. The digger did not even look up, but made a quiet guess as they stood at the grave's edge.

"Is that Ricardo Albañez, the chief of police?"

"Stop digging!" said Ricardo.

The spade flashed down, dug, lifted, poured. "There is a funeral tomorrow. This grave must be empty, open and ready."

"No one has died in the town."

"Someone always dies. So I dig. I have already waited two months for Filomena to pay what she owes. I am a patient man."

"Be still more patient." Ricardo touched the moving, hunching shoulder of the bent man.

"Chief of the police." The digger paused to lean, sweating, upon his spade. "This is my country, the country of the dead. These here tell me nothing, nor does any man. I rule this land with a spade, and a steel mind. I do not like the live ones to come talking, to disturb the silence I have so nicely dug and filled. Do I tell you how to conduct your municipal palace? Well, then. Good night." He resumed his task.

"In the sight of God," said Ricardo, standing straight and stiff, his fists at his sides, "and this woman and her son, you dare to desecrate the husband-father's final bed?"

"It is not final and not his, I but rented it to him." The spade floated high, flashing moonlight. "I did not ask the mother and son here to watch this sad event. And listen to me, Ricardo, police chief, one day you will die. I will bury you. Remember that: *I*. You will be in my hands. Then, oh, *then*."

"Then what?" shouted Ricardo. "You dog, do you threaten me?"

"I dig." The man was very deep now, vanishing in the shadowed grave, sending only his spade up to speak for him again and again in the cold light. "Good night, señor, señora, niño. Good night."

Outside her small adobe hut, Ricardo smoothed his cousin's hair and touched her cheek. "Filomena, ah, God."

"You did what you could."

"That terrible one. When I am dead, what awful indignities might he not work upon my helpless flesh? He would set me upside down in the tomb, hang me by my hair in a far, unseen part of the catacomb. He takes on weight from knowing someday he will have us all. Good night, Filomena. No, not even that. For the night is bad."

He went away down the street.

Inside, among her many children, Filomena sat with face buried in her lap.

Late the next afternoon, in the tilted sunlight, shrieking, the schoolchildren chased Filepe home. He fell, they circled him, laughing.

"Filepe, Filepe, we saw your father today, yes!"

"Where?" they asked themselves shyly.

"In the catacomb!" they gave answer.

"What a lazy man! He just stands there!"

"He never works!"

"He don't speak! Oh, that Juan Díaz!"

Filepe stood violently atremble under the blazed sun, hot tears streaming from his wide and half-blinded eyes.

Within the hut, Filomena heard, and the knife sounds entered her heart. She leaned against the cool wall, wave after dissolving wave of remembrance sweeping her.

In the last month of his life, agonized, coughing, and drenched with midnight perspirations, Juan had stared and whispered only to the raw ceiling above his straw mat.

"What sort of man am I, to starve my children and hunger my wife? What sort of death is this, to die in bed?"

"Hush." She placed her cool hand over his hot mouth. But he talked beneath her fingers. "What has our marriage been but hunger and sickness and now nothing? Ah, God, you are a good woman, and now I leave you with no money even for my funeral!"

And then at last he had clenched his teeth and cried out at the darkness and grown very quiet in the warm candleshine and taken her hands into his own and held them and swore an oath upon them, vowed himself with religious fervor.

"Filomena, listen. I will be with you. Though I have not protected in life, I will protect in death. Though I fed not in life, in death I will bring food. Though I was poor, I will not be poor in the grave. This I know. This I cry out. This I assure you of. In death I will work and do many things. Do not fear. Kiss the little ones. Filomena. Filomena . . ."

And then he had taken a deep breath, a final gasp, like one who settles beneath warm waters. And he had launched himself gently under, still holding his breath, for a testing of endurance through all eternity. They waited for a long time for him to exhale. But this he did not do. He did not reappear above the surface of life again. His body lay like a waxen fruit on the mat, a surprise to the touch. Like a wax apple to the teeth, so was Juan Díaz to all their senses.

And they took him away to the dry earth which was like the greatest mouth of all which held him a long time, draining the bright moistures of his life, drying him like ancient manuscript paper, until he was a mummy as light as chaff, an autumn harvest ready for the wind.

From that time until this, the thought had come and come again to Filomena, how will I feed my lost children, with Juan burning to brown crepe in a silver-tinseled box, how lengthen my children's bones and push forth their teeth in smiles and color their cheeks?

The children screamed again outside, in happy pursuit of Filepe.

Filomena looked to the distant hill, up which bright tourists' cars hummed bearing many people from the United States. Even now they paid a peso each to that dark man with the spade so that they might step down through his catacombs among the standing dead, to see what the sun-dry earth and the hot wind did to *all* bodies in this town.

Filomena watched the tourist cars, and Juan's voice whispered, "Filomena." And again: "This I cry out. In death I will work . . . I will not be poor . . . Filomena . . ." His voice ghosted away. And she swayed and was almost ill, for an idea had come into her mind which was new and terrible and made her heart pound. "Filepe!" she cried suddenly.

And Filepe escaped the jeering children and shut the door on the hot white day and said, "Yes, Mamacita?"

"Sit, niño, we must talk, in the name of the saints, we must!"

She felt her face grow old because the soul grew old behind it, and she said, very slowly, with difficulty, "Tonight we must go in secret to the catacomb."

"Shall we take a knife"—Filepe smiled wildly—"and kill the dark man?"

"No, no, Filepe, listen. . . ."

And he heard the words that she spoke.

And the hours passed and it was a night of churches. It was a night of bells, and singing. Far off in the air of the valley you could hear voices chanting the evening Mass, you could see children walking with lit candles, in a solemn file, 'way over there on the side of the dark hill, and the huge bronze bells were tilting up and showering out their thunderous crashes and bangs that made the dogs spin, dance and bark on the empty roads.

The graveyard lay glistening, all whiteness, all marble snow, all sparkle and glitter of harsh gravel like an eternal fall of hail, crunched under their feet as Filomena and Filepe took their shadows with them, ink-black and constant from the unclouded moon. They glanced over their shoulders in apprehension, but no one cried Halt! They had seen the gravedigger drift, made footless by shadow, down the hill, in answer to a night summons. Now: "Quick, Filepe, the lock!" Together they inserted a long metal rod between padlock hasps and wooden doors which lay flat to the dry earth. Together they seized and pulled. The wood split. The padlock hasps sprang loose. Together they raised the huge doors and flung them back, rattling. Together they peered down into the darkest, most silent night of all. Below, the catacomb waited.

Filomena straightened her shoulders and took a breath. "Now."

And put her foot upon the first step.

In the adobe of Filomena Díaz, her children slept sprawled here or there in the cool night room, comforting each other with the sound of their warm breathing.

Suddenly their eyes sprang wide.

Footsteps, slow and halting, scraped the cobbles outside. The door shot open. For an instant the silhouettes of three people loomed in the white evening sky beyond the door. One child sat up and struck a match.

"No!" Filomena snatched out with one hand to claw the light. The match fell away. She gasped. The door slammed. The room was solid black. To this blackness Filomena said at last:

"Light no candles. Your father has come home."

The thudding, the insistent knocking and pounding shook the door at midnight.

Filomena opened the door.

The gravedigger almost screamed in her face. "There you are! Thief! Robber!"

Behind him stood Ricardo, looking very rumpled and very tired and very old. "Cousin, permit us, I am sorry. Our friend here—"

"I am the friend of no one," cried the gravedigger. "A lock has been broken and a body stolen. To know the identity of the body is to know the thief. I could only bring you here. Arrest her."

"One small moment, please." Ricardo took the man's hand from his arm and turned, bowing gravely to his cousin. "May we enter?"

"There, there!" The gravedigger leaped in, gazed wildly about and pointed to a far wall. "You see?"

But Ricardo would look only at this woman. Very gently he asked her, "Filomena?"

Filomena's face was the face of one who has gone through a long tunnel of night and has come to the other end at last, where lives a shadow of coming day. Her eyes were prepared. Her mouth knew what to do. All the terror was gone now. What remained was as light as the great length of autumn chaff she had carried down the hill with her good son. Nothing more could happen to her ever in her life; this you knew from how she held her body as she said, "We have no mummy here."

"I believe you, cousin, but"—Ricardo cleared his throat uneasily and raised his eyes—"what stands there against the wall?"

"To celebrate the festival of the day of the dead ones"— Filomena did not turn to look where he was looking—"I have taken paper and flour and wire and clay and made of it a life-size toy which looks like the mummies."

"Have you indeed done this?" asked Ricardo, impressed.

"No, no!" The gravedigger almost danced in exasperation.

"With your permission." Ricardo advanced to confront the figure which stood against the wall. He raised his flashlight. "So," he said. "And so."

Filomena looked only out the open door into the late moonlight. "The plan I have for this mummy which I have made with my own hands is good."

"What plan, what?" the gravedigger demanded, turning.

"We will have money to eat with. Would you deny my children this?"

But Ricardo was not listening. Near the far wall, he tilted his head this way and that and rubbed his chin, squinting at the tall shape which enwrapped its own shadow, which kept its own silence, leaning against the adobe.

"A toy," mused Ricardo. "The largest death toy I have ever seen. I have seen man-sized skeletons in windows, and man-sized coffins made of cardboard and filled with candy skulls, yes. But this! I stand in awe, Filomena."

"Awe?" said the gravedigger, his voice rising to a shriek. "This is no toy, this is—"

"Do you swear, Filomena?" said Ricardo, not looking at him. He reached out and tapped a few times on the rust-colored chest of the figure. It made the sound of a lonely drum. "Do you swear this is papier-mâché?"

"By the Virgin, I swear."

"Well, then." Ricardo shrugged, snorted, laughed. "It is simple. If you swear by the Virgin, what more need be said? No court action is necessary. Besides, it might take weeks or months to prove or disprove this is or is not a thing of flour paste and old newspapers colored with brown earth."

"Weeks, months, prove, disprove!" The gravedigger turned in a circle as if to challenge the sanity of the universe held tight and impossible in these four walls. "This 'toy' is my property, mine!"

"The 'toy,'" said Filomena serenely, gazing out at the hills, "if it is a toy, and made by me, must surely belong to me. And even," she went on, quietly communing with the new reserve of peace in her body, "even if it is not a toy, and it is indeed Juan Díaz come home, why, then, does not Juan Díaz belong first to God?"

"How can one argue that?" wondered Ricardo.

The gravedigger was willing to try. But before he had

stuttered forth a half-dozen words, Filomena said, "And after God, in God's eyes, and at God's altar and in God's church, on one of God's holiest days, did not Juan Díaz say that he would be mine throughout his days?"

"Throughout his days—ah, ha, there you are!" said the gravedigger. "But his days are over, and now he is mine!"

"So," said Filomena, "God's property first, and then Filomena Díaz' property, that is if this toy is not a toy and is Juan Díaz, and anyway, landlord of the dead, you evicted your tenant, you so much as said you did not want him, if you love him so dearly and want him, will you pay the new rent and tenant him again?"

But so smothered by rage was the landlord of silence that it gave Ricardo time to step in. "Grave keeper, I see many months and many lawyers, and many points, fine points, to argue this way and that, which include real estate, toy manufactories, God, Filomena, one Juan Díaz wherever he is, hungry children, the conscience of a digger of graves, and so much complication that death's business will suffer. Under the circumstances are you prepared for these long years in and out of court?"

"I am prepared—" said the gravedigger, and paused.

"My good man," said Ricardo, "the other night you gave me some small bit of advice, which I now return to you. I do not tell you how to control your dead. You, now, do not say how I control the living. Your jurisdiction ends at the tombyard gate. Beyond stand my citizens, silent or otherwise. So . . ."

Ricardo thumped the upright figure a last time on its hollow chest. It gave forth the sound of a beating heart, a single strong and vibrant thump which made the gravedigger jerk.

"I pronounce this officially fake, a toy, no mummy at all. We waste time here. Come along, citizen gravedigger. Back to your proper land! Good night, Filomena's children, Filomena, good cousin."

"What about *it*, what about *him?*" said the gravedigger, motionless, pointing.

"Why do you worry?" asked Ricardo. "It goes nowhere. It stays, if you should wish to pursue the law. Do you see it running? You do not. Good night. Good night."

The door slammed. They were gone before Filomena could put out her hand to thank anyone.

She moved in the dark to place a candle at the foot of the tall corn-husk-dry silence. This was a shrine now, she thought, yes. She lit the candle.

"Do not fear, children," she murmured. "To sleep now. To sleep." And Filepe lay down and the others lay back, and at last Filomena herself lay with a single thin blanket over her on the woven mat by the light of the single candle, and her thoughts before she moved into sleep were long thoughts of the many days that made up tomorrow. In the morning, she thought, the tourist cars will sound on the road, and Filepe will move among them, telling them of this place. And there will be a painted sign outside this door: MUSEUM—30 CENTAVOS. And the tourists will come in, because the graveyard is on the hill, but we are first, we are here in the valley, and close at hand and easy to find. And one day soon with these tourists' money we shall mend the roof, and buy great sacks of fresh corn flour, and some tangerines, yes, for the children. And perhaps one day we will all travel to Mexico City, to the very big schools because of what has happened on this night.

For Juan Díaz is truly home, she thought. He is here, he waits for those who would come to see him. And at his feet I will place a bowl into which the tourists will place more money that Juan Díaz himself tried so hard to earn in all his life.

Juan. She raised her eyes. The breathing of the children was hearth-warm about her. Juan, do you see? Do you know? Do you truly understand? Do you forgive, Juan, do you forgive?

The candle flame flickered.

She closed her eyes. Behind her lids she saw the smile of Juan Díaz, and whether it was the smile that death had carved upon his lips, or whether it was a new smile she had given him or imagined for him, she could not say. Enough that she felt him standing tall and alone and on guard, watching over them and proud through the rest of the night.

A dog barked far away in a nameless town.

Only the gravedigger, wide awake in his tombyard, heard.

TO THE CHICAGO ABYSS

Under a pale April sky in a faint wind that blew out of a memory of winter, the old man shuffled into the almost empty park at noon. His slow feet were bandaged with nicotine-stained swathes, his hair was wild, long and gray as was his beard which enclosed a mouth which seemed always atremble with revelation.

Now he gazed back as if he had lost so many things he could not begin to guess there in the tumbled ruin, the tooth-less skyline of the city. Finding nothing, he shuffled on until he found a bench where sat a woman alone. Examining her, he nodded and sat to the far end of the bench and did not look at her again.

He remained, eyes shut, mouth working, for three min-utes, head moving as if his nose were printing a single word on the air. Once it was written, he opened his mouth to pronounce it in a clear, fine voice:

"Coffee."

The woman gasped and stiffened.

The old man's gnarled fingers tumbled in pantomime on his unseen lap.

"Twist the key! Bright-red, yellow-letter can! Compressed air. Hisss! Vacuum pack. Ssst! Like a snake!"

The woman snapped her head about as if slapped, to stare in dreadful fascination at the old man's moving tongue.

"The scent, the odor, the smell. Rich, dark, wondrous Brazilian beans, fresh-ground!"

Leaping up, reeling as if gun-shot, the woman tottered.

The old man flicked his eyes wide. "No! I—"

But she was running, gone.

The old man sighed and walked on through the park until he reached a bench where sat a young man completely in-volved with wrapping dried grass in a small square of thin tissue paper. His thin fingers shaped the grass tenderly, in an almost holy ritual, trembling as he rolled the tube, put it to his mouth and, hypnotically, lit it. He leaned back, squinting deliciously, communing with the strange rank air in his mouth and lungs.

The old man watched the smoke blow away on the noon wind and said, "Chesterfields."

The young man gripped his knees tight.

"Raleighs," said the old man. "Lucky Strikes."

The young man stared at him.

"Kent. Kool. Marlboro," said the old man, not looking at him. "Those were the names. White, red, amber packs, grass green, sky blue, pure gold, with the red slick small ribbon that ran around the top that you pulled to zip away the crinkly cellophane, and the blue government tax stamp—"

"Shut up," said the young man.

"Buy them in drugstores, fountains, subways—"

"Shut up!"

"Gently," said the old man. "It's just, that smoke of yours made me think—"

"Don't think!" The young man jerked so violently his homemade cigarette fell in chaff to his lap. "Now look what you made me do!"

"I'm sorry. It was such a nice friendly day."

"I'm no friend!"

"We're all friends now, or why live?"

"Friends!" the young man snorted, aimlessly plucking at the shredded grass and paper. "Maybe there were 'friends' back in 1970, but now . . ."

"1970. You must have been a baby then. They still had Butterfingers then in bright-yellow wrappers. Baby Ruths. Clark Bars in orange paper. Milky Ways—swallow a universe of stars, comets, meteors. Nice."

"It was never nice." The young man stood suddenly. "What's wrong with you?"

"I remember limes, and lemons, that's what's wrong with me. Do you remember oranges?"

"Damn right. Oranges, hell. You calling me a liar? You want me to feel bad? You nuts? Don't you know the law? You know I could turn you in, you?"

"I know, I know," said the old man, shrugging. "The weather fooled me. It made me want to compare—"

"Compare rumors, that's what they'd say, the police, the

special cops, they'd say it, rumors, you trouble making bastard, you."

He seized the old man's lapels, which ripped so he had to grab another handful, yelling down into his face. "Why don't I just blast the living Jesus out of you? I ain't hurt no one in so long, I . . ."

He shoved the old man. Which gave him the idea to pummel, and when he pummeled he began to punch, and punching made it easy to strike, and soon he rained blows upon the old man, who stood like one caught in thunder and down-poured storm, using only his fingers to ward off blows that fleshed his cheeks, shoulders, his brow, his chin, as the young man shrieked cigarettes, moaned candies, yelled smokes, cried sweets until the old man fell to be kick-rolled and shivering. The young man stopped and began to cry. At the sound, the old man, cuddled, clenched into his pain, took his fingers away from his broken mouth and opened his eyes to gaze with astonishment at his assailant. The young man wept.

"Please . . ." begged the old man.

The young man wept louder, tears falling from his eyes.

"Don't cry," said the old man. "We won't be hungry forever. We'll rebuild the cities. Listen, I didn't mean for you to cry, only to think, Where are we going, what are we doing, what've we done? You weren't hitting me. You meant to hit something else, but I was handy. Look, I'm sitting up. I'm okay."

The young man stopped crying and blinked down at the old man, who forced a bloody smile.

"You . . . you can't go around," said the young man, "making people unhappy. I'll find someone to fix you!"

"Wait!" The old man struggled to his knees. "No!"

But the young man ran wildly off out of the park, yelling.

Crouched alone, the old man felt his bones, found one of his teeth lying red amongst the strewn gravel, handled it sadly.

"Fool," said a voice.

The old man glanced over and up.

A lean man of some forty years stood leaning against a tree nearby, a look of pale weariness and curiosity on his long face.

"Fool," he said again.

The old man gasped. "You were there, all the time, and did *nothing?*"

"What, fight one fool to save another? No." The stranger helped him up and brushed him off. "I do my fighting where it pays. Come on. You're going home with me."

The old man gasped again. "Why?"

"That boy'll be back with the police any second. I don't want you stolen away, you're a very precious commodity. I've heard of you, looked for you for days now. Good grief, and when I find you you're up to your famous tricks. What did you say to the boy made him mad?"

"I said about oranges and lemons, candy, cigarettes. I was just getting ready to recollect in detail wind-up toys, briar pipes and back scratchers, when he dropped the sky on me."

"I almost don't blame him. Half of me wants to hit you itself. Come on, double time. There's a siren, quick!"

And they went swiftly, another way, out of the park.

He drank the homemade wine because it was easiest. The food must wait until his hunger overcame the pain in his broken mouth. He sipped, nodding.

"Good, many thanks, good."

The stranger who had walked him swiftly out of the park sat across from him at the flimsy dining-room table as the stranger's wife placed broken and mended plates on the worn cloth.

"The beating," said the husband at last. "How did it happen!"

At this the wife almost dropped a plate.

"Relax," said the husband. "No one followed us. Go ahead, old man, tell us, why do you behave like a saint panting after martyrdom? You're famous, you know. Everyone's heard about you. Many would like to meet you. Myself, first, I want to know what makes you tick. Well?"

But the old man was only entranced with the vegetables on the chipped plate before him. Twenty-six, no, twenty-eight peas! He counted the impossible sum! He bent to the incredible vegetables like a man praying over his quietest beads. Twenty-eight glorious green peas, plus a few graphs of half-raw spaghetti announcing that today business was fair. But under the line of *pasta*, the cracked line of the plate showed where business for years now was more than terrible. The old man hovered counting above the food like a great and inexplicable buzzard crazily fallen and roosting in this cold apartment, watched by his Samaritan hosts until at last he said, "These twenty-eight peas remind me of a film I saw as a child. A comedian—do you know the word?—a funny man met a lunatic in a midnight house in this film and . . ."

The husband and wife laughed quietly.

"No, that's not the joke yet, sorry," the old man apologized. "The lunatic sat the comedian down to an empty table, no knives, no forks, no food. 'Dinner is served!' he cried. Afraid of murder, the comedian fell in with the make-believe. 'Great!' he cried, pretending to chew steak, vegetables, dessert. He bit nothings. 'Fine!' he swallowed air. 'Wonderful!' Eh . . . you may laugh now."

But the husband and wife, grown still, only looked at their sparsely strewn plates.

The old man shook his head and went on. "The comedian, thinking to impress the madman, exclaimed, 'And these spiced brandy peaches! Superb!' 'Peaches?' screamed the madman, drawing a gun. 'I served no peaches! You must be insane!' And shot the comedian in the behind!"

The old man, in the silence which ensued, picked up the first pea and weighed its lovely bulk upon his bent tin fork. He was about to put it in his mouth when—

There was a sharp rap on the door.

"Special police!" a voice cried.

Silent but trembling, the wife hid the extra plate.

The husband rose calmly to lead the old man to a wall where a panel hissed open, and he stepped in and the panel hissed shut and he stood in darkness hidden away as, beyond, unseen, the apartment door opened. Voices murmured excitedly. The old man could imagine the special police-man in his midnight-blue uniform, with drawn gun, entering to see only the flimsy furniture, the bare walls, the echoing linoleum floor, the glassless, cardboarded-over windows, this thin and oily film of civilization left on an empty shore when the storm tide of war went away.

"I'm looking for an old man," said the tired voice of authority beyond the wall. Strange, thought the old man, even the law sounds tired now. "Patched clothes . . ." But, thought the old man, I thought everyone's clothes were patched! "Dirty. About eighty years old . . ." But isn't every-one dirty, everyone old? the old man cried out to himself.

"If you turn him in, there's a week's rations as reward," said the police voice. "Plus ten cans of vegetables, five cans of soup, bonus."

Real tin cans with bright printed labels, thought the old man. The cans flashed like meteors rushing by in the dark over his eyelids. What a fine reward! Not ten thousand dollars, not twenty thousand dollars, no no, but five incredible cans of real, not imitation soup, and ten, count them, ten brilliant circus-colored cans of exotic vegetables like string beans and sun-yellow corn! Think of it. Think!

There was a long silence in which the old man almost thought he heard faint murmurs of stomachs turning uneasily, slumbering but dreaming of dinners much finer than the hairballs of old illusion gone nightmare and politics gone sour in the long twilight since A. D., Annihilation Day.

"Soup. Vegetables," said the police voice, a final time. "Fifteen solid-pack cans!"

The door slammed.

The boots stomped away through the ramshackle tenement, pounding coffin-lid doors to stir other Lazarus souls alive to cry aloud of bright tins and real soups. The poundings faded. There was a last banging slam.

And at last the hidden panel whispered up. The husband and wife did not look at him as he stepped out. He knew why and wanted to touch their elbows.

"Even I," he said gently, "even I was tempted to turn myself in, to claim the reward, to eat the soup."

Still they would not look at him.

"Why?" he asked. "Why didn't you hand me over? Why?"

The husband, as if suddenly remembering, nodded to his wife. She went to the door, hesitated, her husband nodded again impatiently, and she went out, noiseless as a puff of cobweb. They heard her rustling along the hall, scratching softly at doors, which opened to gasps and murmurs.

"What's she up to? What are *you* up to?" asked the old man.

"You'll find out. Sit. Finish your dinner," said the husband. "Tell me why you're such a fool you make us fools who seek you out and bring you here."

"Why am I such a fool?" The old man sat. The old man munched slowly, taking peas one at a time from the plate which had been returned to him. "Yes, I am a fool. How did I start my foolishness? Years ago I looked at the ruined world, the dictatorships, the desiccated states and nations, and said, 'What can I do? Me, a weak old man, what? Rebuild a devastation? Ha!' But as I lay half asleep one night an old phonograph record played in my head. Two sisters named Duncan sang out of my childhood a song called 'Remembering.' 'Remembering is all I do, dear, so try and remember, too.' I sang the song, and it wasn't a song but a way of life. What did I have to offer a world that was forgetting? My memory! How could this help? By offering a standard of comparison. By telling the young *what once was*, by considering our losses. I found the more I remembered, the more I *could* remember! Depending on who I sat down with I remembered imitation flowers, dial telephones, refrigerators, kazoos (you ever play a kazoo?!), thimbles, bicycle clips, not bicycles, no, but bicycle *clips!* isn't that wild and strange? Antimacassars. Do you know them? Never mind. Once a man asked me to remember just the dashboard dials on a Cadillac. I remembered. I told him in detail. He listened. He cried great tears down his face. Happy tears or sad? I can't say. I only remember. Not litera-ture, no, I never had a head for plays or poems, they slip away, they die. All I am, really, is a trash heap of the mediocre, the third-best-hand-me-down useless and chromed-over slush and junk of a race-track civilization that ran last over a precipice. So all I offer really is scintillant junk, the clamored-after chronometers and absurd machineries of a never-ending river of robots and robot-mad owners. Yet, one way or another, civilization must get back on the road. Those who can offer fine butterfly poetry, let them remember, let them offer. Those who can weave and build butterfly nets, let them weave, let them build. My gift is smaller than both, and perhaps contemptible in the long hoist, climb, jump toward the old and amiably silly peak. But I *must* dream myself worthy. For the things, silly or not, that peo-ple remember are the things they will search for again. I will, then, ulcerate their half-dead desires with vinegar-gnat memory. Then perhaps they'll rattle-bang the Big Clock together again, which is the city, the state and then the world. Let one man want wine, another lounge chairs, a third a batwing glider to soar the March winds on and build bigger electropterodactyls to scour even greater winds, with even greater peoples. Someone wants moron Christmas trees and some wise man goes to cut them. Pack this all together, wheel in want, want in wheel, and I'm just there to oil them, but oil them I do. Ho, once I would have raved, 'Only the best is best, only quality is true!' But roses grow from blood manure. Mediocre must be, so most-excellent can bloom. So I shall be the *best* mediocre there is and fight all who say, Slide under, sink back, dust-wallow, let brambles scurry over your living grave. I shall protest the roving apeman tribes, the sheep-people munching the far fields prayed on by the feudal land-baron wolves who rarefy themselves in the few skyscraper summits and horde un-remembered foods. And these villains I will kill with can opener and corkscrew. I shall run them down with ghosts of Buick, Kissel-Kar and Moon, thrash them with licorice whips until they cry for some sort of unqualified mercy. Can I *do* all this? One can only try."

The old man rummaged the last pea, with the last words, in his mouth, while his Samaritan host simply looked at him with gently amazed eyes, and far off up through the house people moved, doors tapped open and shut, and there was a gathering outside the door of this apartment where now the husband said, "And *you* asked why we didn't turn you in? Do you hear that out there?"

"It sounds like everyone in the apartment house."

"Everyone. Old man, old fool, do you remember . . . motion picture houses, or, better, drive-in movies?"

The old man smiled. "Do *you?*"

"Almost. Look, listen, today, now, if you're going to be a fool, if you want to run risks, do it in the aggregate, in one fell blow. Why waste your breath on one, or two, or even three, if . . ."

The husband opened the door and nodded outside. Silently, one at a time and in couples, the people of the house entered. Entered this room as if entering a synagogue or church or the kind of church known as a movie or the kind of movie known as a drive-in and the hour was growing late in the day, with the sun going down the sky, and soon in the early evening hours, in the dark, the room would be dim and in the one light the voice of the old man would speak and these would listen and hold hands and it would be like the old days with the balconies and the dark, or the cars and the dark, and just the memory, the words, of popcorn, and the words for the gum and the sweet drinks and candy, but the words, anyway, the words . . .

And while the people were coming in and settling on the floor, and the old man watched them, incredulous that he had summoned them here without knowing, the husband said, "Isn't this better than taking a chance in the open?"

"Yes. Strange. I hate pain. I hate being hit and chased. But my tongue moves. I must hear what it has to say. Still this is better."

"Good." The husband pressed a red ticket into his palm. "When this is all over, an hour from now, here is a ticket from a friend of mine in Transportation. One train crosses the country each week. Each week I get a ticket for some idiot I want to help. This week it's you."

The old man read the destination on the folded red paper: " 'Chicago Abyss,' " and added, "Is the Abyss still there?"

"This time next year Lake Michigan may break through the last crust and make a new lake in the pit where the city once was. There's life of sorts around the crater rim, and a branch train goes west once a month. Once you leave here, keep moving, forget you met or know us. I'll give you a small list of people like ourselves. A long time from now, look them up, out in the wilderness. But, for God's sake, in the open, alone for a year, declare a moratorium. Keep your wonderful mouth shut. And here—" The husband gave him a yellow card. "A dentist I know. Tell him to make you a new set of teeth that will only open at mealtimes."

A few people, hearing, laughed, and the old man laughed quietly and the people were in now, dozens of them, and the day was late, and the husband and wife shut the door and stood by it and turned and waited for this last special time when the old man might open his mouth.

The old man stood up.

His audience grew very still.

The train came, rusty and loud at midnight, into a suddenly snow-filled station. Under a cruel dusting of white, the ill-washed people crowded into and through the ancient chair cars, mashing the old man along the corridor and into an empty compartment that had once been a lavatory. Soon the floor was a solid mass of bed roll on which sixteen people twisted and turned in darkness, fighting their way into sleep.

The train rushed forth to white emptiness.

The old man, thinking, Quiet, shut up, no, don't speak, nothing, no, stay still, think, careful, cease! found himself now swayed, joggled, hurled this way and that as he half crouched against a wall. He and just one other were upright in this monster room of dreadful sleep. A few feet away, similarly shoved against the wall, sat an eight-year-old boy with a drawn sick paleness escaping from his cheeks. Full awake, eyes bright, he seemed to watch, he *did* watch, the old man's mouth. The boy gazed because he must. The train hooted, roared, swayed, yelled and ran.

Half an hour passed in a thunderous grinding passage by night under the snow-hidden moon, and the old man's mouth was tight-nailed shut. Another hour, and still boned shut. Another hour, and the muscles around his cheeks began to slacken. Another, and his lips parted to wet themselves. The boy stayed awake. The boy saw. The boy waited. Immense sifts of silence came down the night air outside, tunneled by avalanche train. The travelers, very deep in invoiced terror, numbed by flight, slept each separate, but the boy did not take his eyes away and at last the old man leaned forward, softly.

"Sh. Boy. Your name?"

"Joseph."

The train swayed and groaned in its sleep, a monster floundering through timeless dark toward a morn that could not be imagined.

"Joseph . . ." The old man savored the word, bent forward, his eyes gentle and shining. His face filled with pale beauty. His eyes widened until they seemed blind. He gazed at a distant and hidden thing. He cleared his throat ever so softly. "Ah . . ."

The train roared round a curve. The people rocked in their snowing sleep.

"Well, Joseph," whispered the old man. He lifted his fingers softly in the air. "Once upon a time . . ."

THE ANTHEM SPRINTERS

"There's no doubt of it, Doone's the best."

"Devil take Doone!"

"His reflex is uncanny, his lope on the incline extraordinary, he's off and gone before you reach for your hat."

"Hoolihan's better, any day!"

"Day, hell. Why not *now?*"

I was at the far end of the bar at the top of Grafton Street listening to the tenors singing, the concertinas dying hard, and the arguments prowling the smoke, looking for opposition. The pub was the Four Provinces and it was getting on late at night, for Dublin. So there was the sure threat of everything shutting at once, meaning spigots, accordions, piano lids, soloists, trios, quartets, pubs, sweet shops and cinemas. In a great heave like the Day of Judgment, half Dublin's population would be thrown out into raw lamplight, there to find themselves wanting in gum-machine mirrors. Stunned, their moral and physical sustenance plucked from them, the souls would wander like battered moths for a moment, then wheel about for home.

But now here I was listening to a discussion the heat of which, if not the light, reached me at fifty paces.

"Doone!"

"Hoolihan!"

Then the smallest man at the far end of the bar, turning, saw the curiosity enshrined in my all too open face and shouted, "You're American, of course! And wondering what we're up to? Do you trust my looks? Would you bet as I told you on a sporting event of great local consequence? If 'Yes' is your answer, come here!"

So I strolled my Guinness the length of the Four Provinces to join the shouting men, as one violinist gave up destroying a tune and the pianist hurried over, bringing his chorus with him.

"Name's Timulty!" The little man took my hand.

"Douglas," I said. "I write for the cinema."

"Fillums!" cried everyone.

"Films," I admitted modestly.

"What luck! Beyond belief!" Timulty seized me tighter. "You'll be the best judge ever, as well as bet! Are you much for sports? Do you know, for instance, the cross-country, the four-forty, and such man-on-foot excursions?"

"I've witnessed two Olympic Games."

"Not just fillums, but the world competition!" Timulty gasped. "You're the rare one. Well, now what do you know of the special all-Irish decathlon event which has to do with picture theaters?"

"What event is that?"

"What indeed! Hoolihan!"

An even littler fellow, pocketing his harmonica, leaped forward, smiling. "Hoolihan, that's me. The best Anthem Sprinter in all Ireland!"

"*What* sprinter?" I asked.

"A-n-t-," spelled Hoolihan, much too carefully, "-h-e-m. Anthem. Sprinter. The fastest."

"Since you been in Dublin," Timulty cut in, "have you attended the cinema?"

"Last night," I said, "I saw a Clark Gable film. Night before, an old Charles Laughton—"

"Enough! You're a fanatic, as are all the Irish. If it weren't for cinemas and pubs to keep the poor and workless off the street or in their cups, we'd have pulled the cork and let the isle sink long ago. Well." He clapped his hands. "When the picture ends each night, have you observed a peculiarity of the breed?"

"End of the picture?" I mused. "Hold on! You can't mean the national anthem, can you?"

"*Can* we, boys?" cried Timulty.

"We can!" cried all.

"Any night, every night, for tens of dreadful years, at the end of each damn fillum, as if you'd never heard the baleful tune before," grieved Timulty, "the orchestra strikes up for Ireland. And what happens *then?*"

"Why," said I, falling in with it, "if you're any man at all, you try to get out of the theater in those few precious moments between the end of the film and the start of the anthem."

"You've nailed it!"

"Buy the Yank a drink!"

"After all," I said casually, "I'm in Dublin four months now. The anthem has begun to pale. No disrespect meant," I added hastily.

"And none taken!" said Timulty. "Or given by any of us patriotic I.R.A. veterans, survivors of the Troubles and lovers of country. Still, breathing the same air ten thousand times makes the senses reel. So, as you've noted, in that God-sent three- or four-second interval any audience in its right mind beats it the hell out. And the best of the crowd is—"

"Doone," I said. "Or Hoolihan. Your Anthem Sprinters!"

They smiled at me. I smiled at them.

We were all so proud of my intuition that I bought them a round of Guinness.

Licking the suds from our lips, we regarded each other with benevolence.

"Now," said Timulty, his voice husky with emotion, his eyes squinted off at the scene, "at this very moment, not one hundred yards down the slight hill, in the comfortable dark of the Grafton Street Theatre, seated on the aisle of the fourth row center is—"

"Doone," said I.

"The man's eerie," said Hoolihan, lifting his cap to me.

"Well—" Timulty swallowed his disbelief—"Doone's there all right. He's not seen the fillum before, it's a Deanna Durbin brought back by the asking, and the time is now . . ."

Everyone glanced at the wall clock.

"Ten o'clock!" said the crowd.

"And in just fifteen minutes the cinema will be letting the customers out for good and all."

"And?" I asked.

"And," said Timulty. "And! If we should send Hoolihan here in for a test of speed and agility, Doone would be ready to meet the challenge."

"He didn't go to the show just for an Anthem Sprint, did he?"

"Good grief, no. He went for the Deanna Durbin songs and all. Doone plays the piano here, for sustenance. But if he should casually note the entrance of Hoolihan here, who would make himself conspicuous by his late arrival just across from Doone, well, Doone would know what was up.

They would salute each other and both sit listening to the dear music until FINIS hove in sight."

"Sure." Hoolihan danced lightly on his toes, flexing his elbows. "Let me at him, let me *at* him!"

Timulty peered close at me. "Mr. Douglas, I observe your disbelief. The details of the sport have bewildered you. How is it, you ask, that full-grown men have time for such as this? Well, time is the one thing the Irish have plenty of lying about. With no jobs at hand, what's minor in your country must be made to look major in ours. We have never seen the elephant, but we've learned a bug under a microscope is the greatest beast on earth. So while it hasn't passed the border, the Anthem Sprint's a high-blooded sport once you're in it. Let me nail down the rules!"

"First," said Hoolihan reasonably, "knowing what he knows now, find out if the man wants to bet."

Everyone looked at me to see if their reasoning had been wasted.

"Yes," I said.

All agreed I was better than a human being.

"Introductions are in order," said Timulty. "Here's Fogarty, exit-watcher supreme. Nolan and Clannery, aisle-superintendent judges. Clancy, timekeeper. And general spectators O'Neill, Bannion and the Kelly boys, count 'em! Come on!"

I felt as if a vast street-cleaning machine, one of those brambled monsters all mustache and scouring brush, had seized me. The amiable mob floated me down the hill toward the multiplicity of little blinking lights where the cinema lured us on. Hustling, Timulty shouted the essentials:

"Much depends on the character of the theater, of course!"

"Of course!" I yelled back.

"There be the liberal free thinking theaters with grand aisles, grand exits and even grander, more spacious latrines. Some with so much porcelain, the echoes alone put you in shock. Then there's the parsimonious mousetrap cinemas with aisles that squeeze the breath from you, seats that knock your knees, and doors best sidled out of on your way to the men's lounge in the sweet shop across the alley. Each theater is carefully assessed, before, during and after a sprint, the facts set down. A man is judged then, and his time reckoned good or inglorious, by whether he had to fight his way through men and women *en masse*, or mostly men, mostly women, or, the worst, children at the flypaper matinees. The temptation with children, of course, is lay into them as you'd harvest hay, tossing them in windrows to left and right, so we've stopped that. Now mostly it's nights here at the Grafton!"

The mob stopped. The twinkling theater lights sparkled in our eyes and flushed our cheeks.

"The ideal cinema," said Fogarty.

"Why?" I asked.

"Its aisles," said Clannery, "are neither too wide nor too narrow, its exits well placed, the door hinges oiled, the crowds a proper mixture of sporting bloods and folks who mind enough to leap aside should a Sprinter, squandering his energy, come dashing up the aisle."

I had a sudden thought. "Do you—handicap your runners?"

"We do! Sometimes by shifting exits when the old are known too well. Or we put a summer coat on one, a winter coat on another. Or seat one chap in the sixth row, while the other takes the third. And if a man turns terrible feverish swift, we add the greatest known burden of all—"

"Drink?" I said.

"What else? Now, Doone, being fleet, is a two-handicap man. Nolan!" Timulty held forth a flask. "Run this in. Make Doone take two swigs, big ones."

Nolan ran.

Timulty pointed. "While Hoolihan here, having already gone through all Four Provinces of the pub this night, is amply weighted. Even all!"

"Go now, Hoolihan," said Fogarty. "Let our money be a light burden on you. We'll see you bursting out that exit five minutes from now, victorious and first!"

"Let's synchronize watches!" said Clancy.

"Synchronize my back-behind," said Timulty. "Which of us has more than dirty wrists to stare at? It's you alone, Clancy, has the time. Hoolihan, inside!"

Hoolihan shook hands with us all, as if leaving for a trip around the world. Then, waving, he vanished into the cinema darkness.

At which moment, Nolan burst back out, holding high the half-empty flask. "Doone's handicapped!"

"Fine! Clannery, go check the contestants, be sure they sit opposite each other in the fourth row, as agreed, caps on, coats half buttoned, scarves properly furled. Report back to me."

Clannery ran into the dark.

"The usher, the ticket taker?" I said.

"Are inside, watching the fillum," said Timulty. "So much standing is hard on the feet. They won't interfere."

"It's ten-thirteen," announced Clancy. "In two more minutes—"

"Post time," I said.

"You're a dear lad," admitted Timulty.

Clannery came hot-footing out.

"All set! In the right seats and everything!"

"'Tis almost over! You can tell—toward the end of any fillum the music has a way of getting out of hand."

"It's loud, all right," agreed Clannery. "Full orchestra and chorus behind the singing maid now. I must come tomorrow for the entirety. Lovely."

"Is it?" said Clancy, and the others.

"What's the tune?"

"Ah, off with the tune!" said Timulty. "One minute to go and you ask the tune! Lay the bets. Who's for Doone? Who Hoolihan?" There was a multitudinous jabbering and passing back and forth of money, mostly shillings.

I held out four shillings.

"Doone," I said.

"Without having seen him?"

"A dark horse," I whispered.

"Well said!" Timulty spun about. "Clannery, Nolan, inside, as aisle judges! Watch sharp there's no jumping the FINIS."

In went Clannery and Nolan, happy as boys.

"Make an aisle, now. Mr. Douglas, you over here with me!"

The men rushed to form an aisle on each side of the two closed main entrance-exit doors.

"Fogarty, lay your ear to the door!"

This Fogarty did. His eyes widened.

"The damn music is extra loud!"

One of the Kelly boys nudged his brother. "It will be over soon. Whoever is to die is dying this moment. Whoever is to live is bending over him."

"Louder still!" announced Fogarty, head up against the door panel, hands twitching as if he were adjusting a radio.

"There! That's the grand *ta-ta* for sure that comes just as FINIS or THE END jumps on the screen."

"They're off!" I murmured.

"Stand!" said Timulty.

We all stared at the door.

"There's the anthem!"

" 'Tenshun!"

We all stood erect. Someone saluted.

But still we stared at the door.

"I hear feet running," said Fogarty.

"Whoever it is had a good start before the anthem—"

The door burst wide.

Hoolihan plunged to view, smiling such a smile as only breathless victors know.

"Hoolihan!" cried the winners.

"Doone!" cried the losers. "Where's Doone?"

For, while Hoolihan was first, a competitor was lacking. The crowd was dispersing into the street now.

"The idiot didn't come out the wrong door?"

We waited. The crowd was soon gone.

Timulty ventured first into the empty lobby.

"Doone?"

No one there.

"Could it be he's in *there?*"

Someone flung the men's room door wide. "Doone?"

No echo, no answer.

"Good grief," cried Timulty, "it can't be he's broken a leg and lies on the slope somewhere with the mortal agonies?"

"That's it!"

The island of men, heaving one way, changed gravities and heaved the other, toward the inner door, through it, and down the aisle, myself following.

"Doone!"

Clannery and Nolan were there to meet us and pointed silently down. I jumped into the air twice to see over the mob's head. It was dim in the vast theater. I saw nothing.

"Doone!"

Then at last we were bunched together near the fourth row on the aisle. I heard their boggled exclamations as they saw what I saw:

Doone, still seated in the fourth row on the aisle, his hands folded, his eyes shut.

Dead?

None of that.

A tear, large, luminous and beautiful, fell on his cheek. Another tear, larger and more lustrous, emerged from his other eye. His chin was wet. It was certain he had been crying for some minutes.

The men peered into his face, circling, leaning.

"Doone, are ya sick?"

"Is it fearful news?"

"Ah, God," cried Doone. He shook himself to find the strength, somehow, to speak.

"Ah, God," he said at last, "she has the voice of an angel."

"Angel?"

"That one up there." He nodded.

They turned to stare at the empty silver screen.

"Is it Deanna Durbin?"

Doone sobbed. "The dear dead voice of my grandmother come back—"

"Your grandma's behind!" exclaimed Timulty. "She had no such voice as that!"

"And who's to know, save me?" Doone blew his nose, dabbed at his eyes.

"You mean to say it was just the Durbin lass kept you from the sprint?"

"Just!" said Doone. "Just! Why, it would be sacrilege to bound from a cinema after a recital like that. You might also then jump full tilt across the altar during a wedding, or waltz about at a funeral."

"You could've at least warned us it was no contest." Timulty glared.

"How could I? It just crept over me in a divine sickness. That last bit she sang, 'The Lovely Isle of Innisfree,' was it not, Clannery?"

"What else did she sing?" asked Fogarty.

"What else did she sing?" cried Timulty. "He's just lost half of us our day's wages and you ask what else she sang! Get off!"

"Sure, it's money runs the world," Doone agreed, seated there, closing up his eyes. "But it is music that holds down the friction."

"What's going on there?" cried someone above.

A man leaned down from the balcony, puffing a cigarette. "What's all the rouse?"

"It's the projectionist," whispered Timulty. Aloud: "Hello, Phil, darling! It's only the Team! We've a bit of a problem here, Phil, in ethics, not to say aesthetics. Now, we wonder if, well, could it be possible to run the anthem over."

"Run it over?"

There was a rumble from the winners, a mixing and shoving of elbows.

"A lovely idea," said Doone.

"It is," said Timulty, all guile. "An act of God incapacitated Doone."

"A tenth-run flicker from the year 1937 caught him by the short hairs is all," said Fogarty.

"So the fair thing is—" here Timulty, unperturbed, looked to heaven— "Phil, dear boy, also is the last reel of the Deanna Durbin fillum still there?"

"It ain't in the ladies' room," said Phil, smoking steadily.

"What a wit the boy has. Now, Phil, do you think you could just thread it back through the machine there and give us the FINIS again?"

"Is that what you all want?" asked Phil.

There was a hard moment of indecision. But the thought of another contest was too good to be passed, even though already-won money was at stake. Slowly everyone nodded.

"I'll bet myself, then," Phil called down. "A shilling on Hoolihan!"

The winners laughed and hooted; they looked to win again. Hoolihan waved graciously. The losers turned on their man.

"Do you hear the insult, Doone? Stay awake, man!"

"When the girl sings, damn it, go deaf!"

"Places, everyone!" Timulty jostled about.

"There's no audience," said Hoolihan. "And without them there's no obstacles, no real contest."

"Why,"—Fogarty blinked around—"let's all of us be the audience."

"Fine!" Beaming, everyone threw himself into a seat.

"Better yet," announced Timulty, up front, "Why not make it teams? Doone and Hoolihan, sure, but for every Doone man or Hoolihan man that makes it out before the anthem freezes him on his hobnails, an extra point, right?"

"Done!" cried everyone.

"Pardon," I said. "There's no one outside to judge."

Everyone turned to look at me.

"Ah," said Timulty. "Well. Nolan, outside!"

Nolan trudged up the aisle, cursing.

Phil stuck his head from the projection booth above.

"Are ya clods down there ready?"

"If the girl is and the anthem is!"

And the lights went out.

I found myself seated next in from Doone, who whispered fervently, "Poke me, lad, keep me alert to practicalities instead of ornamentation, eh?"

"Shut up!" said someone. "There's the mystery."

And there indeed it was, the mystery of song and art and life, if you will, the young girl singing on the time-haunted screen.

"We lean on you, Doone," I whispered.

"Eh?" he replied. He smiled ahead. "Ah, look, ain't she lovely? Do you hear?"

"The bet, Doone," I said. "Get ready."

"All right," he groused. "Let me stir my bones. Jesus save me."

"What?"

"I never thought to test. My right leg. Feel. Naw, you can't. It's dead it is!"

"Asleep, you mean?" I said, appalled.

"Dead or asleep, hell, I'm sunk! Lad, lad, you must run for me! Here's my cap and scarf!"

"Your cap—?"

"When victory is yours, show them, and we'll explain you ran to replace this fool leg of mine!"

He clapped the cap on, tied the scarf.

"But look here—" I protested.

"You'll do brave! Just remember, it's FINIS and no sooner! The song's almost up. Are you tensed?"

"God, am I!" I said.

"It's blind passions that win, boy. Plunge straight. If you step on someone, do not look back. There!" Doone held his legs to one side to give clearance. "The song's done. He's kissing her—"

"The FINIS!" I cried.

I leaped into the aisle.

I ran up the slope. I'm first! I thought. I'm ahead! It can't be! There's the door!

I hit the door as the anthem began.

I slammed into the lobby—safe!

I won! I thought, incredulous, with Doone's cap and scarf like victory laurels upon and about me. Won! Won for the Team!

Who's second, third, fourth?

I turned to the door as it swung shut.

Only then did I hear the shouts and yells inside.

Good Lord! I thought, six men have tried the wrong exit at once, someone tripped, fell, someone else piled on. Otherwise, why am I the first and only? There's a fierce silent combat in there this second, the two teams locked in mortal wrestling attitudes, asprawl, akimbo, above and below the seats, that *must* be it!

I've won! I wanted to yell, to break it up.

I threw the doors wide.

I stared into an abyss where nothing stirred.

Nolan came to peer over my shoulder.

"That's the Irish for you," he said, nodding. "Even more than the race, it's the Muse they like."

For what were the voices yelling in the dark?

"Run it again! Over! That last song! Phil!"

"No one move. I'm in heaven. Doone, how right you were!"

Nolan passed me, going in to sit.

I stood for a long moment looking down along at all the rows where the teams of Anthem Sprinters sat, none having stirred, wiping their eyes.

"Phil, darling?" called Timulty, somewhere up front.

"It's done!" said Phil.

"And this time," added Timulty, "*without* the anthem."

Applause for this.

The dim lights flashed off. The screen glowed like a great warm hearth.

I looked back out at the bright sane world of Grafton Street, the Four Provinces pub, the hotels, shops and night-wandering folk. I hesitated.

Then, to the tune of "The Lovely Isle of Innisfree," I took off the cap and scarf, hid these laurels under a seat, and slowly, luxuriously, with all the time in the world, sat myself down. . . .

OUT OF THIS WORLD!

That's the only way to describe Bantam's great series of science fiction classics. These space-age thrillers are filled with terror, fancy and adventure and written by America's most renowned writers of science fiction. Welcome to outer space and have a good trip.

By Ray Bradbury

☐ DANDELION WINE		HP4197	60¢
☐ THE GOLDEN APPLES OF THE SUN		S4867	75¢
☐ THE ILLUSTRATED MAN		S4482	75¢
☐ THE MACHINERIES OF JOY		S5258	75¢
☐ THE MARTIAN CHRONICLES		S4843	75¢
☐ A MEDICINE FOR MELANCHOLY		S5268	75¢
☐ R IS FOR ROCKET		SP5748	75¢
☐ SOMETHING WICKED THIS WAY COMES		S3408	75¢
☐ TIMELESS STORIES FOR TODAY AND TOMORROW		S5372	75¢
☐ ALAS, BABYLON	Pat Frank	SP4841	75¢
☐ A CANTICLE FOR LIEBOWITZ	Walter Miller, Jr.	N5423	95¢
☐ THE TIME MACHINE	H. G. Wells	FP4063	50¢
☐ 20,000 LEAGUES UNDER THE SEA	Jules Verne	HP4448	60¢

By Rod Serling

☐ DEVILS AND DEMONS		H3324	60¢
☐ ROD SERLING'S TRIPLE W		H3493	60¢
☐ STORIES FROM THE TWILIGHT ZONE		HP4419	60¢
☐ MORE STORIES FROM THE TWILIGHT ZONE		HP4829	60¢
☐ NEW STORIES FROM THE TWILIGHT ZONE		HP5211	60¢
☐ STAR TREK	James Blish	H5629	60¢
☐ STAR TREK II	James Blish	H5529	60¢
☐ STAR TREK III	James Blish	H5761	60¢

Ask for them at your local bookseller or use this handy coupon:

Wait 'til you see what *else* we've got in store for you!

Send for your FREE catalog of Bantam Bestsellers today!

This money-saving catalog lists hundreds of best-sellers originally priced from $3.75 to $15.00— yours now in Bantam paperback editions for just 50¢ to $1.95! Here is a great opportunity to read the good books you've missed and add to your private library at huge savings! The catalog is FREE! So don't delay—send for yours today!